I0619178

Georgette Alden Starts Over

Deslisle Publications

Georgette Alden Starts Over

By

Annie Hoff

CLIMAX, SK
CANADA

Copyright 2018 by Annie Hoff
December 2018
ISBN 978-1-989276-07-5
Cover Art by Petra's Art
Produced in Canada

Dedication

For Carolyn. who believed in this book right from the start and always told me that ice cream was good for you. I miss you, my friend.

Chapter One

Georgette Alden was disappointed at waking up in her own bed the morning after Electra Holmes was killed. She had imagined waking up in a private suite at St. Luke's hospital surrounded by massive bouquets from well-wishers and a copy of the *New York Post* left discreetly on the night table. Not that Georgette gave two cents for a rag like the *Post*, but it did excel in gossip. In the scenario she envisioned, the paper was opened to the gossip page and the headline read: *Despondent Star Attempts to Take Her Life.*

To achieve the desired scenario, Georgette had swallowed down four Xanax with the quarter bottle of Chardonnay stashed in her refrigerator next to a half-eaten Portobello burger and the wilted remains of an arugula salad. This was the only food in her refrigerator and also all that was left to remind her of the party at Harvey Bristol's townhouse. At the party, Georgette had imbibed half a bottle of the Pinot Grigio Harvey had flown in from his vineyard in Italy. Harvey had accompanied her back to her apartment for sex that was sweaty and discomforting. Pity sex. It was after this Georgette decided on staging an attempted suicide.

By morning, Harvey was nowhere to be found and nothing had come of the attempt except for a long lie in —lie in a term she borrowed from her ex-husband the

Brit—and a blinding headache. To remedy the latter, Georgette stumbled to the bathroom and found a bottle of aspirin in the medicine cabinet next to the empty Xanax container. She downed three of the little white pills and considered swallowing the rest of them. But the timing was all wrong. Georgette had been an actress for over thirty years. If she'd learned anything at all from her profession, it was that timing was everything.

Though now, aspirin swallowed, stray gray hairs plucked, Georgette faced another sort of timing problem. What was she to do with all these hours in the day? It hadn't occurred to her, before this moment, how embedded she was in her routine. Without the driver coming to pick her up and take her to Rockefeller Center, without the morning make-up chair, the rehearsal and the final shoot, who was she?

She tried to envision ways she might spend the day. Baking cookies? Cookies were fattening and besides, she hated to clean up messes. Watching television? Dear Lord, no. She did not want to tune in to *Our Time Tomorrow* only to see herself on the TV screen. The daytime drama, which had been called a soap opera when Georgette first began her acting career, was filmed three weeks in advance. Three weeks ago, Electra had been alive and well.

So alive and well, in fact, Georgette would be blindsided by her untimely demise. The very thought made Georgette shiver as she remembered Jerome Conlan, the sniveling young snot of a director, handing her the week's script. She had stormed Harvey's office after reading it.

"You cannot possibly be serious about pushing Electra off a cliff," she had said or, more to the point, shouted.

Harvey had come from behind a desk piled high with God knows what and had calmly and firmly shut the office door. "You must have seen it coming, Georgie. The storyline has been headed for a showdown between Electra and Angora for some time now."

"It should be Electra shoving Angora off a cliff, not the other way around."

Harvey sighed deeply and offered Georgette a chair, which she did not take. "We have discussed this. It's better for the show this way."

"Electra is the heart and soul of the show. Electra is *Our Time Tomorrow*," said Georgette. Meaning, of course, she was the heart and soul of the show because she had played the part of Electra for thirty-one years.

Harvey took the crystal paperweight Georgette had given him for Hanukkah, turned it over in his hand and pocketed it. "It's time for new blood. The audience wants young and sexy. It's the way of the world. I'm sorry, Georgie. We *have* talked about this."

It dawned on Georgette that Harvey had pocketed the paperweight so she wouldn't hurl it through the clouded glass office door. She would have done just that had the opportunity presented itself. As it was, she was reduced to shouting "Thirty-one years!" before turning on her heel, exiting the office and slamming the door for a satisfying if somewhat incomplete glass rattle.

She had considered quitting. Damned if she was going to let the silly young ingénue who played Angora push her off a cliff either physically or metaphorically. But her professionalism got the best of her. She would see it through to the end, even if it ended with poor Electra lying on a boulder with a broken neck.

The end had come and now, who was she? It felt as though she were no one at all. No. There was plenty she could do. She would not allow herself to think like one defeated. She could visit her son Richard in London, even if it meant putting up with that twit of a girl he lived with. She could go to the museums. One could spend days wandering the halls of the Metropolitan. She could go to Central Park and feed the squirrels. Georgette got back into bed and pulled the covers over her head. She would do all those things. But first, she would take a well-deserved nap.

The nap turned into a tussle with the duvet. It was too warm with it on and too cold with it off. Damn those hot flashes anyway. They served as an unpleasant reminder that Georgette was now a woman of a certain age, an age that meant acting roles would be scarce as apples in the Antarctic. Damn the young and the sexy.

Georgette gave up the quest for sleep and trundled to the kitchen to hunt for coffee. She found a half empty jar of instant and managed to chisel enough free from the rock that had formed in the jar to eke out a tablespoonful. She sniffed the crystals, which smelled of nothing at all, and decided this was not what coffee should smell like. Had it expired? Holding the jar at arm's length, she searched for an expiration date. Damn the miniscule print. Forget the coffee. She threw the jar into the trash.

She would get herself dressed and walk down to that cute little coffee shop on the corner. What was it called? Alehandro's? Alabamo's? With all the ethnic names littering the city, you needed a translator to go anywhere at all. The coffee shop had good coffee. She'd had her driver stop to buy her a cup and a croissant every Friday before picking her up to go to the studio.

Georgette took out her makeup kit and began careful applications. She would wear the yellow silk blouse she'd bought at Sak's last week. It would look stunning with black trousers. She would never, she vowed, become one of those women who thought it was fine and dandy to parade around in old *I Love New York* sweat shirts and sneakers. No matter that she was only planning to walk to the corner, buy coffee, and walk back. If she did anything at all, she would do it with panache. She chose a silvery scarf and a pair of black suede pumps to complete the ensemble. The pumps were a bit more casual than she would have liked, but she was walking and they were the closest thing to walking shoes in her closet.

The day was overcast and warm, a perfectly lovely day for a stroll. Georgette turned up the street. On the corner, where she had imagined the coffee shop to be, was a Food Emporium. She supposed she could go there to get coffee, but she had her heart set on the little café. And she would have sworn it was here. Then it dawned on her: she should have turned left instead of right when exiting the apartment. Well, fine. Another block's walk would do her a world of good. In fact, she would walk the long way around the block. She could use the exercise.

The sky began to rumble as if agreeing with Georgette in taking the longer route. As she turned the first corner, the fresh air she'd been enjoying began to swirl, sending a few newspapers flying through the air as though they'd grown wings. The drops began after the third turn, growing thicker and wetter with each step. Why had she not thought to bring an umbrella? She should have prepared for contingencies.

There, on the corner not twenty feet ahead, was the coffee shop. The skies opened like a faucet; buckets of cold rain began rinsing the sidewalk of debris. Georgette jogged towards the shop and made it inside as a lightning bolt arched over the building. The young woman behind the counter glanced at her with some sympathy and Georgette realized she must look as wet as she felt. She rushed to the lady's room and locked the door. The woman in the mirror looked like she'd taken a shower fully dressed—her hair hung in loose strings around her shoulders and the mascara she had so carefully applied ran in rivulets down either cheek. Georgette didn't dare look down at her feet for fear of finding her suede pumps ruined beyond repair. She wondered momentarily if there was a way to sneak out the back unseen.

No! She had come for coffee and coffee she would have. A little rain was not going to deter her. She fixed her makeup and dried her hair as best she could in the close quarters of the bathroom. Then, unlatching the door, she sallied forth to make her purchase.

She had no sooner settled at a wobbly table near the back with a large cappuccino and a low-fat blueberry scone when the door jangled and in walked Peggy what's-her-name.

Peggy was Georgette's neighbor and Georgette could never remember the woman's last name. It was one of those double names like Osso-Bucco or Crème-Brule. Peggy folded her umbrella and nodded to the young women behind the counter. "Oh my! What weather!" she exclaimed as though rain were a new invention and this her first experience with it.

The last thing Georgette wanted was to talk to the woman. Too late. Peggy Martini-Rossi was already waving as though Georgette were a taxi that needed to be flagged down. "Hello! I haven't seen you in here before! I love this little café! So cozy!"

The headache from which Georgette had not yet fully recovered began thumping like a steel band at her temples. "How are you?" she managed.

"Oh, a little wet! But then a little rain never hurt anyone!" Peggy sat down without being invited. "Say, aren't you usually at work this time of day?"

"I've been—" Georgette closed her eyes and sighed. Maybe a bit of sympathy would help her through. "I've been terminated."

"How very awful! Why, I used to watch you on *No Time Like Tomorrow* when I was just a girl."

A girl? Peggy was sixty if she was a day. So much for sympathy. "*Our Time Tomorrow.*"

"Well, my." To her credit, Peggy did look as though she'd been hammered physically by Georgette's news.

"They dumped my character off a cliff without as much as a how-de-do."

"Awful, awful, awful! Just terrible! You poor dear! Whatever will you do?" Even Peggy's concern sounded like it should be served with a side order of marshmallow fluff.

"I'm looking forward to some time off. A change of

scenery might be just the thing I need."

"Say! I've got it!" Peggy's small gray eyes brightened. Georgette didn't think Peggy having ideas was a good thing. But, alas, Peggy was already expounding. "I volunteer at a homeless shelter! You could, too! Giving back to the community is a wonderful thing! Makes you feel scrubbed all over!"

Georgette tried to picture tweedy Peggy being scrubbed to a pink sheen with a giant loofah. Her imagination failed her. "A homeless shelter? For the indigent?"

"Oh, goodness! All sorts of people need charity! Anyhoo, you could join in. I'm on the board. I serve lunch on Tuesday afternoons!"

Georgette nearly spit out her cappuccino. Spending an afternoon in Peggy's company would be intolerable. Spending it in her company among sour smelling street people was hell's own punishment. "I'll give it some consideration."

Peggy took a sip of her coffee. Then, nearly hammering the cup to the table, looked at Georgette with shiny eyes again. "I've thought of something even better."

Georgette smiled through gritted teeth. What was next, a dumpster dive for *Save the Children*?

"Helping Hands, that's the charity which runs the shelter? Plans on doing some of those public announcement spots on the local New York stations. We've raised enough to shoot a commercial, but having a big star like you in it would put us on the map. You could be our own Angelina Jolie! Or—who's the other one always supporting good works?"

"Madonna?" offered Georgette. Her teeth had stopped grinding together and the pounding in her temples was beginning to recede. Maybe there was something to this charity business after all.

"Yes, yes. Exactly! You could be our own Madonna!" Peggy beamed. Then the light dimmed. "Though we wouldn't be able to pay you much."

Georgette waved a hand in the air. "I doubt very much that Angelina or Madonna get paid for their good works."

"So you'd do it? For free? Oh bless my stars, that would be wonderful! There's a board meeting this very afternoon. Did I tell you I'm on the board? They will be thrilled beyond measure!"

***

Georgette didn't hear from Peggy for a few days after Georgette had agreed to the public announcement spots. She couldn't imagine why the woman hadn't come knocking the afternoon of the meeting. She'd been so enthusiastic. Well, why shouldn't she be? Georgette was a celebrity and she was willing to volunteer her time. The board of Helping Hands would be thrilled, why wouldn't they be?

Finally, on Thursday, the doorbell rang and there stood Peggy Winston-Salem in a sweater that looked as though it had been crocheted by a troop of blind chimpanzees. Her smile was so wide her teeth practically fell out from between her lips. "Good news! You've got an interview."

"An interview?" Georgette hadn't thought she'd needed to apply for the spot. "Whatever for?"

Peggy's teeth retracted back between her lips. "Well, it's a formality, really. Mr. Rodriquez is dying to meet you! You're a shoo- in!"

"Who is Mr. Rodriquez?" Georgette pictured a slick-haired Columbian drug lord, and then amended the thought.

"He's a lovely man. He's the director. And not only of the shelter in Harlem, where I'm active, but of a dozen shelters scattered all over the city!" Peggy's face lit beatifically, as though this Rodriquez man were the second coming. *Well, fine. We all must idolize someone.* "I've set up a meeting for tomorrow morning at his office, if that's all right. We can change it if it's not convenient."

Georgette was tempted to say it wasn't, but frankly she had nothing planned for tomorrow except another long lie in. "Yes, well. I suppose I can make time."

"Oh wonderful! His office is at the shelter. You'll adore him. I'm sure you two will hit it off!"

Chapter Two

Peggy picked Georgette up as promised the following day then proceeded to prattle on endlessly about the lovely spring weather. Well, it *was* a beautiful day, Georgette conceded as much; daffodils and tulips blooming in street carts, the trees all greening. But dear God, the woman would have made Wordsworth cringe with her salutations.

They found a parking space after four turns around one of the hundred street blocks in Harlem. Georgette tried to avoid this part of the city. Evidence of why it should be avoided was all around, buildings that looked like disheveled old men, one step from falling in upon themselves. A sign on one such building had "Helping Hands" painted in somber black letters over a pair of open hands that looked to Georgette as though they might want to snatch your purse rather than offer assistance. The building was, at least, the best maintained of its neighbors.

The lobby reeked of cleanliness; a sort of disinfectant smell double-layered with ammonia. Georgette supposed this was a good thing. One no doubt had to work double time to keep germs at bay in a place such as this.

Peggy led the way down a hall of closed doors and stopped at one, distinguishable from the others only because the word "Director" was stenciled on it in white lettering, and knocked lightly, her ear to the door as though there were a mystery to be solved inside. A deep voice said, "Come in." After which, she opened the door a crack, stuck her head inside, and said "Tony? I've brought Ms. Alden!"

It was Tony and not Mr. Rodriquez, was it? And what, exactly, was Peggy implying? Being brought made Georgette feel like a cup of coffee. She might have grumbled about it aloud had Peggy not stepped out of the way revealing a bookshelf-lined office with a desk facing outward near the center wall. The desk was messier than Harvey Bristol's, something Georgette hadn't thought possible. Behind the desk sat the most beautiful man Georgette had ever laid eyes on.

Georgette couldn't have said what made him beautiful. She was accustomed to handsome men. She had worked on a daytime drama for over thirty years where handsome men were a commodity as common as a bar of soap. Tony Rodriquez was neither young nor perfect. His hair had gone silver at the temples. But there was something in the large lipid brown eyes set into olive skin that seemed to glow. His very presence made Georgette feel light all over—she could have wafted into the room on the spring air. It was small wonder that Peggy Simon-Schuster was smitten.

Tony Rodriquez eyed Georgette in a most gratifying way, as though she were the perfect ring at Tiffany's. She hadn't been gazed upon by someone who wasn't acting a part in a good long while and damned if she didn't like it a good great deal. She sallied forth, a million watt smile lighting her face. "Mr. Rodriquez. What a pleasure."

She expected him to stand. Old fashioned, she supposed, but once upon a time a gentleman would have stood when a lady entered the room. Tony Rodriquez most certainly appeared to be a gentleman, but gave no more than a bright smile and a nod in her direction.

The reason for his seemingly boorish behavior became apparent a moment later. "Won't you have a seat?" He motioned to an empty chair before wheeling around the front of the desk in a wheelchair. It took Georgette a full minute to register this: the man was in a wheelchair. He hadn't stood because he couldn't. She sat down quickly, feeling glad the chair, the regular chair, not the one with wheels, was there to catch her. She caught her breath and remembered she was an actress. Hadn't there been a wheelchair-bound man on *Our Time Tomorrow*? Yes, Brock Brockton. It had been a long time ago, maybe twenty years, but Georgette remembered the story line. Brock Brockton, the handsome young brain surgeon had been shot in a crossfire when terrorists invaded the hospital. Electra had been recovering from a brain tumor. Brock Brockton had saved her life. Because, at the time, Electra was still young and sexy enough for miraculous recoveries, thought Georgette sourly. She chased the thought away. It had no bearing on now, when the very handsome and wheelchair-bound Tony Rodriquez was wheeling up to her and saying, "Please, call me Tony." His voice would have made Pavarotti weep.

"And you must call me Georgette."

"Georgette." Her name rolled off the man's tongue as though it tasted like fresh strawberries. His handshake was soft and firm, as it should be. "Peggy, could you give us a moment?"

"Oh, of course." Was she still here? Why, it seemed she was standing in the doorway looking as though her puppy had chewed through a favorite pair of shoes. It was a new look for Peggy Phillip-Morris and Georgette had to admit it didn't suit her nearly as well as terminally cheerful.

Tony wheeled over to the door and shut it gently. Georgette watched with fascination as the muscles in his forearms corded. He caught her looking and she felt heat rise to her face. "Such strong arms." Had she just said it aloud?

"Thanks." He smiled at her again and she felt her heart thump even as she told herself to stop gawking.

She crossed her legs then uncrossed them again. "So, Georgette." Good lord, the man had wonderful eyes. "Why are you here?"

The question caught her entirely off guard. "Why am I here?"

"An actress of your caliber. Why would you want to do a local public announcement spot that will be seen by three or four insomniacs and a couple of house cats?"

Peggy had quite clearly said channel five, had she not? Or had Georgette assumed? "New York is a big city. Local means a lot more than a handful of people."

"True. But my point is, we're small potatoes. Hell, we're practically no potatoes. And you—" Tony gestured towards her with a flourish. Damned if she didn't like it.

"I enjoy giving back to the community."

"Have you done a lot of volunteer work?"

"Not per se. I've been extremely busy. But I'm currently on hiatus. It's the perfect time to get involved." Why was she selling this? She should have stalked out. But she found she wanted the job. Moreover, she wanted to do it well if only to impress Tony Rodriquez. She pressed on. "My character, Electra, ran a Braille school for orphans for a while."

Tony laughed. "You really want to do this?"

"Of course."

"Then we have a slight problem." What problem? She was volunteering. What more could they want? "Mollie and Saul Hammerstein are our biggest donors. We couldn't survive without their largess. Mollie fancies herself an actress. She's apparently a headliner over in Cos Cob."

Now it was Georgette's turn to laugh. "Don't tell me. She played Maria in the Cos Cob production of *Sound of Music?*"

Tony smirked. "Worse. She was Dolly in *Hello Dolly.*"

"Well, surely she understands the need for someone—professional."

"Would that she did. But I think, if you decide to do this, you may well have a co-star."

Georgette should have said no. The last thing she needed was some suburbanite from Cos Cob gumming up the works. But it was a good cause. And she did have the time. "Co-star it is," she said.

Tony watched as Georgette walked out of the office. The woman had great legs. Georgette Alden. When Peggy had suggested her, he'd felt flush as a school boy. *Our Time Tomorrow* was his guilty secret; he'd begun watching it every Friday in his dorm room at Fordham years ago. A lot of the guys had watched, mostly so they could ogle the sexy bad girl, Electra Holmes, and the sweet girl next door, Tamara Oden. There were opinion polls and beer-fueled arguments over who you'd rather bang. Tony had always opted for dark-haired Electra. The name suited her; she was like a live wire. He imagined touching her would make your heart race.

Of course, that had been a long time ago. Even so, he'd told Peggy to bring her in for an interview. Not because he'd really need to interview her for a volunteer spot, but because it was the fulfillment of a long held adolescent fantasy.

Georgette hadn't disappointed. She was older, sure, but who wasn't? In real life, you could feel the buzz she created the minute she walked into the room.

He hadn't felt that kind of buzz in a very long time. Not since Sophia had died in the car accident that had taken his ability to walk. That had been ten years ago. For ten years, he'd lived like a monk though the wheelchair hadn't, as he'd thought it would, kept women away. They liked the idea of a tragic hero. Tony hated the role.

For the past ten years, he'd put his passion into making Helping Hands a success. The charity had sustained him in the dark days after the accident and he'd thrown himself into work. He'd given up on relationships, or at least on the idea of ever having another one until Georgette Alden had appeared in his office and forced him to rethink his notions about abstinence.

He hadn't counted on her saying yes to the project. He thought, soon as he explained about Mollie Hammerstein, Georgette would decide it was too much trouble. Maybe he hadn't explained well enough. Mollie was one of those brash women who sucked all the air from a room. He hadn't explained that part. He hadn't wanted to because, in truth, he wanted to see Georgette again.

Mollie Hammerstein hated the very thought of Georgette Alden doing the spot. She had argued against bringing her in at the meeting, calling her an outsider and an unnecessary complication. Well, Mollie was right that Georgette may well complicate things. Tony was going to have to do some fast spinning to sell Mollie on the idea of co-starring. Reluctantly, he picked up the phone and dialed the Hammerstein's number.

"Mollie. Great news! Georgette Alden has agreed to do the spots with you." His cheery announcement was greeted by silence. "She's so looking forward to working with you."

"I thought I was to do the spots."

"Of course. You'll do the spots with Ms. Alden. It's a wonderful opportunity."

Mollie snuffled in a way that suggested it wasn't wonderful it all. "Too many cooks."

"No, no. It will be wonderful. You'll see. I'll get back to you with the details." He hung up before Mollie could raise any more objections. He would go to the shoots himself to assure there was no trouble. Who was he kidding? He would go to the shoots so he could be in the same room with Georgette Alden, the Mollie Hammersteins of the world be damned.

There was a voice mail on her phone from Harvey

Bristol. Georgette's hopes jumped to all sorts of conclusions. They would bring Electra back as a ghost to haunt that awful little snip, Athena. Or they would invent a long-lost twin for Electra, come to town to find the sister she'd been separated from at birth. Georgette dialed Harvey's number.

"I just wanted to check in with my favorite girl."

"Favorite girl? Since when?"

"Since forever. Come have dinner with me tomorrow night."

She supposed, afterwards, that she shouldn't have gone. But Harvey was an old friend, or so she insisted to herself. He had produced *Our Time Tomorrow* for as long as she had been part of the show. If Georgette were being totally honest, though, she would have admitted that if Harvey were to bring Electra back to life, it would be just like him to make the announcement at a five-star restaurant over foie gras.

She should have known better. The restaurant was a trendy new mid-town bistro that seemed to specialize in tiny tables and over-priced, under-proportioned entrees. The wine was top notch, of course. Harvey ordered a bottle. By the time dinner, such that it was, was served, they were well into the second bottle.

"I hope you don't plan on asking me back to the show," Georgette said as she finished her entrée in three bites. Wine always loosened her tongue. So far, dinner had passed without a single mention of *Our Time Tomorrow* or Electra's part in it. "I'm going to be very busy." The waiter swam over to them with the dessert cart. At least it seemed he was swimming. The entire room swam. "I'm doing volunteer work."

Harvey coughed and used his napkin to catch the wine that flew from his mouth. "You must be joking."

"Why would I joke? I'm doing public announcement spots for a terrific organization. Helping Hands. Perhaps you've heard of it?"

"Can't say I have." Harvey pointed to an apricot tart.

It wasn't mentioned again. Harvey Bristol was good at dismissing anything that held no interest for him. It was a trait Georgette had always despised. She didn't bring it up again herself. Last thing she needed was for Harvey to add a coffee stain to the wine stain in his napkin.

Neither did Harvey mention Electra. By the cab ride home, Georgette came to realize Harvey was not about to mention Electra. Another subject dismissed with ease.

"Are you going to ask me in?" Harvey asked when the cab pulled up to her apartment house. Georgette had a notion of what would happen if she asked Harvey up. The last time, the result had been a consideration of attempted suicide. Well, she'd been distraught. She'd thought a roll on the mattress with Harvey would ease her mind. Not that Harvey would win any awards for his technique. But sex with Harvey was a no-strings-attached sort of affair that could usually lift her out of a funk and could occasionally get her what she wanted.

She stood now weighing her options. The meter was, quite literally, running. Sex with Harvey could lead to a conversation about Electra or about her career in general and she didn't particularly want to go upstairs alone. "Would you care to come in?" she asked.

Harvey smiled and paid the cabby. "I thought you'd never ask."

Georgette's head spun as she unlocked the apartment door. How much wine had she consumed, exactly? Harvey grabbed her by the waist and began dancing her about the room. "Rumba with me Georgie. Shake those sweet hips. Ah, no, no. First, first, we should take off our clothes. Naked rumba." Harvey giggled like a school girl. How much wine had *he* consumed?

"The room is spinning."

"Nonsense, Georgie. I am spinning you. We are spinning crazy fools."

Just when she was ready to beg him to stop

because the dinner, light though it was, threatened to find its way back out, he kissed her. His tongue felt like an old dish rag polishing her teeth as it invaded her mouth. Georgette swallowed the thought and the gorge away.

Harvey began fumbling with her buttons. At least the room had stopped spinning. He took her hand and dragged her to the bedroom and the fumbling began again in earnest, zippers and socks and sleeves and condoms. When the fumbling came to its conclusion and Harvey was perched atop her on the bed, Tony Rodriquez and his deep brown eyes waltzed into her brain. Could a man in a wheelchair still satisfy a woman? Her hair caught in Harvey's wristwatch, the one thing he hadn't fumbled with, and yanked her sharply back to the situation at hand. They finished in record time and Georgette leaned back on the pillow and thought again of Tony's corded forearms.

"What's wrong?" Harvey was already sitting up and pushing a leg through his boxers.

Maybe it was time to be honest with Harvey Bristol. "I don't know that I can do this anymore."

Harvey stood, pulled up the boxers and turned to face her. "What this?"

"You know perfectly well what this." Georgette got up and put on her robe.

"Georgie, you know I adore you.' He zipped his trousers.

"Then prove it. Give Electra another chance. A miraculous recovery after the cliff dive. She could be paralyzed. In a wheelchair. It would be a marvelous story line."

Harvey sighed and buttoned his shirt. "Please don't mix business with pleasure."

"Fine. It would please me if we didn't see each other anymore."

"Okay, baby doll." Harvey pulled on a sock. "I get it. You've got to punish me for killing off your character. Okay, fine. Consider me punished. I'm sorry."

Georgette pointed an accusing forefinger at him. "You are not sorry. You've never been sorry about anything in your whole life."

"And you know how to ruin a perfect evening."

Georgette turned her back to him. "You've gotten what you came for. Now go."

"You are impossible, Georgie." Harvey kissed her on the forehead. She hated when he did that, it made her feel like a toddler having a tantrum. "Thanks for a pleasant evening." And he was out the door.

"Pleasant? I'll give you pleasant!" Georgette considered throwing the crystal vase with the roses he'd sent earlier out after him. But the vase had cost a small fortune and Harvey Bristol wasn't worth it.

"We'll need a director." Mollie Hammerstein had a way of asserting herself as an expert in everything the board addressed. Tony hated the way she'd commandeered this Tuesday's board meeting, not that it was anything new. The day had been a particularly difficult one. The kitchen in the South Bronx shelter was short of help and short of food donations. Someone had left a lighted cigarette on a couch in the lobby of the Harlem shelter that had destroyed the cushions. It was sheer luck someone caught it early enough to keep the place from burning down. And now, instead of going home for the evening, ordering some Chinese and watching reruns of "Law and Order", Tony was forced to endure a power struggle with Mollie Hammerstein.

"Where do we find a director?" Peggy Smythe-Bolton looked supremely happy with the question she'd formulated. Then again, Peggy looked happy most of the time. At the moment, her cheeriness was nearly as annoying as Mollie's bossiness.

"Maybe Ms. Alden could help us," Tony said. Mollie shot him a sour look as expected. He glanced over at Peggy, whose look had also turned sour. That was not expected. He soldiered on anyway. "She's a professional actress. I'm sure she has connections. She knows about these things."

"She is that." Tony could have kissed Saul Hammerstein for agreeing with him. How he lived with Mollie, Tony could only imagine. He would not have traded places with the man.

"She's on some frivolous soap opera," Mollie shot back. "Hardly serious about her craft." Tony wanted to remind her they were doing a sixty second public announcement spot that would not be in the running for an Emmy, daytime or otherwise. He glanced to Saul, hoping for more backup. Saul, no doubt sensing his saying anything further would only add to marital misery, simply nodded.

Enough with these people. No matter they funded the organization heavily. It was still his organization and he would be in charge. "She has more experience than any of us. We will ask her."

"I don't know how helpful she would be." Peggy glanced at Mollie. Why was everyone always glancing at the woman as though she might either throw them a bone or chop off their fingers?

Well, she wouldn't get to him. He was already imagining Georgette leaning over his desk. The smell of her perfume wafting past his nose, the lovely curve of her breasts as they disappeared into her blouse. "We need someone professional. Ms. Alden has very generously offered to volunteer her time." He smiled at Peggy hoping he could win her over. "She's your friend. Would you please ask her on our behalf?"

Peggy looked uneasy. "She's not my friend, really. Just a neighbor."

Why were these people so exasperating? "Fine, I'll call her myself." He rather liked the idea.

"No, no. Don't trouble yourself. I'll ask her," said Peggy. With that, Mollie got up and walked out of the conference room. *Good*, thought Tony. *The meeting would be easier to finish with her gone.*

Chapter Three

Another dozen red roses arrived at Georgette's door with a card. *"Thanks for a climatic evening- Harvey."* She nearly threw the flowers in the trash. A dozen red roses? How cliché could you get? Ah well, at least they would replace the ones wilting in the vase.

She was putting the flowers in water when the doorbell rang again. She hoped it wasn't Harvey. Then again, she would have liked to give him another piece of her mind. This time she would throw the bouquet at him. She'd take them out of the vase first.

It wasn't Harvey at any rate, but a dour-looking Peggy Oscar-Meyer. "I have a question for you." The cheer had gone from Peggy's voice. It startled Georgette. It surprised her even more that she wished it would come back. It wouldn't do to have Peggy Yankee-Doodle in a snit.

"Won't you come in?" Georgette had coffee, real coffee not those awful crystals, and a French press to brew it in. The woman at the café had given her instructions on how to brew it and she'd managed to make a decent cup earlier. She was willing to make Peggy a cup if it would wipe the scowl from the woman's face.

The scowl did not go away. "I haven't the time." Hadn't the time? Did do-gooding take up all twenty-four hours of Peggy's day? "Mr. Rodriquez asked me to speak with you."

Perhaps the scowl didn't matter. The mention of Tony's name brightened the room considerably. Although Georgette did note Peggy had called him Mr. Rodriquez, which no doubt had something to do with her mood.

Georgette worked to keep from beaming. "Oh?"

"Yes. He—we actually, the board at Helping Hands—were hoping you might help find a director for the spots?"

"Of course!" It was something she could do. She would be able, with her vast experience, to come up with at least one director hungry enough to do a spot for good will. Wouldn't she? "I'll get right on it!"

"Good." Peggy turned without another word. And Georgette noted, as she shut the door, that the exclamation points had transferred from Peggy's speech to her own.

***

In truth, the only directors Georgette knew were the ones she'd worked with on the show. None of them had been killed off and so they were all still working and unlikely to work for free. And besides, she wasn't about to call the snot who had directed Electra off a cliff. No, he was not a man she cared to speak with again, let alone work with again. She had seen the look on his face when he'd handed her the final script. Smug little bastard, he had smiled. Smiled! He'd been happy to have a hand in murdering Electra.

The most obvious person to call was Harvey. After last Saturday, she was ready to sign a pact with herself to never see or speak with him again either. But Harvey was a producer and he did know a lot of directors. It wouldn't be so awful to have coffee—or something—with Harvey if it meant impressing Tony. After a moment's hesitation she dialed his number.

"You got the flowers?"

"Yes. Thank you. They're lovely." She managed not to choke on the words, though saying them made her teeth hurt.

"I do think a lot of you, Georgie."

"Then prove it."

She could hear him sigh. Georgette knew he hated repeated arguments as much as he hated leftovers. "I can't bring Electra back to life."

"Can you lend me a director?"

"A director? What for?"

"The public announcement spots."

"What public announcement spots?" It was Georgette's turn to sigh. Did the man listen to nothing?

"I told you about them over dinner." Georgette remembered Harvey spitting wine into his napkin. She had an image of him missing the napkin, the wine staining his silk tie. She rather liked the idea.

"You are not really thinking about working for nothing."

"It's hardly nothing. It's for charity."

"Charity." It sounded a lot less noble when Harvey uttered it.

"Do you know of any directors who would volunteer for a good cause?"

"Volunteer? You're joking."

"I'm dead serious. Since you value our friendship so highly, I would think you could do me this one teeny favor."

Georgette waited as he mulled it over.

"Okay. I'll come up with something."

Tony kept his therapy appointments religiously, though after ten years he was no closer to walking than he had been when he'd started. He couldn't have survived without Vida Morrison. Vida was tall, mocha skinned, and, in many ways, foreboding. If it wasn't for her pushing he would never have gotten out of bed. Now, ten years later, he was training for the wheelchair division of the New York City Marathon. This, too, would never have happened without Vida's gentle and steady pressure.

"You got your application in?" she asked as she handed him the barbells.

"Better than that. I'm going to race for Helping Hands. We'll raise some money."

Vida raised her eyebrows and smirked at him. "Your do-gooding knows no bounds. I think you might be a superhero."

Tony laughed as he began his lifts. "You going to do street training with me?"

"Wouldn't miss it."

Vida was the most straightforward person Tony had ever known. She had become far more than his therapist. She was his friend. And yet, as he did his reps, he found it hard to find a way to ask the questions that had been on his mind ever since Georgette Alden had wafted into his office.

He had long ago gotten over being self-conscious about the chair. Vida had been a big part of that. For the first six months after the accident, all Tony had wanted to do was take pain killers and sleep his life away. He missed more appointments with Vida than he kept. Then, one day when he hadn't shown up for therapy, his doorbell rang. There stood Vida, all six intimidating feet of her. "The way I see it," she said. "You can shoot yourself now and get it over with or you can start getting your shit together."

Maybe he'd been ready to get his shit together. He started going to therapy regularly. Vida made him wheel around Central Park, made him do so many arm curls that his muscles ached, made him swim laps three times a week. He had thrown himself into work and exercise. And slowly, he'd gotten his life back. The only part of his life he hadn't gotten back was the relationship part. He'd lost Sophia. He couldn't replace her and he was pretty sure he didn't want to. And now he was attracted to someone who was more than likely unattainable.

"What's with you?" Vida asked. "You're about five

million miles away."

"Sorry."

"Trouble at work?"

"A woman. I've met a woman."

"Well, it's about friggin' time."

"Thing is, I feel about fourteen around her. I've got a bad crush and I don't know what to do about it."

"Ask her out."

"Just like that? I barely know her."

"That's why you need to ask her out. Jeez, you are out of practice."

"And then what?"

"And then what? Then you go to dinner. You talk. You go to the park. You kiss her good night."

"And eventually—" Tony tried hard not to feel sorry for himself.

"Eventually, if she cares about you, it'll be fine."

"How can you be so damn sure?"

Vida took the barbells from him. "Because you are a terrific guy and if I didn't already have a girlfriend I'd date you myself."

"I'm not even sure she's interested. She's way out of my league."

"Honey, you are the league. The show, the big time, the real deal." Vida gave his chair a push. "You need to be more confident."

"I'm plenty confident."

"Yeah? Prove it. Park. Tomorrow. Be there. I plan on handing you your ass."

***

Georgette got a call from Harvey the next day. "I got you a director. Am I a great guy or am I a great guy?"

"So soon? That's terrific. I don't know how to thank you." Georgette was sure Harvey would come up with a list of ways in which she could express her gratitude. The thought did not alter the flutter she felt down to her toes. She could tell Tony she'd gotten a director. He'd asked her for a favor and she was about to deliver like the takeout pizza man. She could go see him this very afternoon.

"I'm sure you'll think of something." Harvey's throaty laugh made her plummet back down to earth.

"Well, who is it?"

"Kent Markham."

Georgette wracked her brain to remember a Kent Markham. Nothing but blank space and then—Kent Markham had been a director at *Our Time Tomorrow* not long after she'd started. He'd seemed very old to her at the time. Of course, she was barely out of her teens, anyone would have seemed old. "Is he still alive?"

"Hell, yes. Alive and looking for ways to fill the time."

"How old is he exactly?"

"I don't know, Georgie. You of all people should know better than to let someone's age sell them short."

"*I* should know better?" Georgette bit her tongue. It wouldn't do to let Harvey get the best of her.

"So anyway, you're welcome."

After she hung up, something else about Kent Markham floated into her brain. She called Harvey back. "He's the guy who went to prison."

"That was years ago. He was a terrific director."

"He ran his car through the display window of a butcher shop or something, right? Something about not eating animals?"

"He maintains it was an accident. Besides, he's older and wiser now. He's mellowed."

"Exactly how old and mellow is he?" asked Georgette, running into the breach of the age inferno yet again.

"I don't know. Maybe eighty. Eighty-five."

"Do I hear ninety?"

"Eighty-nine. Tops."

"Great. I ask for a director and you hunt up an eighty-nine-year-old ex-con. One little favor. You'd think—"

"One little favor? Directors who will work for free don't grow on trees, you know."

"No. Apparently, they grow in prisons." Georgette hung up before Harvey could answer. Damned if she would let the man call her ungrateful.

Well, fine. Kent Markham it was. She'd have to break the news to Tony gently. Her day brightened. She'd have to break the news to Tony. Which meant she had an excuse to go and see Tony.

Georgette had forgotten Tuesday was the day Peggy Coconut-Macaroon volunteered at the Helping Hands shelter. She ran smack dab into the woman in the lobby. It was late afternoon and Peggy was putting on a sweater, though the weather was warm and Georgette couldn't figure out why Peggy would need a sweater, unless she enjoyed looking like an ad for the Alpaca Association. Georgette herself had chosen to wear a sleeveless red silk blouse that, top buttons left open, showed just a touch of cleavage paired with a black pencil skirt slit just above the knee along one side. She had chosen carefully, the idea being to look interested but not downright desperate.

She thought she'd chosen well until the smile pasted to Peggy's face faded as her eyes trailed from Georgette's face to her couture. "What a surprise, seeing you here." She sounded as though it were an unpleasant surprise.

"I've come to see Tony. Is he in?"

Peggy crossed her arms, her face set in a scowl. "Why in the world would you need to see Tony?"

"I've found a director for the spots. Isn't that wonderful? I came to give Tony the good news."

"You do have a phone? Couldn't you have called? No sense in coming all the way here to talk to him."

Georgette could not imagine what had gotten into the women. She would be damned if she let Peggy Hokey-Pokey get the best of her. "Do you have a problem with my being here?"

"It's a free country."

"As I recall, you were the one who asked me to do this project. I agreed out of the kindness of my own heart."

"Kindness my foot," muttered Peggy.

"I'm sorry?" Georgette wasn't sure she'd heard right.

"Kindness my foot. I don't think you have the right motivation. I think you're hoping Tony Rodriquez will ogle you."

"Excuse me?"

Peggy was nodding furiously. "Yes. Ogle. Don't tell me you don't know men ogle you. Women like you—" Peggy squeezed her lips together as though preventing anything further from falling out of them. A move that didn't work, because she added "And now you've set your mark on poor Tony Rodriquez."

"What are you talking about?" In truth, Georgette knew exactly what Peggy Ralston-Purina was talking about. And all right, she liked men and she liked Tony. What was wrong with that?

"You want to lure him into your web. The last thing he needs is a woman like you."

A woman like her? It took all of Georgette's resolve not to slap Peggy for her affront. Just because she wore sweaters woven in third world countries did not mean she had a right to insult women with better fashion sense. "When did you become Tony Rodriquez's keeper?"

Peggy shook her finger in Georgette's face. "You keep your claws away from him."

Tony wheeled around the corner. His look told her she had dressed right, the Peggy Sears-Roebucks of the world be damned. "Something wrong?" he asked.

"No, nothing." Georgette turned her back on Peggy and gave Tony her best hundred-watt smile. "I dropped by to talk to you about the commercial."

"Great! Why don't we go back to my office?" Peggy put her hand to Tony's arm and Tony patted it absently.

"I'll see you at the meeting tomorrow, Peggy?"

"Of course." Peggy shot Georgette a look that could have melted her shoes. "I'll see you tomorrow."

Georgette followed Tony back into his office. "So. You wanted to see me?" God, his smile could start a nuclear reaction.

"Yes. I've got a director for the spots."

"Oh. Okay. Well, that's terrific." The smile lost a few sparkle points.

"I'm really glad to be doing the spots. I think what you do here is special and I'm thrilled to be a part of it."

"Well, good. I'm glad you're glad." The smile had all but turned into a frown. It stung a little. Maybe she should just come out and tell him she thought he was terrific. She had said the shelter was terrific and most men she knew, no, all the men she knew, liked it when you complimented their work. So why wasn't he acting as though he liked it?

She had misread him. He was a nice man who cared about people. Peggy was wrong. There was no ogle. Maybe she had lost her sexy along with her young as Harvey had suggested. Well, fine. She could still have the pleasure of working with Tony Rodriquez. She would just need to put aside the fact that he made her skin feel like it had caught fire every time he looked at her.

She decided now was not the time to tell him about Kent Markham's sketchy past. She wrote down Kent's name and number and handed it to Tony. "I can call him if you like. We've worked together before."

"That would be great. If you'd call him."

"Okay. I'll let you know. You'll let me know when we're to start shooting?"

"Yes. Sure. I'll let you know."

She turned to walk out of his office when she heard him call her name. "Georgette?" She swung around to see a pained look in his eyes. "Thank you," he said.

***

Why, oh why had he let her walk out of the office? He heard Vida's voice in his head. "Just ask her to dinner. What have you got to lose?" His pride? Worst thing that could happen was she would say no. She'd say no and he would bow out of handling the commercial spots himself. But no would be terrible. He wasn't ready for no.

He'd been on a handful of dates since his accident. The women he'd seen all admired him, they gushed about his courage and fortitude and, at first; he'd been taken in by the gushing. But soon enough, the reality of his situation replaced whatever fantasy they contrived in their heads. And the reality was more than any of them were willing to deal with.

So he'd stopped dating. He and Sophia had had a dozen terrific years together. Maybe that was all anyone could ask for. He kept busy. At work, he didn't have anything he needed to prove. He was still strong enough to wheel his chair through a twenty-six mile marathon. And yet. Something about Georgette Alden—no, everything about Georgette—made him want her down to the creak in his bones. So why hadn't he tried? Why had he acted like a tongue-tied school boy?

Peggy Smythe-Bolton poked her head through the half-opened office door and startled him from his reverie. "I thought you'd gone home," he said.

"Oh," Peggy bit her lip. An unpleasant habit, that. "I was on my way out. Just wanted to pop in and make sure you were okay."

"Why wouldn't I be?"

Peggy shrugged. "No reason. No reason at all."

"Good." Another thought occurred to him. "Why were you arguing with Georgette Alden earlier?"

"Arguing? We weren't arguing." Peggy smiled and shrugged and bit her lip all at the same time. "I think Mollie might be right, though. Georgette Alden might make things difficult."

Tony felt heat flush to his face. Why couldn't anyone around here be supportive? "She's a professional. It was a terrific idea to bring her in." He spoke more stridently than he'd intended and Peggy's eyes welled. She blinked a few times. "I thought you liked Georgette," he said more softly.

"She seems very good at catching people up in her personal drama." Peggy blinked again. "I'm sorry. I've spoken out of turn. It's just that—well. You should have seen her at the coffee shop the day I asked her to do the commercial. She looked like a kitten left out in the rain. So beleaguered and lost and...and now she shows up at all hours parading about in low cut blouses and skirts with slits up to her you know what. I think she's after you."

"I don't think she's after me, Peggy." Damned if the thought didn't have some appeal.

"She's...Just last Saturday she had a man in her apartment. They looked mighty cozy in the hall. He was practically drooling on her. Then he left an hour later."

He should have read Peggy the riot act for spying on Georgette, but he was too galled by the thought of another man pawing Georgette.

"It's late," Peggy said before he could answer her charge. "I've said too much."

"Yes. You have. Georgette Alden is doing the spots. It's nice of her to do them. I think we should all remember that and maybe treat her with some civility, don't you?"

"Yes. Of course."

The relief Tony felt when Peggy walked out of his office was soon replaced with a nagging uneasiness over Peggy's words. A man drooling all over Georgette. He wanted to find the man and take him by the throat. He had no claim on her and maybe it was just Peggy's jealousy talking. Peggy was jealous of Georgette, that was clear. Why wouldn't she be? Georgette was gorgeous. No doubt the man all over her like a blanket in her hallway was gorgeous, too. How could he compete with the men who must fill Georgette's life? He didn't stand a chance.

Chapter Four

Georgette decided a pre-emptive strike might be necessary—she would go to see Kent Markham herself. She was, she decided on the cab ride back from Harlem, not about to let a doddering ex-con rain on her public announcement spots.

Kent lived in a high rise for the elderly a few blocks from Georgette's building. He answered the door wearing florescent green yoga pants and a matching shirt that looked like a pajama top without buttons. His feet were bare, long toes with cracked yellow nails topping off long feet at the base of spindly legs that gave him a sort of aging Big Bird look. Georgette made a mental note to get a pedicure and soon.

"Come in, dear Georgette. Do come in!" Kent put a gnarled hand on Georgette's elbow and led her through his hall to a small and barely furnished room with a futon to one side and a yoga mat on the other. "Last time I saw you, you were just a slip of a girl." Kent put both hands to Georgette's shoulders and held her out at arm's length. "And now? You are a magnificent and mature woman."

Georgette didn't particularly like the word mature, especially since it came out of the mouth of a man who had matured beyond all expectation.

"So." Kent clapped his hands together and bowed at her before gesturing to the futon. "Won't you sit down? I have some delightful oolong tea. I will fetch us each up a cup."

"Delightful," repeated Georgette as she watched his skinny frame disappear into the kitchen area.

He called back to her, "How long has it been since we've worked together?"

"A few years? Quite a few," Georgette answered. The only response this time was a clanging noise. Kent probably hadn't heard her and besides, it was awkward holding a conversation through two rooms. Georgette put a hand to either side of her on the futon's velvet cover. It was soft, but who knew what hid inside the nap. She put her hands on her lap.

Kent came back with two steaming cups of greenish tea and handed her one. Instead of sitting beside her, he sat Indian style on the yoga mat. He raised his cup to salute her and she took a sip of strong and bitter tea.

Kent was looking at her in a way that Georgette was sure could be described as ogling. Yes, he was most definitely ogling. She remembered something else about Kent Markham—he had tried to seduce every actress on *Our Time Tomorrow*. He had succeeded more than once with some of the women, who thought sleeping with the director would help their careers. It hadn't helped to get them anything but a roll in the hay with Kent. Georgette had known as much from the start. She hadn't let him seduce her then and she was certainly not about to let him seduce her now.

"I'm happy to shoot the commercial spots if you'll do me a small favor." Kent smiled at her. She wondered if he still had his own teeth.

"Favor? What kind of favor?"

"A personal favor." *Great. Here it comes.* Georgette took another sip of bitter tea. "Help me free the penguins."

The tea spurted out of Georgette's mouth, sprinkling her blue linen blouse. At least she'd chosen a washable fabric. Kent was spry for an octogenarian. He was in the kitchen and back two seconds later with a handful of paper towels.

Georgette dabbed at the spots. "Did you say penguins?" It had occurred to Georgette, in the brief moment Kent was in the kitchen, that penguins might be some sort of quaint euphemism connected to his ogling.

"Yes," Kent said, taking the paper towels and going to deposit them in the kitchen, "from the Bronx Zoo." Kent came back and plopped down on the yoga mat.

"Excuse me for asking, but why would you want to take penguins from the Bronx Zoo?"

"Why?" Kent jumped up again and began pacing. "Because penguins are sentient beings and they deserve better than to be confined in enclosures! Don't be fooled by how comfortable those enclosures may look. A prison is a prison."

Georgette blinked. Kent's impassioned speech left her speechless.

"How would you like to spend your life in an enclosure?"

Georgette tried to remember the penguin enclosure at the zoo. She had only a vague recollection, but animal cruelty did not come to mind when she thought about it. How horrible could it be to be fed, watered, and sheltered with your nearest and dearest? Georgette noted the crazed look in Kent's eyes and knew he wouldn't share her point of view. "Why penguins?" she asked. "Why not gorillas or tigers?"

"Of course, all sentient beings deserve to be free. But we have to start somewhere. We will free the penguins to make a statement and let the world know about all the poor enslaved animals in need of liberation. Join us, Georgette. Join the cause!"

"There's a cause?"

"Of course there's a cause. And I figure it to be a fair trade. I help you with the poor indigents who need shelter and you help me to free the wild things."

"Does your cause have a name?" Georgette couldn't quite believe there was a group dedicated to freeing penguins.

"Of course it has a name. The Wild Things Project. We have a website."

"And how do you plan to free these penguins?"

"The details are unimportant. It's the passion that counts!"

Georgette nodded, speechless again.

"So you'll join us? And I'll shoot your public service announcements. One good cause helping another!"

"Sure," Georgette said. "Let's go free some penguins."

Georgette had no intention of helping to vandalize the Bronx Zoo. Kent Markham was a loon, but he'd also been a good director who could, with any luck at all, still direct. Georgette figured she could get Kent to do the spots then slowly worm her way out of any free the penguins commitment. She hadn't really promised him anything anyway. She hadn't given her word and she certainly hadn't signed anything. Kent was old and crazy to boot. He would no doubt forget about the penguins.

She was curious enough about the project to check out the Wild Things website and was surprised to find that such a group actually existed. On the home page was a photo collage of goofy looking people with all sorts of animals, most of them the harmless kind you might find at the petting zoo. The site contained a lot of information about zoo abuse and the same speech Kent had given was quoted nearly word for word.

The free-the-penguins project had its own separate page with a picture of the Bronx Zoo penguin enclosure and a caption that said, "Help wildlife be wild." A second picture showed penguins in what Georgette presumed was their natural habitat. Why would those poor creatures want to go back to such a harsh and inhospitable place? Just because you were born in Antarctica didn't mean you wanted to stay there. She'd been born in New Jersey and she had no desire to live there anymore.

***

Tony was on a roll, quite literally. He clocked ten miles in his racing chair in the same amount of time it took Vida to do three. He waited for her at the bridge near the children's zoo and handed her water. "Who's got whose ass again?" There weren't many advantages to being in a wheelchair, but he had to say he liked the fact that he could wheel more than twice as fast as she could run. And damn if he didn't love to tease her about it.

"You're going to have to haul that chariot a whole lot faster if you don't want to be blown away by the competition in November." Vida smirked at him.

"You're going to have to do a whole lot of running if you plan on finishing the race at all, woman."

Vida finished the water, tossed the bottle in the trash and put her hands on either side of his wheelchair. "I'll race you to Starbuck's. Last one there gets the coffee."

"You're on."

They raced, as they always did, with Tony going the long way around and Vida taking the short route. Traffic was heavy and the light slow at his end of the street and she beat him by half a block. He bought them each coffees and a couple of bagels to go with them.

"So you ask her yet?" Vida spread cream cheese on her bagel.

"I don't work that fast."

Vida pointed the bagel at him. "You don't work at all, you mean."

Tony spread his portion of cream cheese. "I think I blew it."

"Why? What did you do, call her up and breathe heavily into the phone?"

"She came to my office yesterday and I had my chance and didn't take it. She told me she'd found a director and like an idiot I said "well, that's just swell" and so ended the conversation."

Vida started to laugh.

"This is so not funny."

"Yes, funny. Also pathetic."

Tony scowled at her. "I do not need your sarcasm right now."

"Not sarcasm. Honest opinion. You need someone to tell you to go for it. You're a grown man not a fifteen-year-old boy."

"Great. Why don't you coach me? I can install you in my bedroom closet."

"I wouldn't worry about the bedroom, honey. You haven't even made it into the hallway yet."

Tony put his bagel down. "I should get going."

Vida put her hand to his wheelchair. "I'm sorry, that was over the line. Let's start over, okay? How's that woman you like?"

Tony sighed. "I've got it bad. I know it. It's stupid of me, acting like I'm in junior high. But Georgette Alden, God, Georgette Alden has been my fantasy since I was eighteen."

"Okay, you lost me."

"She was on this soap, *Our Time Tomorrow*. If you tell anybody this, I'll deny it, but I've been watching her since college. Or watching her character, Electra Holmes."

"You do understand that she's not Electra Holmes?"

"She's better than Electra ever could be. She's gorgeous, she's vibrant. And I feel like an adolescent with a bad crush when I'm around her and there's nothing I can do about it."

"What do you want to do about it?"

"What I want has about as much to do with reality as does Electra Holmes."

"You want to bang her."

"When did you get so crude?"

"Sorry, Tony, but that is what we're talking about here, right?"

"Okay, yes. There's more to it than that. But yes, that's what we're talking about."

"You know that there are ways to have sex, even in the chair?"

"Yes, Vida. I read the pamphlets and watched the video. You've got to admit it ain't exactly romantic. Oh darling, I'll just grab my pills and paraphernalia and we'll get down to it."

Vida slapped his arm so hard that it stung. "Stop it. Feeling sorry for yourself isn't going to get you anything. If she cares, it doesn't matter. You've got to stop letting it get in the way."

"It does matter, Vida. It matters a whole lot."

"So all you want from this woman is a roll in the sack so you can fulfill some adolescent fantasy? I got to say, that's disappointing. I thought you were better than that."

"It's not all I want." Tony felt the heat rise to his face. Last time he'd gotten angry at Vida, he'd started racing marathons. Maybe anger wasn't such a bad thing. He did want more, but why wouldn't he want this one thing, the one thing he couldn't have?

Chapter Five

Peggy Chicken-Noodle rang the doorbell at dawn. It wasn't dawn, really. It just seemed that way. Georgette had spent over thirty working years getting up before the sun. She did not enjoy getting up before the sun. And now here was this woman—a woman who had insulted her no less—ringing the doorbell mercilessly.

Georgette threw on a robe and stood gaping as Peggy, dressed in her usual tourist to the Amazon gear, thrust a looseleaf notebook at her.

"The script for the commercial," Peggy said. "I thought you might want to take a look."

Peggy seemed to have made the transition back to her old cheery self and Georgette wasn't quite sure what to make of her. "Won't you come in?"

"It's—my way of saying sorry," Peggy said. Or some such, Georgette's ears hadn't come fully awake yet. "I misspoke yesterday. Tony said we—meaning the board—ought to be civil. He's right. We are a perfectly civil group and you are a professional and we are lucky to have you."

Tony had said all that? Georgette's ears were suddenly wide awake.

"Well, aren't you going to read it?"

"Now? You want me to read it right now?

"Well, sure. Mollie already has her lines memorized. Would you like me to read with you?"

Reading a script with Peggy Simon-Garfunkel was

about as appealing as cleaning out the gunk in the back of the refrigerator but the woman *had* come to Georgette's door with an apology on her lips. Peggy's enthusiasm had, God help them all, been restored. And, God help her, Peggy's enthusiasm was starting to grow on Georgette.

Besides, it would be good to know what was in the script. If she was going to be forced into working with the Mollie woman, she might better have a leg up on the commercial. It was what any professional would do.

Georgette made coffee and she and Peggy settled into the living room. Peggy thought to bring two copies of the script so they could work through it together, which did not surprise Georgette in the least. Peggy was exactly the sort of woman who would plan for contingencies.

"I'll do Mollie's lines." Peggy took a pair of reading glasses from her pocket and put them on. Georgette hoped the font was large enough that she could avoid her own reading glasses. Alas, no. She had to go to the bedroom and hunt them down. "Mollie's first," Peggy said when they had both settled in again. Of course she was, thought Georgette.

"Bring us your poor, your underfed, your unwashed homeless masses," Peggy read.

Georgette pulled off her glasses. "Has someone paid a visit to the Statue of Liberty recently?"

Peggy didn't answer. She turned back to the page. "We will shelter you, clothe you, and give you hot soup." She looked up. "Your turn."

Georgette put her glasses back on. "Chicken soup on Mondays and Wednesdays. Vegetable soup on Tuesdays and Thursdays. Friday is tomato soup day. And on the weekend, a choice of mushroom barley and minestrone." Georgette pulled off her glasses again. "Who wrote this?" She almost added drivel but managed to restrain herself.

"Mollie and I did. We sat down last night and it went so smoothly! One hour and presto!" Peggy smile turned to a frown. "Is there a problem?"

Georgette had been on daytime television for over thirty years. God knows, there had been some plots hung together by a string. Occasionally there had been writing that was overwrought and superfluous. But never in all those years had she come across words so trite they left an aftertaste in her mouth. She glanced up from the page and there sat Peggy Tutti-Frutti, her gray eyes magnified under the glass of her lenses, looking eager as a school girl. "Maybe it...it could use a little tweaking," Georgette said.

Peggy's magnified eyes blinked as she tried to take in the critique. "We timed it. It's exactly one minute when you include the music. We're doing that song, *Angel*. The one Sarah McLachlan did? She used it in that animal commercial."

Georgette willed herself not to groan. "You know, professional scripts always get edited. It's part of the process. Maybe this could do with some editing, that's all."

"I could talk to Mollie, if you think— We can't really afford an editor. All these costs! Who knew?"

"Maybe we should talk to Mollie. We could probably edit it together. Keep the good parts." Georgette scanned through the script looking for a good part. "This last bit about ten locations in the New York metropolitan area is very informative."

Peggy beamed. "Yes. Informative is important, don't you think?"

"Absolutely. Really, when you think about it, information is the biggest reason for doing the spots. We need lots of information."

"Like the bit about the soup?"

This time, Georgette couldn't suppress the groan.

The last person Tony wanted to see sitting across from his desk was Mollie Hammerstein. Yet there she sat, scowling at him after having stormed into his office and throwing a binder on his desk. She had a look that could frighten linebackers.

"Well?" she demanded, tapping her forefinger on the arm of the chair. "I suppose you've heard the latest travesty."

Tony worked to keep the furrow from his forehead. "No, Mollie. I don't suppose I have."

"I talked to Peggy this morning. Now *she* wants to change the script."

"Peggy wants to change the script?"

Mollie looked at him as though he was a half-eaten fish stick. "Not Peggy. The actress."

"Georgette Alden?" Tony swore Mollie twitched at the mention of Georgette's name. "Why would Georgette, Ms. Alden, want to change the script?"

"That," said Mollie with a flourish fit for a queen, "is exactly what I'd like to know."

"Would you like me to talk to her?" Tony hated getting into the middle of Mollie's drama. Yet, it would be an excuse to talk to Georgette, which might actually add some sunlight to what had been a glum day so far.

"I don't see why we need *her.* But if you insist, as you seem to, that we do, then talking some sense into the woman is the least you can do." With that, Mollie stood up, wrapped herself in her pashmina, and stalked off to find her next victim.

If only Mollie weren't involved in the project, life would be just about perfect. But Mollie was involved— more than involved, the idea for public announcement spots had been Mollie's in the first place—and Tony would have to put up with her. Besides, the spots, which Tony had at first assumed (and not without reason) would be a bigger pain than they were worth, had brought Georgette into his life. That might be worth putting up with Mollie and her tempests. Yes, it would definitely be worth it. He could talk to Georgette again today. If only he hadn't messed it up so badly the last time he'd seen her.

He picked up the binder. "Public Announcement

Spot" was written on the cover page in Peggy's neat block print. He wasn't sure why Georgette would want to change it. Maybe she was as good at making up crises as was Mollie. Given the electric current he felt every time he was in the same room with Georgette, he figured she was pretty good at generating drama.

He put the binder down and picked up the phone, remembering the heady scent of Georgette's perfume, the soft curve of a shoulder under her blouse. Hell, he had it bad. She could put him on a platter and serve him for lunch and he'd be smiling all the way to the table. He doubted he even registered on Georgette's radar. Her date book was full of handsome, rich men. She hardly had time to have him for lunch.

He put the phone down. "What did he have to lose?" Vida had asked. "Everything and nothing" should have been his answer. Well, if he was going to lose he might as well do it big. Never mind the phone call. He'd pay Georgette Alden a personal visit.

When the doorman—Norm or Earl, she could never remember which was which—called up to say she had a visitor, Georgette had visions of Mollie Hammerstein storming her apartment. She'd had a rather unnerving phone call from Mollie not an hour earlier in which Mollie nearly threatened her if so much as a word of the public announcement spot was changed.

"It's a man," Norm or Earl said over the intercom. "He's incapacitated," added the doorman in a low key akin to a whisper.

"He's drunk?" Georgette's imaginings turned from Mollie to a drunken Harvey demanding she sleep with him on the spot.

"No. He's in a wheelchair."

"Oh," The vision of Harvey disappeared and Georgette did a small inner cheer at the thought of Tony come to visit. "Send him up, then."

She jogged to her bedroom and shut the door.

Why, oh why had she chosen this afternoon to try the infernal Zumba DVD she'd ordered on Amazon? She had been half way through the first hour when the intercom had buzzed and as a result she looked as though she'd been working in the fields all morning. That is, if field workers wore Dior sweats. Her face was flushed, her hair was a windstorm tied back at the nape of her sweaty neck.

She ripped open the door of her walk-in closet and began rummaging through clothes, evaluating each piece and, finding each lacking, tossing it aside. She had made it through three pairs of slacks, several shirts, and a poncho and was appraising a slinky red cocktail dress when the doorbell rang. What had she been thinking? Style could not be accomplished in the amount of time it took to ride an elevator from the lobby to her apartment. She undid the band holding her hair, grabbed a brush and ran it hastily through the wreck while at the same time saying "Coming!" and going to answer the door.

Putting down the brush, she put on her most dazzling smile and opened the door. "What a nice surprise. Come in."

Tony stared up at her open mouthed before looking away. Georgette didn't know what to make of it. "Should I come back?" he asked his lap.

"Of course not," Georgette said the moment before she realized that, in her haste to change, she had unzipped her exercise jacket. Not one for those awful sports bra contraptions, she wore a Victoria's Secret underwire made of gossamer silk that was nearly transparent. She hastily zipped the jacket. Georgette was not a fan of embarrassing situations, yet she reasoned that had she chosen to show her underwear off to anyone it would be Tony. So where was the harm? "I was exercising," she explained.

When Tony looked up, his lipid brown eyes carried a hint of amusement. ""I'm sorry I interrupted your exercise."

"I'm not sure I even like Zumba."

His eyes grew warm. "I'm sorry to interrupt your Zumba. It seems we have a bit of a problem."

"Not Zumba related, I take it?"

That got Tony to laugh. She liked it when he laughed and hoped she could do it again. "Mollie Hammerstein tells me you want to change the public announcement script."

"And she's not happy. She called me this morning."

"Why would you want to change it?"

"Have you read it?" It occurred to Georgette that they were still standing at the door. When had she become so rude? All right, maybe not rude. Distracted. Tony's presence in her hallway was very distracting. "Won't you come in? Peggy left a copy here. You should have a look."

She led the way to her living room and dug through a pile of magazines. Tony maneuvered his chair through the hall and came up behind her. Had she backed up she would have ended up in his lap. The thought made her page right past the script and she buried it back into the pile. A second go-round unearthed it. She handed it to Tony.

"Should I look for anything in particular?" Tony asked. "I'm no expert on scripts."

"You don't need expertise." Georgette watched with growing satisfaction as Tony's expression went from curious to bemused to something resembling mortification.

He closed the script and shook his head, a scant smile on his lips. "That was, quite possibly, the worst thing I've ever read."

"Not worth the paper it's printed on?"

"The only good thing I can say about it is it's short." Tony broke into a grin and it made Georgette warm all over.

"So you understand why I suggested changes."

"God, yes. But—"

"Mollie," Georgette finished for him.

"Mollie," Tony agreed. "She seems to think it's dandy just the way it is. She and Peggy did work hard on it."

"Peggy said it flowed out easily. I think she was okay with tweaking it a little."

"I think Mollie can be brought around. We have to convince her it was her idea to change it."

"She practically threatened to sue me if I changed so much as a word."

Tony licked the corner of his lip; she wondered if it was a habit. A very endearing habit. "We have to get her to change them."

"I don't think it would be possible for me to persuade her to cross the street."

Tony laughed again. "You may have a point. Though I think you can be very persuasive, Ms. Alden."

"It's Georgette. Can I persuade you to have coffee with me?"

Tony seemed to hesitate. Had she pushed too hard? It was hardly a shove to ask the man if he wanted coffee, was it? Then he said, "I'd love some coffee. See, that was easy." The lines alongside his eyes crinkled in a way that made Georgette want to kiss them.

Tony watched Georgette's backside sway towards her kitchen. She was lovely coming and going and he was about to have coffee in her apartment. Okay, so it wasn't dinner and more, but it was a start.

He took a look around the setting, hoping it would tell him more about the woman who raised his temperature by stepping into his airspace. The furniture was done in deep tones of green and gold; the word regal came to mind. The windows were draped in damask, the walls papered in soft shades of eggshell. All impressive, much like Georgette herself. Then there was the art work, which looked museum-worthy and spoke of collections and wealth. The thought niggled at him.

"I didn't know how you like it, so I brought

everything." Georgette startled him from his reverie. She was carrying a silver tray with an ornate coffee pot and two china cups perched on it. The word wealth scuttled through Tony's brain again. He chased it away as she placed the tray on a mahogany coffee table. "Well, how do you want it?" Georgette asked, putting him at ease once again.

"Hint of cream, no sugar."

She poured from the pot, her red nails shining against the surface. "I like mine strong, dark, and hot." Georgette grinned at him as she handed him the cup. His pulse rate rose. Was she flirting? He wouldn't mind in the least if she were.

He held the delicate cup precariously with both hands, dreading the possibility of breaking it. "You have a lovely apartment."

"What, this old thing?" Georgette waved her hand playfully towards the walls. "My husband bought it for me. I had it furnished to his taste and I'm just too much of a stick in the mud to change it."

Tony put the cup carefully into the saucer, hoping his surprise wouldn't be evident. "Husband?" He'd never imagined a husband. He didn't like the imagining.

"Ex-husband actually." Georgette smiled in a most gratifying way. "Nigel and I have been divorced for over twenty years. And still I sit amongst his furnishings."

"You've never thought to change it?"

"Quite honestly, I like it. It's become more mine than his over the years. And I really couldn't replace it."

"Too sentimental?"

"Too expensive. Nigel spared no cost."

Tony picked up the cup again and took a sip. He thought about his own apartment on the west side. It wasn't a bad place; comfortable and in a decent neighborhood, but it was no match for priceless artwork and antiques.

Tony Rodriquez had no idea he was heart-stopping,

which made him all the more attractive. Georgette felt her pulse rate spurt up whenever the man glanced in her direction; he made her feel so at ease she wanted nothing more than to bask in his presence like a cat in a spot of sun. If anyone could tame Mollie the shrew, it was this man. Any woman would be bound to melt like heated butter at the sound of his voice.

"I should go." This came as an unwelcome notion. She had assumed he'd been enjoying her company.

"So soon?"

"I really need to get back to work." He held out his hand. "Thanks for coffee." The man had wonderful hands, soft and big and warm. Georgette had a momentary image of those hands roaming freely over her body. She suppressed a shudder. Now those marvelous hands went to the wheels of his chair maneuvering towards the hallway and the door and away from her.

"Thank you for offering to talk to Mollie." She hoped he'd stop wheeling so she could be with him for one minute longer.

He didn't. "No problem. Though I do think you could take her."

"She frightens me." There, that stopped him.

He turned his eyes to her, questioning. "I don't imagine you'd be scared of anything."

"Oh, you'd be surprised. Then again, you're so very brave. You think everyone's the same."

"Because of the chair?" His eyes clouded and Georgette feared she'd said something to chase him away.

"No. Because of the center. Running all those shelters. It's quite an undertaking."

His shoulders loosened. "Well, it's my job." With one last smile, he was in the elevator and then he was gone.

Tony didn't know what he was going to say to

Mollie Hammerstein. He rehearsed speeches in his head, but couldn't seem to find the single point that would make her accept the changes to the script. Unless they could scrap it entirely. Could he get her to do that?

He was preoccupied as he wheeled around the park and was still preoccupied when Vida came running up to his chair. "What's up?" she asked

"The public announcement spot. It's causing more trouble than it's worth."

"Your crush bailing on you?"

He began wheeling towards the street as Vida walked alongside. "She's not my crush. And no, this is a related matter." Vida listened to him go on about Mollie and the script all the way to Starbucks.

"Is the script really that bad?" she asked as they ordered coffee.

"Oh hell, if *I* could tell it was bad it must be God awful."

"So how come your actress can't take care of it?" Vida pulled out the chair so he could wheel to the table.

"She asked me to do it."

"And you, bright shining knight, will take up the quest." Vida raised her cup to him.

"It's not like that." Tony frowned at his own cup. "Besides, winning Georgette is a lost cause."

Vida put down her cup and raised her eyes towards the ceiling. "I thought you were going to stop acting like a tongue-tied schoolboy around her. We had the talk, remember?"

"I went to her apartment."

Vida raised her eyebrows. "Ooh, progress. Do tell."

"She's got art work worth millions on her walls. She's got vases from the Ming Dynasty. She's got rugs hand woven by twelfth century Persians."

"So she's got nice digs. She got the money and you got the honey."

"She likes nice things. She as much as said so. I can't buy her antique tapestries and Picassos."

"You can't afford her?"

"Why does it always sound so bad when you say it?" Tony frowned at his friend.

Vida frowned back. "Because it is bad, sweetums."

Maybe Vida was right. Maybe he was making too much of Georgette's possessions. They were just things, after all. Maybe he should ask her to dinner. No strings, no commitments, and if she said no, so be it. He'd be no worse off than he was now.

He was staring at the phone on his desk, working up the nerve to make the call and chiding himself that the call was so hard to make when Mollie stormed the office once again. Her face was red and her pout made Tony wonder if she practiced tantrums in front of the mirror.

"That woman is ruining the PA spot," she said without as much as a hello.

Tony forced a smile. "Won't you have a seat, Mollie? Can I get you some coffee?"

"What you can get is rid of that...that *actress*!" Mollie sat down as though being pushed into the chair.

"I'm surprised. I thought you had buried the hatchet. Just this morning Peggy was telling me how you planned to get together to write a wonderful script." It was an out and out lie. Mollie stopped huffing and stared at him in a way that could pull paint off the wall. Tony winced inwardly and kept the smile pasted to his face.

Mollie would probably bite his head off, but what the heck. "Peggy tells me that you want to keep working at it until it's perfect. I know how much it means to you. And that you'd take on some of Ms. Alden's suggestions? Even given the way you feel about her? I've got to say, Mollie, you are the heart and soul of generosity and diplomacy."

Mollie's face went from pout to bewilderment. He was halfway there. One more little push ought to do it.

"I'm so grateful to you for taking on the challenge. I don't know the first thing about PA spots. Between your expertise and Peggy's organizational skills, it's bound to help the center in ways I can't even begin to imagine."

"Well, we do our best." Bewilderment had turned to smiling satisfaction.

Tony breathed a quiet sigh of relief. "Of course, if Ms. Alden is too much of a burden..."

"She does have notoriety, I suppose." Mollie flipped her hand into the air.

"I suppose she does. But is her celebrity worth all the trouble of working with her? I mean, I know she's brought in a professional director and her notoriety will get us noticed. Maybe."

Mollie sighed a deeply resigned sigh. "Commercials do use celebrity endorsements all the time. I suppose the clients who would use our services love that show she was on. And if it can bring in donations for Helping Hands...I suppose it is the price we must pay."

"I imagine you're right. I do appreciate the sacrifice."

Tony folded his hands and said a silent prayer of thanks as Mollie turned and left the office. When he'd told Georgette all he had to do was make Mollie think the changes were her own, he hadn't been sure he could pull it off. But it had been easy. So easy, in fact, it made him wonder if there wasn't some devil's dilemma lurking in the shadows. And then he thought of it: he couldn't possibly ask Georgette out to dinner now. If he did, he would blow over the house of cards he'd just built with Mollie. He wasn't sure if he was disappointed or relieved at the thought.

Chapter Six

Georgette's son, Richard, called as she was shutting off the TV after having finished the Zumba DVD. She'd felt a nearly unbearable charge of emotion after Tony left, feelings she thought might be rectified by a long sweaty workout. She *was* feeling better and when the phone rang she picked it up with a cheery hello.

"Why Mumsy, aren't you the chipper one?" Richard said from the other end of the line.

"I've been exercising."

"Exertion can overcome so many obstacles." For a single moment, Georgette imagined her son might offer up sympathy about Electra's terrible fate. The funeral had been broadcast a few days earlier, although Richard may not have known that. He soon cleared away any idea of his being at all attuned to her life. "I could do with a spot of exercise myself. We've been positively cooped up on those tiny seats for hours."

Georgette wondered again if the boy was a changeling. He had grown up stateside, prep school at Eaton and then four years at Dartmouth. He'd been living in England for several years now and to hear him on the phone, you'd think he'd spent his life on the other side of the pond.

"We've decided to visit for a few days," Richard was saying. Visit? We? We no doubt meant he was bringing the Twit. What was the girl's name? Began with a p...

"You and Petula are certainly welcome." Georgette

was nothing if not gracious.

"Poppy." Richard sounded mildly irritated. She would have to write the girl's name down somewhere and memorize it before the visit.

"You and Poppy are most welcome," Georgette amended.

"Brilliant! We'll see you in an hour." An hour? Had she misheard? Perhaps he'd meant to say "Friday" or "next week." "Oh and Mummy? Would you be a darling and send the car to Kennedy to fetch us?"

"You're at Kennedy? Now?"

"Yes. Waiting for the luggage. You'll have to dispatch the driver immediately."

"I don't have a driver." There was what Georgette imagined as a shocked silence on the other end of the line. "The one I had came with work and I haven't had time to hire another."

"Well, we can take a town car, I suppose."

Georgette ended the call feeling a vague sense of annoyance. Not that she wasn't happy Richard was coming to visit. She loved her son and she hadn't seen him since she'd traveled to England last fall, when he'd introduced her to the Twit. Poppy. The girl's name was Poppy. She repeated it several times so she'd remember.

The cleaning woman had come and gone, so Georgette had to make up the bed in the guest bedroom herself. She was pulling the sheet over the mattress when the doorbell rang.

Peggy Barnum-Bailey seemed to have a way with bad timing. "I've brought the script so we can work on it!" Peggy blinked, her eyes magnified through those huge glasses she wore for reading. "You look a bit flustered."

"Do I?" Georgette pulled back the strand of hair that had come loose from where she'd tied it at the nape of her neck. "I was exercising"

Peggy nodded. "I can come back."

The thought of Peggy leaving became strangely unbearable. She could not face getting ready for Richard alone. "No, come in." She flung the door open and Peggy stepped inside, still blinking like an owl. "I do admit I'm a bit frazzled. My son Richard is coming. I suppose I'll have to make dinner. I never cook. I have no idea what to make." Georgette's eyes welled. My goodness, why was she getting so emotional?

"I didn't know you had a son," Peggy said.

Of course she had a son! She'd lived in the building since Richard was a toddler. Peggy had moved into the apartment next door when Richard was still a boy. Well, he *had* been away at Eaton. She and Nigel had both insisted on the best education. Certainly, he'd been to visit though. How could Peggy not have noticed a boy in a school uniform? "He lives near London. He's come to visit and called from the airport, giving me no more than a moment's notice. He is very busy and he loves to surprise." Georgette wasn't at all sure the last part was true. She tried to remember if Richard had ever surprised her.

Peggy checked the practical-looking watch strapped to her wrist and Georgette wondered if she were keeping her from something. But then Peggy said, "Traffic being what it is, it will take a good hour to get here from the airport."

"I haven't any food in the house and he's bringing his girlfriend."

"This is New York. You don't need to cook."

"I want to be a good mother. I wouldn't want anyone to mistake me for Cornelia Pepperwood."

"Cornelia Pepperwood?"

"She's the one who sold her children on *Our Time Tomorrow*. Terrible woman."

"Well, you have no intention of selling your son, do you?" Peggy put a hand on Georgette's shoulder. "I'll tell you what. I'll go down to the Food Emporium. It's just around the corner and they have all sorts of take out. Anything you like, they'll have it all cooked and ready."

"You'd do that for me?" Georgette had labored under the distinct feeling Peggy didn't much like her, a feeling intensified by the words they'd had over Tony.

"It's what neighbors do. You'd do the same for me."

Georgette nodded her head in agreement, though had she been honest, she would have to admit she would never have done the same for Peggy.

Peggy, it turned out, was a wizard at getting ready for company. She went to the Food Emporium and brought back several take-out boxes of curried chicken, which she then transferred to her own casserole dishes so they would be ready to pop into Georgette's oven for reheating. She found a tablecloth in Georgette's china cabinet and set the table with the Lenox china Georgette seldom used. She even went so far as to drag the vacuum from the hall closet and run it over the Persian rugs, though the cleaning woman had done it not five hours before and Georgette couldn't for her life imagine where dirt would have come from in such a short space of time.

Meanwhile, Georgette put on the pearl necklace Nigel had given her when they were first married and examined herself in the mirror. She was trying to decide whether the necklace was too matronly or just motherly enough when the doorman buzzed up to announce Richard and the girl—she really had to remember to call her Poppy and not the Twit—were in the lobby.

"I should be going, " Peggy said, slamming the door on the vacuum she'd stuffed back into the closet.

"Leave the script." Georgette felt she owed her neighbor some generosity. "I'll look it over this evening."

"Don't worry about a silly little thing like that." Peggy pulled a piece of stray lint from her sweater. "You'll be much too busy. Mollie and I can handle it."

Given the last script, Georgette wasn't sure Mollie and Peggy could handle it. Moreover, she wasn't sure she wanted them too. If she was going to be invested in the project, she wanted it done right. She was about to say something when the doorbell rang.

The man at the door bore little resemblance to the school picture Georgette had standing on her sideboard. The pudgy boy with a cowlick that couldn't be tamed had grown into an attractive young man. Lanky in a shirt and jeans, dark hair cut short and a pair of stylish glasses, he could have passed as one of the hedge fund managers who worked on Wall Street. Behind Richard stood a diminutive young woman with long blonde hair, eyes made up to pop out of her face by an overabundance of mascara and eyeliner, and a shirt that showed off breasts far too large to be natural on so boyish a figure.

Air kisses were exchanged, along with the mandatory questions about flights and weather. The whole while, Georgette eyed the young couple. The woman, Poppy, was wheeling a suitcase the size of a steamer trunk.

"How wonderful that you've come to visit!" Georgette had all but forgotten Peggy was still in the apartment. Yet here she was striding into the hallway with an outstretched hand. Richard and the girl stared at her as though she were a side show curiosity.

Georgette made hasty introductions and, again the mandated information about traffic was exchanged.

"I've really got to be getting on," Peggy said, nearly tripping over the massive suitcase that blocked the hallway passage to the door. The girl moved the suitcase aside and Peggy scurried from the apartment, shutting the still-opened front door behind her with a delicate thump.

The niceties exhausted, the air in the room threatened to fill with a noxious silence. Georgette rushed into the breach. "Let me show you to your room. You'll want to freshen up and, in the meantime, I'll get dinner started."

"You cooked?" Richard looked as though he couldn't have been more astounded if she'd said she whittled her own furniture.

"Brilliant," said the girl, giving Richard the tiniest

of shoves.

Georgette led them to the guest room and shut the door behind them before making her way to the kitchen. What was it Peggy had said about reheating? Thirty minutes at 350 degrees? Or was it fifty minutes at 300 degrees? Georgette noticed the post-it note tagged to the top of the casserole dish. Yes, the first was correct. Peggy was a regular Girl Scout and at the moment Georgette could have kissed her for her efficiency.

If only Peggy had left directions for how to use the oven, all would be well. Georgette examined the controls at the top of the range. Good Lord, one needed a pilot's license to work the damn thing. She had just found the button for bake, pushed it and been rewarded with a satisfying beep, when Poppy came into the kitchen. She'd changed into a pair of jeans so tight they looked as though they'd been spray painted on and a halter top that left her mid-drift uncovered to show off a tiny diamond in her pierced navel. Georgette shoved the casserole into the still cold oven and smiled at the girl.

"Smells marvelous," Poppy said. Clearly, she had no sense of smell as the only scent in the room was Georgette's Chanel #5. None-the-less, Georgette nodded in agreement.

"This apartment is fantastic!" the girl continued.

"Thank you." Georgette had never been at a loss for words. Yet, just now, she *had* lost them. It wasn't going to easy dealing with this Poppy person, whose entire vocabulary consisted of brilliant, marvelous, and fantastic. She would try. If only for Richard's sake, she would try.

"Dinner will be ready in half an hour," she announced.

"I can't get over it, Mumsy cooking." Richard had entered the room looking dapper in a fresh creased pair of chinos and a blue shirt. Magic, thought Georgette, that he had been able to pack his clothes without wrinkling them. "You're becoming quite domestic," Richard continued, putting an arm around her shoulder. "It must be the neighbor's influence."

"Who, Peggy?" Georgette was not yet ready to concede dinner would not be happening had it not been for Peggy's intercession.

"Did you get a load of the sweater she was wearing? Does she raise Angora rabbits in the back garden?" Richard asked.

Though Georgette had often thought such things of Peggy herself, she found them less than pleasant coming from out of the mouth of her only child. "Peggy's a good neighbor."

"I'm sure, Mumsy. She probably knits her own vests from the fur of the bunnies she raises."

"She's been very helpful since Electra's untimely demise."

"You mean the character you played on the telly?" This was the first full-fledged sentence Poppy had spoken. Georgette wished she'd chosen another, given the way the girl was wrinkling her nose as though *Our Time Tomorrow* had an unpleasant odor.

"I have, as you might well imagine, been a bit at odds since they murdered her."

"Murdered? Come now, Mumsy. It was just a silly character on a bit of twaddle. Hardly a cause for mourning."

Georgette felt the gorge rise in her throat. "That bit of twaddle paid for Eaton and Dartmouth."

"Really? I thought my father's fortune paid for them." Richard raised his eyebrows in a way that made her remember why she and Nigel had divorced and, at that moment, she didn't much like the young man standing in her kitchen. She may have loved him. But she didn't like him much.

What Richard said was, at least in part, true. Nigel was a wealthy man, the only son of a wealthy family. His father had been an earl and Nigel had inherited the title along with a large estate in Hampshire. Georgette met him when she was a fresh-faced girl from New Jersey who'd managed to land a starring role in a brand new soap opera. The soap had been on for a year by then and both it and Georgette—or Electra anyway—enjoyed tremendous popularity. With popularity came a tremendous amount of money. Though if she thought about it now, Georgette would have admitted it wasn't really much money by Manhattan standards. There were invitations to all sorts of affairs by producers and directors, older men who liked to wear her on their arm like a Rolex.

It was at such an affair that she met Nigel, this one a fund raiser at the Metropolitan Museum of Art's Cloisters. She'd been the guest of Ted Gorande who, Georgette found out later, was tolerated by the movers and shakers of Manhattan only because of a fortune in real estate. He was the friend of one of the show's producers. She knew it to be a command performance. Georgette may have been young and easily impressed, but she wasn't naïve. She'd heard all the rumors about Ted and, while it was true gossips often exaggerated; she also knew there was some truth to what was said. Ted Gorande would want more than a pretty young actress hanging off his arm for the evening. He wouldn't be satisfied until he'd gotten her into his bed, called her a cab come morning, and stuffed her into it while wishing her a pleasant Sunday.

Georgette had no intention of spending a moment in the bed of a man she could barely tolerate. She allowed him to take her arm at the affair and introduce her to all his colleagues. Then, once they had been thoroughly impressed and scandalized, she broke free. She planned on keeping as much distance as possible between her and Ted. With any luck, he'd drink too much champagne and forget about her. Then she could call a cab herself and head back to the tiny walkup she rented on West 45th Street.

It was May, one of those balmy spring evenings with a sky so clear a million stars canvassed it. She walked out to the edge of the property, to an overhang overlooking the Hudson, and gazed down at the river. Behind her arose the sound of clinking glass and muted laughter. Ahead, a boat whistle moaned softly. A sliver of moon rose over the dark water. A sense of peace overcame her and Georgette pulled off her heels, sat down in the grass, and sighed.

"Lovely, isn't it?" a British accent accosted her from out of the dark. Georgette shot up. It would not do to have anyone, particularly not a male anyone, find her lounging in the grass. She raised a foot to put her shoe back on. "Allow me." The man came out of the shadows. Flaxen haired, dark eyed, he looked like the handsome prince out of the fairy tales Georgette loved as a girl. The man knelt before her, took her other shoe, and slipped it onto her foot. Georgette was rendered speechless.

The man bowed. "Prince Charming at your service."

That made her grin. "Do you make a point of helping women with their shoes?"

He put his hands into his trouser pockets and looked her over ."I only help the pretty ones." He pulled one hand back out of his pocket and held it out to her. "Would you like to dance?"

Still stunned, Georgette allowed him to pull her into the circle of his arms. Soft music flowed from the party. They danced under the stars until the music stopped. "I'm very rude," he said, not letting her go. "I haven't introduced myself. Nigel Hathgrove Waddington Benningsworth."

"That's a lot of name." She stepped back and curtsied, "I am Georgette Anne Alden."

He pulled her into his arms again and whispered into her ear. "I have a secret to confess. I knew precisely who you were. I followed you outside." He raised his eyebrows as though daring her to think he was anything but dashing.

So began a whirlwind romance. They went out in dazzling style; he took her to clubs and Broadway shows and five star restaurants. He took her cruising on the

Hudson and on a wild ride at Coney Island. Georgette was so smitten she couldn't see straight.

A month after they'd begun dating, Nigel came to her door with a dozen roses and a ring from Tiffany's. He got down on one knee. "Marry me."

She'd been young enough and foolish enough to marry the young prince who had swept her off her feet. Now the only product of the marriage that remained was standing in her kitchen insulting her life's work. Well, the boy didn't know any better. He had been spoiled by his father's money.

Richard was, of course, right in assuming his father's money had paid for his education. Not that Georgette didn't have money of her own. She was the daughter of a truck driver in Camden. Her blue collar bones made her pragmatic and she had saved a large chunk of her handsome salary, plenty enough to live out her days in comfort and style. Yet her plenty was a pittance compared to Nigel's plenty. Nigel had an estate the size of Central Park, a house with over eighty rooms, a staff of thirty, and an income that appeared as though by magic through investments made.

"You do have drinkies?" Poppy interrupted Georgette's thoughts. Drinkies? Where in the world had Richard found her? Certainly not through Nigel. Her ex had become a stuffy old trout and his second wife, the lady of the manor, was so ramrod straight it made Georgette's spine hurt to think on it. Neither of them would approve of Ms. Drinkie. Which was, it came to Georgette as a revelation, why she should take the girl under her wing. Poppy would be malleable, a tabula rosa, and Georgette was looking for projects to occupy her time.

Georgette opened the wine and poured them each a glass. "Do you like to shop?" She asked, handing Poppy a glass.

"Shopping is brilliant." Poppy took a sip. Richard

cleared his throat and shot the girl a hard stare. Poppy swallowed and continued, "I like park walks better. All the things you can do free like. Much better than running through stores, isn't it?"

Georgette was taken aback at the girl's turnabout. She would have sworn when she said the word *shopping,* Poppy's eyes had lit. Then suddenly, she became an advocate of squirrel feeding. It made no sense. "I'll check on dinner," she said, unwilling to delve too deeply into Poppy's multiple personalities.

Once in the kitchen, Georgette hunted down the two cow-shaped potholders Peggy had left behind with the casserole dish. She opened the oven door and stood back, expecting a furnace blast to assault her. No hot air flowed out. Georgette peered into the dark oven cave. Tentatively, she put a finger to the casserole. It was stone cold. That couldn't be right. She had pressed the buttons. They had dinged. Wasn't that all there was to it? Georgette stared at the stove and was still staring when Poppy and Richard came into the kitchen.

"Problem, Mumsy?'

"Seems the oven isn't working properly."

Poppy took the casserole from the oven. "It's still cold, isn't it?"

"Of course it's cold." Georgette took a moment to regain her calm. She would cure Poppy of rhetorical questions at another time. "I don't understand it." So much for Peggy's silly ideas. She should have just taken them out to eat.

"We'll get it sorted, won't we, Richie?" The girl examined the stove and put her head in the cold oven.

Richie? Georgette glanced at her son, who either didn't notice or didn't mind the hideous nickname. Poppy pulled her head back out and began pushing the stove buttons. She waited a moment and peered into the oven again. "It's working now. Shall I pop it back in?"

"Thirty minutes at 350 degrees." Georgette recited the instructions Peggy had left.

"No trouble then. We'll have another drinkie, shall

we?'

"Mumsy has the finest selection of wines, don't you, darling?"

Georgette pointed to the wine cooler next to the refrigerator. "I like to keep it well stocked. Nothing compared to your father's cellar, though." She turned to Poppy. "Have you been to Hillcrest House?" If they were going to make polite conversation, she might as well have at it.

Another warning glance shot from Richard to Poppy. "It's a brill estate," Poppy said.

They went back to the living room and Richard refilled their glasses. Georgette sat on the couch. Poppy parked herself on the hassock. Richard did not sit. He took a deep sip of wine. "I have some rather distressing news."

Poppy's eyes darted between mother and son. "Couldn't it wait, love? We only just arrived, didn't we?"

Richard examined his wineglass. The tension in the room was palpable and tension was something Georgette could never abide. Richard took another sip. "It's about Hillcrest, you see."

"What about Hillcrest?" Georgette had no interest in Nigel's estate. But Richard was his father's only heir. The house would be his someday and the boy was very keen on his inheritance. It was the reason he had moved to England. Georgette wasn't terribly happy about her son becoming British. Then again, he would have a large inheritance and he would want for nothing and that was no small thing.

"Father may sell."

"Sell Hillcrest?" The news stunned Georgette. In the few years they had been married, Nigel had spoken longingly of his estate. He could not wait to go back to England and occupy the house he inherited. It was one of the reasons they had divorced. Georgette loved New York. She loved acting. Tempting as it might be to become mistress of a large estate in Hampshire and spend her days attending garden parties, Georgette had no intention or desire to leave the States.

"You're an actress," Nigel had argued, spitting the word actress as though he equated it with street walker.

"I like being an actress," she had replied. And so began the argument that eventually pounded a wedge between them.

Nigel finally gave her an ultimatum; he was going to live at Hillcrest. Was she coming along or not? The provocation had been the final sledgehammer blow to a marriage that had been splintering. She stayed in New York with Richard and the nanny.

Nigel had taken little interest in the boy until he reached the age of majority. Then he had insisted that the heir apparent come live in England. Richard had no misgivings about moving to England or about inheriting an earldom and all that the inheritance entailed.

It was because of this that the words 'sell Hillcrest' hung heavily in the air now. "I can't imagine it," Georgette said. "Why would your father sell his estate?'

Richard put down the wine glass. "He may have no choice in the matter."

"No other choice?" To Georgette's mind, men like Nigel always had choices. Being born with an entire set of silverware in your mouth gave one choices.

"He's made a few mistakes."

"What sort of mistakes?" Georgette would not have thought the possibility of Hillcrest being sold would hit her so hard.

"The sort one makes with investments."

"A few bad investments are hardly enough to bring down an empire. If anyone is too rich to foil it's your father. Besides, the family is invested in all sorts of stogy old endeavors. I remember from my provisional days as her ladyship."

"Father decided to be more...innovative...with his investments."

Poppy snorted at this and Georgette cast a hard stare at her, which caused the girl to purse her lips. "Your father may have been a terrible husband, but he was as cautious as a red light when it came to family money."

Richard examined his hands as though he'd never noticed them before. "He may have gotten some bad advice." He put his fingers to his lips.

"Please don't tell me you've begun chewing your nails again." Richard had a terrible habit of biting his nails to nubs as a child. It had taken the nanny, the strict one from Eastern Europe, to cure him by painting them with a bitter tasting substance she had found in some catalog or other.

"Sorry." Richard folded his hands into his lap.

It dawned on Georgette there was something the boy wasn't telling her. "Did you advise your father to make those investments?"

Richard put his head in his hands. Georgette's heart dropped like a runaway elevator. The last thing she'd wanted was for her inference to be right.

Poppy came over to the chair, sat on the arm, and put her hand to Richard's shoulder. "You mustn't blame him. It was Cousin Alex's influence."

Georgette glared at the girl and watched as she turned a satisfying shade of crimson. "Who, pray tell, is Cousin Alex?"

Poppy patted Richard's shoulder as though she were burping a baby. Richard, head still in hands, was unresponsive. "He's my second cousin once removed. He and Richie went to Oxford together. He started a company called Vacu-Sit. They were going to manufacture Hoovers."

"Hoovers? You mean vacuum cleaners?'

"Yeah, like that. Only these ones were to be special, you see. They were ride-ons."

"Ride-ons?" If Georgette hadn't been upset over bad investments she would have grinned at the thought.

"It's a brill idea, actually," Poppy said. "But you need a stack of dosh, don't you? To start up?"

"You need more than dosh." Richard had taken his head out of his hands and looked so forlorn that

Georgette nearly went over to pat him on the back herself. "You need more than a brilliant idea."

"It was a brill idea," Poppy repeated.

Richard got up and began pacing. "It might or might not be. Alex certainly thought it was a fabulous idea. He had us all convinced." He glanced over at Poppy. "Or shall I say fooled? He had no idea how to build them and no idea how to market them. The only thing he knew was how to finance them."

"It was a scam?" Georgette asked.

Richard looked as though he might start to cry. "He had a brilliant presentation, complete with a team of engineers and a plan that would have made CFOs weep for joy. He was going to sell them to seniors." Richard refilled his wine glass until the wine nearly overflowed the glass. "He didn't mention that a single machine would cost ten thousand pounds. Or that they were far too large to use in most living rooms, let alone the small rooms of a pensioner.

"As soon as investments were made, Alex disappeared like a bad magic trick. We found him living in Panama. On our funds."

"He had no intention of building the vacuums?"

"His intentions were good," Poppy said. "Just not thought through is all. Once he realized—" A hard look from Richard made her stop her defense.

"And your father invested in this nonsense?"

"Rather heavily."

"Heavily enough to lose Hillcrest?" Georgette could not believe that this was all there was to the story. It wasn't like Nigel to invest willy-nilly. She would have questioned Richard further but just them the fire alarm went off. Georgette ran to the kitchen. As soon as she opened the door, a dark cloud of smoke escaped the room and overtook her.

Chapter Seven

"Silly thing, really." Peggy held the script to her chest as she addressed the board of Helping Hands.

"A fire isn't silly." The thought of Georgette brought to the hospital for smoke inhalation, even if she was treated and released, upset Tony and he didn't like Peggy brushing it off as though it were nothing.

"No harm, no foul. It was just a little bit of smoke from the oven in Georgette's kitchen. She's fine. The apartment needed a good airing. Though I can't say I blame her for taking her company to the Hamptons for a few days." Peggy cast a furtive glance at Mollie as she put the script down on the conference table.

Mollie hadn't said a word as Peggy explained the circumstances. Until now. "I take it Miss Alden won't be able to do the spots?"

It wasn't enough that Georgette was nearly done in by smoke inhalation. Now Mollie had to use it as a wedge to pry her out of the spots. God, the woman was as irritating as poison ivy. Tony fisted his hands on his lap and worked to keep his voice even. "Why would you think that, Mollie?"

"Well, we need to start shooting next week. Who knows when she'll be back? We have the studio next Thursday, it's all been arranged." Mollie looked like a cat who'd swallowed the goldfish. Hell, she looked like she'd gobbled the entire koi pond.

"Next week?" Peggy asked. From the tone of her

voice, it was apparent Mollie hadn't chosen to share the schedule with her.

"Yes. My sister's husband knows someone with a rather large studio in Paterson. It will be perfect and she's arranged for us to have it for next Thursday."

Saul snorted. Mollie gave him the stink eye and Tony's suspicion grew. "How much is this going to cost us?"

"Not a single penny," said Mollie.

"It won't cost *you* a single penny," added Saul under his breath. The stink eye came again and Saul frowned at it.

"Jane is doing it as a favor. Because she knows what a wonderful cause Helping Hands is."

Saul snorted again. Tony wanted to know more about what Saul had to give Jane for her to be so magnanimous. But he knew Saul wouldn't be dumb enough to disclose it.

"How long is Ms. Alden going to stay in the Hamptons?" Tony asked.

"I'm not sure. She didn't say," said Peggy.

"Could you find out, please?" This caused a hard stare from Mollie, which he ignored, and a blank stare from Peggy, which made him want to shake her. "Do you have a way to contact her?"

Peggy brightened. "Yes! She gave me her cell number. For emergencies, you see."

"Why don't you call her?"

Peggy smiled and nodded. "I could do that."

"How about now?"

"What, right now? In the middle of a meeting?"

Tony sighed. "Since Mollie has been so kind as to find us a studio, we need to find out as soon as possible, don't you think?"

Peggy pulled out her cell phone, fumbled with the keys, and pressed the phone to her ear. She listened and then left a message. "It went right to voice mail. I can try again later."

"Voice mail? We need someone reliable. Not

someone who turns off the cell phone whenever it doesn't suit her to answer." Mollie glared at Peggy, who quickly tucked her phone back into her purse.

Tony wanted to take his own cell phone and hit Mollie over the head with it. She had already ruined a perfectly lovely Friday afternoon by calling an emergency meeting over this nonsense.

"We have to film next Thursday. That's in less than a week. We can't wait forever for Ms. Alden to decide to come back." Mollie turned to Peggy. "Do you have her land line number in Hampton?" Peggy shook her head. "Well, this is just ducky. Though I suppose I could find someone from—"

"No!" Tony was surprised at the force of his voice. So was everyone else at the table. A wonderful terrible idea occurred to him. Maybe there was a way to make lemonade out of these lemons after all. "Do you have Ms. Alden's address in the Hamptons?" he asked Peggy.

"Yes, why?"

"I was planning a weekend out there anyway. A friend has a beach house. Why don't I go talk to her?" For once Mollie was speechless. *Good.* "I think this meeting is adjourned."

He hadn't planned on going to the Hamptons. He didn't know anyone with a house there, beach or otherwise. Well, not quite anyway. Georgette had a house there. Still and all, what he'd told his board was, pretty much, an out and out lie.

Molly eyed him suspiciously as he wheeled out of the conference room. She'd lost this particular battle, but Tony felt sure she was still set on waging a war.

Vida answered the phone on the third ring. Not bad for a Friday night. "Tell me you're wimping out on me tomorrow. I know it's supposed to rain." She'd planned a half-marathon run, thirteen miles through the park, for them in the morning.

"I've got a proposition." Tony wasn't adverse to

Vida's challenges, but he had a whole different sort of challenge in mind.

"I'm listening."

"We postpone for a week." He heard Vida scoff on her end of the line. "And you drive me to Hampton tomorrow."

"Why would I drive you to Hampton in the rain?"

"Personal matter."

"Does it have to do with a certain woman?"

"Yes."

There was a moment of silence in which Tony figured Vida was trying to figure out whether to laugh at him or to chew him out. He decided he'd better sweeten the deal. "I'll spring for ice cream."

"You'll spring for dinner," Vida said.

Tony smiled.

Vida arrived at Tony's door at dawn on Saturday morning. He was still in the T-shirt and shorts he'd slept in. He had, in fact, been asleep when the intercom buzzed and it had taken him a while to get into his chair and answer the door.

"I said morning," Tony grumbled as he let her in. "Five o'clock isn't morning."

Vida eyed his wrinkled T-shirt and sighed. "It is if you want to beat the traffic on the Long Island Expressway."

"You want coffee?"

"No. I want you to get dressed. You can buy me a coffee on the road."

"This favor is going to cost me, isn't it?" Tony wheeled back to the bedroom.

"Anything to help you get laid, sweetums."

Tony stopped and turned the chair to face her. "Don't, okay?"

"I still can't tease you about the lady on the TV screen?"

"No. I have no idea what I'm doing. I've gone completely insane."

Vida put a hand to his shoulder. "Infatuation will do that to a person."

"No, really? What am I doing? Dragging you out to Hampton in the pouring rain to see her on some lame excuse. If I was thinking clearly, I'd let Peggy and Mollie handle it. God knows it would get both of them off my back."

"Oh, I don't know. I've met Peggy. I bet she'd like to handle you."

Tony wheeled to the bedroom again. "Please don't. She'd knit me a sweater vest."

"She called my office to complain I was working you too hard."

"You do work me too hard." Tony pulled slacks and shirt from his closet. The shirt still had the tags, a purchase he'd made at Macy's yesterday afternoon, going all the way down to 34th street. He pulled them off, and looked over his shoulder to make sure Vida hadn't seen him do it. Last thing he needed was teasing about the new duds; he already felt like an idiot for trying to impress Georgette with them.

Vida was sitting on the couch, not paying attention to his wardrobe. He dressed and came back out to the living room. "Where's your bag?" she asked.

"What bag?"

"You said weekend. Weekend is two days."

"Sorry, you misunderstood. I meant to go out and come back today."

"Sheesh." Vida shook her head as she opened the door. "You really don't believe you'll ever get lucky, do you?"

Chapter Eight

The beach house was feet from a wide sand beach and, on hot summer days, cooling breezes came up and danced through the windows. Unfortunately, it was neither summer nor hot. It was April and the weather had turned from sweet spring to shades of late autumn, a cold hard rain pelting the roof shingles and an equally cold wind rattling the windows and sneaking in through the cracks in the sill. The ocean was out there somewhere, buried under a mass of fog and clouds.

The house had been built in the 1940's and the furnace hadn't been replaced. It had radiators that hissed and clunked as though angry gremlins were banging on it with hammers. This, and Poppy's vacant looks and Richard's sour ones, did little to improve Georgette's mood. Neither did the thought that Richard hadn't told her the whole of the story concerning his inheritance and Nigel's estate. She feared she would soon hear from Nigel and she had spent the past twenty years trying hard not to hear from her ex-husband. The only communication they had was in regard to the son they shared. Now, if it was as Georgette feared, that Richard had done something to jeopardize Nigel's precious estate and his standing in the community around it, her ex would let her know he blamed her for everything.

If Richard had any more to say about the financial ruin of Hillcrest or the ruin of his own future, he hadn't indicated. His lips were sealed tight, quite literally, as Poppy prattled on about how she loved walking along the wild ocean during a storm. "It's so thrilling, really, isn't it?"

Richard was barely paying her any attention. He had gathered his laptop and was putting on his raincoat. "I can't believe this place doesn't have Wi-Fi. And my mobile has no signal."

"Service is a little spotty." Georgette had never minded. She had, in the past, come here to escape being at the beck and call of producers and directors and publicists.

Richard didn't share her sentiment. "Spotty doesn't begin to describe it. I saw a coffee shop down in the village. Maybe they can get me connected."

"You should stay here, darling!" Poppy hooked her arm into Richard's and led him to the window. "Take me walking in the rain."

Richard moved Poppy's hand from his arm. "Don't be daft."

Georgette felt a rush of sympathy for the girl. Sure, she had been a near constant annoyance, what with her inane questions and statements. She reminded Georgette of a fly, buzzing around the room while one was trying to rest. But none of that excused her son's boorish behavior. "I think walking in the rain sounds fabulous," she said.

Richard stared at his mother. "You can't be serious."

Well, she wasn't. She just wanted to come to the girl's defense. Now the gauntlet had been thrown and she'd be damned if she backed from the challenge. She went to the coat closet and pulled two slickers out from the back, frumpy things in a God-awful shade of yellow. Georgette hated the thought of looking like a wet ducky. Still, she handed one to Poppy. "Have a wonderful Internet session," she said to her son. "Maybe you can find some sound investments."

The last bit might cause her some regret later, and

Richard's jaw dropped when she said it. She wasn't the least sorry. She had heard the anxious whispered argument between Richard and Poppy through the thin wall that separated their two bedrooms. And, although she hadn't heard all the words exchanged, "not so terrible" had come from Poppy's end of the row clearly enough as had the "you don't have a clue" that had been Richard's response.

Georgette put on the awful slicker and a pair of flip flops and asked Poppy if she were ready. A cold rain assaulted them as soon as they were out the door. They braved the elements and began walking along the beach. Wind kicked up the sand and pelted them, forcing them to watch their feet. They walked on for ten minutes or so before Poppy turned to Georgette. "Maybe we ought to go back."

Georgette would have liked nothing better, but stubbornness prevailed. She pretended she hadn't heard the girl and continued. Five minutes later a swell came up unawares, the surf soaking both of them to the knees. What was she trying to prove? Richard would be long gone by the time they got back. She turned around. "We should get back."

Between the rogue wave, the pelting rain, and the sand, Georgette was limp and exhausted by the time they reached the house. She had never felt quite so glad to be back indoors and, judging by sigh Poppy let out, the girl felt much the same.

Poppy took off her rain-soaked clothes on the way to the bedroom and was naked by the time she got to the door, the clothes trailing behind her like wet breadcrumbs. She put on a robe and began toweling her hair. "That was exciting, wasn't it?"

Exciting? Georgette could scarcely believe her ears. Maybe the girl would find pneumonia exciting, too. Before she could say something she might regret later, Georgette marched off to the bathroom and shut the door firmly behind her. She peeled off her drenched clothes, jumped into the shower, turned the water on full blast and made it hot as she could stand.

Water cascaded down her over tense shoulders. She could have stayed under the stream all day and so took her time lathering up and rinsing. She lathered and rinsed a second time and was letting the water pelt her face when she heard a familiar voice. "God, you are lovely when wet."

Georgette's eyes had been closed and her thoughts miles away. She pulled back from the water to find Harvey Bristol looking her over as though she were on display in a deli case. "Go away." She closed the curtain between them with such force she nearly tore it from the rings.

"Baby doll, I've seen it before. Not that I don't enjoy an encore."

"Maybe you didn't hear me. Go away." She stuck her head back under the flow and counted to ten. A peek around the curtain told her she had made herself clear. She shut off the water and stepped from the shower. She sneezed a few times as she dried herself off; the walk had done more harm than she had imagined and there was the slightest scratch in her throat. Harvey, Poppy, rain and a cold in one day was just too much to bear. She wrapped the towel around herself, ready for a long nap that might help the day get better.

Harvey was lying on the bed. Thank God he was still fully clothed. Georgette stared at him. "Who let you in anyway?"

"This is my house. I have a key."

That was, unfortunately, the truth of the matter. Georgette had rented the house from Harvey on a few occasions and had been his houseguest on a few others. When the apartment filled with smoke, all she could think about was a quick getaway and Harvey's beach house seemed the perfect solution. She had, in her defense, offered to pay rent for the week. Harvey had declined the money. Of course, he'd want some sort of recompense. She might have known.

"That still doesn't give you the right to walk into

the bathroom while I'm showering. It's an invasion of privacy."

"I wanted to surprise you. Not so long ago you would have been happy to have me leer at you in the shower."

"Times change."

"You've changed." Harvey reached out and took her arm. "You're not still mad about Electra, are you? You've got to learn to let go."

"I am still mad. You threw over thirty years of my life in one reckless moment."

"What if I told you I could give it back?"

"You're bringing back Electra?"

"Not exactly."

Georgette's hope sunk as quickly as it had risen. It was just like Harvey—he'd say anything to get her into bed with him and then he'd reverse direction. Well, if he thought for a minute she was going to take off her towel and climb under the sheets, he had another thing coming. Those days were gone. "I didn't come as a bonus with the house. Please leave so I can get dressed."

"Why don't you listen to my proposition? Then you can decide if you want to get dressed."

Georgette marched to the bedroom door and, holding the towel with one hand, yanked the door open with the other. "I'm going to get dressed. Then I'll decide if I want to listen to your proposition."

Harvey got up and went to her. He caressed her shoulder with one hand and kissed her neck before walking out. Georgette slammed the door at his retreating back. "Cocky bastard," she said to the door. She used to like that Harvey was a cocky bastard. Now, it only made her angry and a little sad. She'd had enough of cocky bastards to last her a life time.

She pulled on a pair of slacks and a loose sweater that covered her completely. She was not about to give any sort of signal to Harvey except stop. She brushed her hair, her thoughts drifting toward Tony and how he'd caught her in her workout clothes. Now there was a real hero—no cocky bastard was Tony Rodriquez, though maybe he could use just a touch of Harvey's bravado. At least, with Harvey, she knew where she stood.

She found him in the kitchen with Poppy, regaling her with stories about the network. The girl took to his charming repartee like a honeybee to pollen. "Harvey is doing a Lifetime movie," she told Georgette.

"Is that so?" It occurred to her this was his proposition. She wouldn't mind starring in a Lifetime movie. She'd done it before, years ago, when she'd played the mistress of a powerful tycoon who ended up going back to his long suffering wife.

"It's to be the story of a bond trader who finds happiness as a goat herder." Poppy was gushing like an open faucet. She seemed totally unaware of the way he was ogling Poppy's breasts. Which were, Georgette noted, poorly hidden under a T-shirt without benefit of a bra.

Georgette poured herself a cup of coffee from a freshly made pot. At least the girl was good at something besides showing off her breasts. "Does this movie have anything to do with your proposition?"

"In a way, yes."

Georgette's hopes soared again. She sat at the kitchen table. "I'm listening."

"ColorCare Hair is sponsoring the movie."

"ColorCare Hair covers the gray?" asked Poppy. "They're super! They sell it at Tesco's even."

Harvey nodded at the girl, his eyes still planted on her breasts. "And in every damned store in North America, South America, Australia and Siberia." He flipped his gaze to Georgette. "They want you to be their spokeswoman."

Georgette's hopes sunk again. Starring role in a movie had just become spokesperson for old lady dye. "Why would I want to do that?"

"For God's sake, Georgie. It's national spokeswoman. It would make you a ton of money for starters and it's great exposure."

"As what? A woman who covers her gray?"

"As the sensuous mature woman every woman aspires to become."

Okay, she didn't like the mature part. But the sensuous and aspiring part had appeal. A series of hair commercials would hardly make up for Electra's murder, but it was something. "I suppose you'll want my eternal gratitude."

⁓

Tony watched raindrops splatter against the passenger side window of Vida's SUV. Last night, he'd lain back in bed and imagined a day on the beach with Georgette. She'd been heart stopping in a blue bathing suit, a one-piece—for some inexplicable reason his imagination had refused to put her in a bikini, though it could well envision peeling her out of the one-piece—the suit and her skin both wet with salt water. The rain managed to spoil his fantasy and the windshield wipers seemed to taunt him, whispering *you fool, you fool,* with every swipe.

Vida switched on the radio. The weather report was ominous, the storm would get worse before it got better, with some winds gusting to hurricane strength and a high tide surge that could wash out roads and cause damage to beach front homes. Tony switched off the disembodied voice of the meteorologist. "Maybe we should turn back."

"We're ten miles from the Hamptons. We might as well keep on going." Vida glanced at him. "You grateful I made you pack an overnight bag?"

"I'm sorry I asked you take me to the Hamptons in the middle of a storm."

"Anything for love."

"Seriously." Tony turned from the window to look at Vida's profile. "I'm sorry I got you into this. Driving the length of the L.I.E. isn't anyone's idea of a good time. Not even on a nice day."

Vida turned to look at him for a second. "I'm proud of you," she said before turning her attention back to the road. This came so far out of left field that Tony let go a cough. "I mean it. You're going after what you want. It may not be the right thing to want, but hell, that's not the point."

Tony was turning over the praise when the second part of what Vida had said slapped him like a cold ocean wave. "You don't think I should want Georgette Alden?"

"I didn't say that. You can't help that you're attracted to her. I looked her up online. Hell, I'm attracted to her too. You'd have to be blind not to be. I think it's terrific you're willing to give this a shot. But..." Vida sighed. "Don't take this the wrong way. But you're really not hung up on her because of some adolescent fantasy, are you?"

Tony felt the slightest sting of annoyance. They'd had this conversation and he really didn't want to have it again. "I know the difference between fantasy and reality."

"I know you do. I guess I just don't want you to be disappointed to find out Georgette Alden puts her panties on one leg at a time just like the rest of us mere mortals."

"You had to bring up her panties, didn't you?" Tony grinned at Vida and Vida grinned back.

By the time they pulled off the highway and into the village of Hampton, most of the day had passed and Tony wondered again at his sanity, spending an entire day stuck in traffic in the rain to pay Georgette an unexpected visit must classify as nuts. Still, they were here now and so he found the address Peggy had given him and plugged it into the GPS. A few minutes later, they were parked in the driveway of a two story beach house with a gabled roof and gingerbread trim. Getting into the wheelchair in the pouring rain was a trial. He and Vida were both soaked despite the quick way in which they managed the transfer. There was no ramp, so Vida had to haul him step by undignified step to the porch. By the time they got to the door, Tony was so dejected that he was ready to tell Vida they ought to forget the whole deal. The door swung open wide before he could and he was staring up at a thin young woman, her oversized breasts barely covered by a tank top.

The woman stared back. "Who are you?" Her British accent made the question sound ruder than it might have been.

It was enough to make Vida, who had been grumbling about ramps and inconsiderateness all the way through the porch step ordeal, take the last step up the threshold and stare down at the woman. "We are wet. We are tired. The least you could do is show a little courtesy."

The woman backed up a step. "I'm already in the shit for letting the bloke in. I don't want to make matters worse, do I?"

"Who is it, Poppy?" Georgette came out into the foyer. She looked great in gray slacks and a red sweater that showed off her raven hair. Tony felt his skin heat. Vida was right. He had it bad.

"I can't rightly say."

"You can't—" Georgette stopped short. God, she was beautiful. "Tony?"

"Yes. It's me." Okay, that was dumb.

"Well, don't stay out in the rain, come on in." Vida lifted Tony up the step and the threshold. He watched as Georgette's smile faded just a little. Was she only pretending she was happy to see him ? He chased the thought away.

"Would you like some tea? Coffee? Something stronger to help weather the storm?" Georgette asked as she led them into a living room filled with Victorian furniture. A man was lighting a fire in the grate of an ornate marble fireplace. He stood up when they entered. Tony noted he wasn't particularly tall, but he was handsome enough to pass as George Clooney's brother. "This is my friend, Harvey Bristol," Georgette said. "Harvey, this is Tony Rodriquez. He's the head of

Helping Hands?" This seemed to draw a blank from Harvey. "The PA spots I told you about?"

Still a blank, but Harvey covered well, smiling and holding out his hand. "Of course. Welcome to Mi Casa."

Mi Casa? That couldn't be right. Peggy said "her place in the Hamptons," hadn't she? Or had Tony misunderstood? Or maybe they owned the house together? Tony didn't like that theory at all. Then another thought clobbered him. Peggy had mentioned a man pawing Georgette in the hallway of her apartment building. Tony decided he didn't like Harvey Bristol.

Further introductions were made and the young woman, Poppy, went off to get them all coffee. Was she the maid? Tony wondered. Georgette fetched two towels and he and Vida blotted their clothes and moved closer to the fire. He eyed Harvey as Poppy came back with a tray. The man's eyes were firmly planted on Poppy's barely covered boobs. It was hard not to look—the girl practically had them in a display case. But to stare at them when you already had the gorgeous and curvy Georgette?

Tony took the mug of coffee Poppy offered him. He swallowed back the urge to run Harvey over with his wheelchair and then grab Georgette, set her on his lap and wheel away. *Stop. Georgette and this Harvey guy are probably in a relationship. You're going to have to stop thinking this way.* He took a sip of coffee. "Anyway, Vida and I were in the Hamptons for the weekend." He saw Vida roll her eyes the slightest bit from the corner of his own eye. "And Peggy said you were here. I thought we'd drop by to talk about the PA spots."

Georgette's smile seemed to dim down another notch. Did she not want to do the spots after all? "Mollie has booked us a studio. But it's only available next Thursday. Will that work for you? And for the director?"

"Sure, we should be back in the city by then," Georgette said.

At the same time that Harvey said, "Impossible."

"Is there a problem?" Tony asked.

"Little bit, my friend. Georgette has to meet with the advertising department at ColorCare Hair on Thursday."

"ColorCare Hair covers the gray?" asked Vida.

"That's the one." Harvey smiled at Vida as though she was his prized pupil. "Georgette has agreed to be their next spokesperson."

Georgette frowned at Harvey. "I haven't said yes yet."

"But you will." Harvey was smug. Tony hated smug.

"If and when I do, I'm sure we can work around the PA spots. I did promise Tony and his board."

At least she would do the spots, thought Tony. She'd promised. He wished he had more to offer her. Even Harvey's commercial spots were better than his.

Georgette didn't take her eyes off Vida. If she took her eyes off Vida she would ogle Tony and she was too confused to ogle Tony at the moment. The woman was a statement—an Amazon with flawless mocha skin, she was a work of art. She reminded Vida of Paris McClinton, the tough cop with the heart of gold on *Our Time Tomorrow*. Paris had been Electra's foil, but Georgette had liked Lynn Bowman, the actress who played her. She'd been disappointed when Paris became a vice cop in Hawaii so Lynn could pursue a movie career. At any rate, it hadn't been Paris who stole Electra's man. It had been the other way around.

She hadn't thought about Tony having a girlfriend. She didn't like the thought of Tony having a girlfriend and especially not this girlfriend, who looked like she could take on an entire battalion of Electras.

Harvey was petting Georgette's hair like she were a prize winning poodle. He talked to Tony as if the man were the village idiot just because he happened to be in a wheelchair. Georgette had always known Harvey wasn't the world's greatest guy, but had he always been such an insufferable ass?

"I'll be there for the PA spots next Thursday. I'm sure the hair people can wait."

Harvey shot her a look that could have been bottled and labeled poison. "May I see you in the kitchen, please?" He took her arm and nearly dragged her into the other room and shut the door. "Do you have any idea what I had to do to get the ColorCare people to consider you?"

"You didn't sell your soul. You don't have one."

Harvey ignored the remark. "You cannot be serious about choosing a PA spot for some two-bit charity over a national commercial spot. The rain must have melted your brain tissue."

"Helping Hands is not some two-bit charity. They do great work. And I promised Tony."

"You like him." This came like an accusation out of Harvey's mouth. It sounded so adolescent that it made Georgette laugh. "Jeez, Georgie. The guy is in a wheelchair, or hadn't you noticed? I know how hot your libido runs."

Georgette slapped him. She would have asked him to leave if this wasn't his house. Harvey, mouth opened, put his hand to his cheek. And then the lights went out.

It wasn't fully dark yet, but the gray day made everything dim and the lack of electricity made it even dimmer. A thunderclap rumbled and shook the windowpanes. It felt like a warning and Tony turned to Vida. "If we're going to get back to the city, we should get going soon."

"I thought you were here for the weekend." Georgette took the paper with the address of the studio on it from him.

"We are here for the weekend." Vida shot him an unreadable look he was sure she would interpret for him once they were back on the road.

"With the weather bad as it is, I think we might

better just fold." Tony shot his own look back.

The knock on the door seemed a second sign, made more ominous when Poppy opened the door to two police officers. Georgette blanched when she saw them and this made Tony want to hold her.

Harvey, the bastard, didn't even seem to notice Georgette's distress. "What are you fellows doing out here on such a horrid afternoon?"

"We're evacuating everyone from the shore road," said the elder of the two officers, who looked like he was only a few years from retiring. "I'm afraid we're going to have to ask you folks to leave."

"Leave?" Poppy asked.

The younger officer, a guy in his twenties had been staring at Poppy's breasts. He turned away, his face crimson with the realization that everyone in the room was aware of his preoccupation. "They're predicting a storm surge. It could wash out the roads and cause some damage. We want to make sure no one's hurt. It's a precaution."

"That's ridiculous." Harvey was, once again, proving to Tony what a pompous idiot he was. "This house has been here for eighty years. A big bad storm isn't going to blow it down."

The younger officer took a step back from Harvey's bluster while the older man frowned deeply. "That may be, but we still need to evacuate. The last few storms have caused damage and as my partner said, we don't want anyone getting hurt."

Harvey puffed out his chest ready to confront both officers again. If Tony had learned anything as a director of homeless shelters, it was that you needed to stop these kinds of confrontations before they got out of hand. "Well then, maybe we all ought to go back to the city."

"That may be difficult, sir," said the younger officer. "We've closed some of the roads and traffic out of town is backed up for miles."

Harvey crossed his arms. "So where, exactly, do

you expect us to go?"

"There's a lovely inn in the village. Seacrest, I think it's called." Georgette turned to the officers. "Can we have a little time? I'll have to repack."

The officers, both of them, seemed mesmerized. "Sure, if you don't take too long." The older one tipped his cap.

The only one not under Georgette's spell, it seemed, was Harvey. He turned to her as soon as the officers left, his face still puffed out in anger. "That old inn charges extra for drafts and peeling paint."

"We don't have much choice, Harvey. I know you prefer young and sexy, but you can't always get what you want." Georgette flounced out of the room and Harvey looked as though she'd slapped him.

Poppy called after her. "What about Richard?" Georgette stopped halfway up the stairs and considered. "I'm sure he's warm and dry at the café. We'll get him on our way to the inn."

Chapter Nine

Tony and Vida, already packed and ready, left for the Seacrest Inn soon after. "That was interesting," Vida said as they pulled onto the street.

"She's interesting," said Tony. "You can see why—"

"You lust after her. Hell, yes. If she gave off any more electricity, she would kill people." Vida turned to concentrate on the dark road, which was already a hazard of lake-sized puddles.

Tony wasn't ready to stop talking. His head was full of Georgette and if it was possible, he was even more attracted to her now than he had been before coming to Hampton. "But you think I'm a fool."

"I wouldn't go that far. You're a man and, speaking as your therapist, it's reassuring to know you can still get lusty."

"Only I get lusty over the unobtainable. She's in a relationship."

"You mean that Harvey guy? You could take him."

"Clearly, he has money and clout. And clearly there is something going on between him and Georgette."

"And also clearly—she's not that into him."

Tony wished that he could read hints of "not that into him" with some clarity. He hoped, fervently, that Vida was a better sign reader than he was.

෴

It was decided Poppy would go to the café and pick

up Richard while Georgette and Harvey went ahead and got rooms for them all at the Seacrest Inn. Harvey was still grumbling about leaving.

"You would rather stay here, without electricity, and brave the storm?" Georgette asked him once Poppy had left.

"I shouldn't have to stay in a musty inn with fake antiques." Harvey cocked his head as though he were assessing her value as an antique. "You might convince me if you'll share a room with me."

"What? And have you complain about antiques all night? I don't think so."

"You're a hard woman, Georgie."

Georgette was not about to relent. She didn't want to share a room, let alone a bed with Harvey. Now that he was no longer her boss, she had the ability to look at him with fresh eyes and she wasn't crazy about what she saw. She didn't like to think of herself as an opportunist, but she had been, hadn't she? The only reason she'd ever given Harvey anything but a cold shoulder was because of what he could do for her. She winced at the thought. Well, that was over now. It was true, despite her claims otherwise, she wanted the commercial spot he'd gotten her. It would mean income and national exposure. But she would give it all up in a heartbeat if it meant breaking a promise to Tony. Wouldn't she?

"I'm leaving now. Where are the keys to your Mercedes?"

"I'm not letting you drive my Mercedes."

"Then you'll take me to the inn like a good boy."

He sighed deeply and found the keys. He wasn't going to stay and get swept away by the ocean after all.

The Seacrest Inn was inviting despite what Harvey had said about it. It had a cozy common room with chairs you could sink into and a fire burning in a fieldstone hearth. Dried flowers hung from rafters overhead.

Georgette shook off her umbrella and went to the

desk, figuring how many rooms they needed. One for Richard and Poppy—she hoped Richard could tear himself away from the café, he'd have to once they closed at any rate, one for herself. Harvey could get his own room. As for Tony and Vida—were they coming here? Tony had mumbled something about not making a reservation and Vida had said something like "I told you so" before they'd left.

Tony showing up at the beach house unannounced would have been perfect if only Harvey and Poppy and Vida hadn't been there. Vida—what was Georgette to make of the beautiful mocha Amazon?

Georgette got so far lost in her thoughts, which included a fantasy of sharing a room with Tony while the Amazon slept elsewhere (with Harvey perhaps?) that she barely heard the desk clerk. She threw the young man a hard stare and said "What?"

The clerk went three shade of red. "I'm so sorry. It's the storm. We're completely booked."

"Then where are we to go?" Georgette asked as Harvey, who had dropped her at the door before parking the car, walked into the lobby like a bear who'd been woken from hibernation during a rainstorm.

"No rooms," she told him as he came to the desk.

"There is a makeshift shelter set up at the high school," the clerk said. "I can give you the address."

Harvey examined the clerk as though the young man had grown a second head. "You expect me to sleep on a cot in some high school auditorium like some kind of homeless waif?"

"I think it's the gym, sir. Where the cots are?"

Harvey looked like he might punch the poor clerk. He might well have had the door not opened again. Vida was struggling to get the wheelchair over the threshold. "Does nobody here believe in ramps?" she asked when Georgette came to help.

Tony took the wheels into his powerful arms, and wheeled towards the desk. "I'll do the rest myself." He didn't sound too happy with Vida and looked nearly as angry as Harvey.

The anger must have been catching, because Georgette felt it, too. "They are completely booked," she told Tony.

Harvey was arguing with the clerk, threatening law suits and various other forms of unpleasantness. Georgette had to admire the clerk's fortitude. He just kept saying, "I'm sorry, sir. There's nothing I can do." She also admired the fact that he hadn't tried to spear Harvey with the pen on his desk. Something Georgette probably would have done in his position.

"I'm going back to the house," Harvey said, when he finally came to realize this was one battle he wouldn't win.

"Suit yourself," Georgette said. "I myself am not afraid of spending the night in a high school gym. It will be an adventure."

Harvey snorted. "Right. You're going to sleep on a cot next to a bunch of snoring strangers. News flash— they don't have room service and there's no ocean view."

Georgette hated Harvey at the moment. No, hate implied she cared what he thought. Of course she liked nice things. Who didn't? But to insinuate she was incapable of functioning without someone waiting on her hand and foot? He didn't know her very well. She was the daughter of a truck driver, for God's sake. Not some hot-house princess.

Tony wasn't crazy about the idea of sleeping in a school gym. The chair would be a bigger impediment there than it was at home. He'd need help getting in and out, the cot would slip along the floor if Vida, or someone, wasn't there to anchor it, and he couldn't wheel up stairs no matter the weather. He hated the lack of independence. Moreover, he hated the idea of Georgette seeing him at his most vulnerable. He would have to admit, though, that sleeping in the same room with her had a certain appeal.

The gym wasn't as crowded as he'd thought it would be. There was a long folding table just outside the door with a couple of folding chairs and a bunch of papers stacked on them. A young woman with a tag that said, "Lydia, Red Cross Volunteer" stuck to her T-shirt put a few of these papers onto a clipboard and handed them to Vida. "We're a handicapped facility," she spoke over his head as though he weren't there.

"Good to hear," he said, wanting to speak up for himself. Lydia smiled at him, a little too indulgently for his taste.

"I think I can get you those two cots near the door. You'll be closer to the restrooms that way."

Tony was going to ask Lydia if she thought he had bladder trouble, but Vida shot him a look and said, "That would be perfect."

"That would be perfect," Tony mimicked rolling his eyes as they set their things on the two cots appropriated for them.

"Get over it. You will not grumble about this, hear me?"

"I know. I owe you. I'll let you beat me in our next race."

Vida stopped to look towards the door where Georgette had just walked in. It seemed to Tony as though theirs was not the only conversation that stopped on Georgette's account.

Vida winked at him. "You're going to owe me even more, lover. I'm about to make your dreams come true." With that, she walked over to Georgette, who was being handed a clipboard by Lydia. Vida said a few words and Lydia smiled over at him and nodded.

Tony nodded back. A few minutes later, Georgette was walking over to his cot with Vida.

"Seems I've snagged the cot right next to yours," Georgette said, setting her bag on the cot next to Tony's.

Vida to the right of him and Georgette to the left, it was going to be an interesting night. "Good. I hate to sleep alone." Tony had meant it as a joke, but the minute the words fell from his mouth he heard how awkward they sounded. Georgette bit her lip. She was lovely when she bit her lip.

Vida laughed. "We'll have a sleepover. Anybody bring snacks and teen magazines?"

"Shoot, I left my nail polish at home. Or we could have done each other's nails," Georgette said. Tony would put up with pink nails if Georgette painted them.

Tony grabbed his shaving kit. "Since we're so close to the rest rooms, I might as well brush my teeth." He wheeled off and Georgette found herself left alone with Vida.

"I think I forgot my toothbrush," Vida said.

"I might have an extra." Georgette hunted through her bag and pulled out a still wrapped pink brush. "Here you go. Compliments of the house." She nodded towards the door. "He's pretty remarkable, isn't he?" Tony's chair disappeared around the corner.

"How so?"

"He's...smooth, I guess. It can't be easy for him, having to deal with situations like this."

Vida stopped pulling the wrap off the new toothbrush to study her and Georgette wondered if she'd said something offensive. She certainly hadn't meant to be offensive. "Tony's had to deal with a lot of things. And yeah, he's pretty remarkable." With that Vida picked up her makeup bag. "Thanks for the toothbrush," she said and she was out the door after Tony.

Was she storming off? Georgette couldn't quite read the woman—joking one minute and dead serious the next. Maybe Vida had figured out Georgette was attracted to Tony. She *was* attracted—he was capable and kind and he had those great limpid dark eyes. Not to mention a pair of arms that would make any woman swoon. Electra Holmes would have acted on her feelings in a heartbeat, no matter that it hurt Vida. But Georgette drew the line at other women's lovers.

Her musings were about to take another roll through her head when she saw Poppy and Richard. Lydia, the Red Cross volunteer, handed a clipboard to Richard and told them something with arms waving around.

Georgette walked over and Richard turned to her. "It's not the Ritz, is it?" It seemed like a rhetorical question so Georgette didn't answer. Richard nodded towards Lydia, "The concierge over there informs us that we'll be staying in the cafeteria. I've always wanted to sleep with the smell of canned corn wafting through the air."

Poppy gave him a little shove. "It won't be so bad, now will it? It's an adventure."

Richard scoffed. "Some adventures I could do without."

Georgette didn't know which was worse, Richard's churlishness or Poppy's lemonade-from-lemons attitude. She was glad they wouldn't be staying in the gym and then felt ashamed that she felt glad. She pointed to the cot where her bag rested. "I'll be in bed number three if you need me."

"You mean if eau-de-fish sticks gives me nightmares?" Richard asked. Vida had returned to her cot, nearest the door. Richard's attention turned to her. "The dark goddess could comfort me."

Georgette was about ready to take her boy aside and remind him that it was impolite to lust after another woman aloud with your girlfriend standing next to you. But Poppy seemed to take it all in good stride, punching Richard lightly on the arm. "I know her. She's called Vida and I daresay I have a better chance with her than you."

Where in the world did the girl get her notions? Though Georgette half hoped those notions had some merit, she considered the source. Poppy thought rides on vacuum cleaners were a 'brill' idea. She was hardly an expert on anything.

Georgette grabbed her overnight bag and went to

the rest room. There was something unsettling about washing up in a public bathroom. She cut her ablutions short; brushing her teeth and removing her makeup. She rinsed her face and thought about the public sleeping arrangements and Vida and Tony—sleeping on the cot next to hers. She fished her lipsticks from the bag, decided on cherry red to match her nails and reapplied. Then she took out the mascara. She was about to apply the wand to her eyelashes when she remembered how she'd looked like a ravaged raccoon the last time she'd slept with eye makeup on. She closed the tube. Last thing she wanted to do was scare Tony when he awoke.

Next came an inner debate about clothes. Georgette had thought to pack a nightgown, a frilly, shear thing that she'd bought at Victoria's Secret. She chided herself for thinking this would be appropriate attire for a sleepover with a hundred strangers. She went to the stall, took off her bra and put her sweater back on. She'd leave on her slacks as well even though it meant she'd be a rumpled mess before this ordeal was over.

The lights in the gym had been dimmed and the large room swam in a blue florescence that made everyone look anemic. A family of six had moved into the cots next to hers. They had pushed six cots together in a sort of huddle and had pushed Georgette's cot closer to Tony's. The space between her cot and his was nearly erased, a defile that could easily be reached across. Under other circumstances, Georgette would have marched over to Lydia and demanded her private space back. Tony was already tucked into his cot, his head within easy reach of her pillow, so Georgette silently thanked the family and hoped that lack of makeup and bad lighting didn't make her look like she ought to be featured in a horror film.

Vida had already fallen asleep on her cot. Georgette walked past her, smiled at Tony and climbed into her own bed. "Sleep well."

He sighed and blinked at the ceiling. "You too."

She lay down and closed her eyes. A toddler cried and was soothed by a soft feminine voice. There were whispers and footsteps as people settled into their spots. Then the room quieted to coughs and snores. Georgette counted backwards from three hundred and got all the way to zero. She tried telling each of her extremities to relax, starting with her toes and moving to her ankles and legs, then to her fingers and hands and arms. None of her body parts listened to her directive. The cot mattress was thin and the cot frame dug into her back. The sheets were scratchy and smelled of laundry. The pillow was rock hard.

Georgette rolled to her side and punched the pillow a few times in a futile effort to fluff it. "You can't sleep either?" Tony's whisper was like a rich hot cup of cocoa. She turned to her other side to see him watching her, his lipid eyes a reflection of his voice.

"No," she said. "It's not the Ritz, is it?"

Tony laughed softly. "It's not even the Dew Drop Inn."

"Makes me think about how awful it must be to be in a homeless shelter." Had those words really dropped from her mouth? She quickly amended them by adding, "Not that Helping Hands doesn't do great work—"

"It's okay. I know what you mean. No one wants to sleep among a hundred snoring strangers who haven't washed in a while."

"Well, yes. But it's better than sleeping on the street. Or out in a storm, I'd think."

"I'd love to expand Helping Hands to include a jobs program and help people find homes in their communities."

"That's a wonderful idea."

"But our funds are limited. Some of our clients don't mind being homeless, but a lot of them just don't have any means at all."

"They got caught in something beyond their control?" Georgette thought for a moment about Electra being written off the show. Had they killed the character off back when Georgette was just starting out, she would have been out of money. And maybe out on the street, who knew?

"Yes. That's why the PA spots are important. We need to raise awareness."

An idea hit Georgette so hard that she sat up on the cot. "We should do a documentary. That would really raise awareness."

"*We* should?" Tony raised his eyebrows.

"I could produce it. I don't have a lot of experience, but I do have connections and I think it would be wonderful to try. We could find a director." She lay back down, caught up in the excitement of her wonderful new idea.

Tony smiled at her; his eyes were beautiful even in this awful light. "I'm hungry. Perhaps we could talk about it over snacks? I saw some vending machines out in the hall." He struggled to sit up in the cot and looked uneasily to the wheel chair that sat in the space between him and Vida.

Georgette's first thought was to offer to help him into the chair, but then she remembered the way he'd looked when Vida had wheeled him into the gym, the way he'd said, "I can still do the bathroom by myself," as though warning Vida away. She fished out her purse from under the cot. "I'm buying. What's your pleasure? Chips? Pretzels? An assortment of fine cheese snacks?"

Tony smiled. "I have a hankering for barbeque chips. You think they have those or are they too exotic?"

"I'll see what I can do," Georgette said.

Tony watched Georgette walk off on stocking feet and for about the hundredth time since he'd laid eyes on her, he wished fervently that his legs still worked the way they were supposed to. He wished he could run off after her, catch her in the hall. They would examine the contents of the vending machine and laugh about the choices. They would sit on the floor in the hall with their backs to the wall and share snacks like a couple of teenagers.

That line of wishful thinking would get him nowhere except into a deep gully of depression. He could hear Vida's voice is in his head "What are you complaining about?" she would ask him. "You have Georgette Alden, beautiful vibrant Georgette, camped out on a cot within touching distance. She is right now buying you snacks. So shut up and enjoy the moment."

Tony glanced over at his sleeping friend. She was curled on the cot with one hand under her pillow. He had to admire her ability to sleep in this place. And he also wanted to thank her for being such a sound sleeper and giving him time alone with Georgette.

Georgette—who was walking towards him now, her arms laden with goodies. She dumped the pile of snacks on his cot. "No barbeque chips. I didn't know what else you wanted, so I got everything."

"You bought out the vending machine?" Tony grinned ear to ear.

"I did not." Georgette put her hand to her hip and feigned indignation. "I bought one of each. Then I ran out of change."

"I'm bowled over." He was.

Georgette sat at the foot of his cot and began sorting through the goodies. "We have all the basic food groups—chips, cookies, chocolate and life savers." She held up a Slim Jim. "And these. I'm not sure how they fit into the food pyramid."

"It's a food pie plate now." He took the Slim Jim from her. "This supplies essential protein to the diet and contains a full day's worth of fat and salt." He peeled back the plastic, broke the Slim Jim in half and handed half to Georgette. "Here's to good food."

Georgette touched her half to Tony's. "And great company."

Tony couldn't remember feeling this happy in a long time. He devoured his half and tore into a bag of chips. He would eat all the snacks she'd brought, no matter that it would probably mean he'd have to live with indigestion for the rest of the night and well into tomorrow. A little bout of intestinal discomfort was a small price to pay for the wonder of Georgette's company.

Georgette nibbled at the Slim Jim. "Interesting consistency."

Tony offered her a chip. "This pairs well with the smoky sausage flavor."

Georgette jumped up. "I forgot the drinks! There's a soda machine next to the snacks. Alas, I am out of change."

Tony fished his wallet from an overnight bag. "Drinks are on me. I think we might need them after the salt fest."

"I think you're right. Cola? Or shall I bring an assortment?"

"Cola would be perfect." Tony wanted to add something about Georgette being perfect, too. He ate another chip instead.

Georgette was gone and back in a few minutes. They devoured a second bag of chips and some pretzels. "We should save the candy bars for dessert."

"Or breakfast."

"Good golly. I hope we'll be out of here by breakfast."

The statement panged at Tony's heart. He wanted to stay forever in the gym with Georgette. Clearly, she didn't share his sentiment. "Well, I'm sure the storm will clear out before long."

"Will you go back to the city when the roads open?"

"I think so. You?"

Georgette sighed deeply. "Yes. I'm sure the apartment is fine by now. Cleaners came in yesterday." She took a sip of soda. "I suppose I should go check on Harvey first. He decided to stay at the house, the fool."

Harvey in the conversation felt like a bright hard pinch to wake Tony out of his reverie. Georgette was not his girlfriend. She was barely even a friend. "Are you worried about him?"

"About Harvey?" Georgette snorted out a laugh. "He's the most self-serving son of a bitch that ever lived." She took another chip. "I didn't just say that out loud, did I?"

"I'm afraid you did. Should I alert the media?"

Georgette sighed. "He thinks a TV commercial is going to make up for what he did to Electra. As if."

Georgette's eyes flared and it seemed she was off somewhere. Tony wasn't sure he should encourage her. Though, honestly, he liked hearing her talk trash about Harvey. "What did he do?"

"He's the producer of *Our Time Tomorrow*. He's the one who signed off on her death. He told me they wanted young and sexy. Young and sexy, can you imagine? I poured my heart and soul into that show and then I get discarded like an old pair of boots." Georgette blinked, her face flushed. "Oh God, I'm sorry. I shouldn't rant at you."

"Don't be sorry. It's fine." Tony wanted to tell her how alive he felt with her sitting on his cot. He wanted to tell her how happy he was to listen to her rants and eat junk food with her. He would have told her if he had any nerve at all. Or if Vida hadn't chosen that moment to wake up.

⁓

Vida sat up and blinked a few times, as though she didn't quite know where she was. Georgette marveled that she could have slept so deeply and then wished that she'd stayed asleep so she could have more time with Tony. She got off Tony's cot to sit on her own.

"What's all this?" Vida pointed to the snack assortment piled out on Tony's cot. "You had a party and didn't invite me?" Georgette might have thought Vida was angry and hurt, but her tone and smile said otherwise.

"We knew you'd take our sugar fix away." Tony

turned to Georgette. "Vida is a tyrant when it comes to nutrition. She thinks this stuff ought to be illegal." He handed Vida a chocolate bar. "But she can be bribed."

"No jail time." Vida unwrapped the candy bar. "But you're going to have to train twice as hard next week."

"Slave driver."

Vida looked at Georgette. "He thinks he's going to be able to wheel in the marathon on this diet. I don't think so."

"Marathon?" Georgette asked.

"This guy wheels in the NYC marathon, wheelchair division. He had a chance to beat his last year's time." Vida pointed the candy bar at Tony. "If he keeps eating this stuff, he'll be lucky if he finishes."

Georgette didn't know what to think. "I didn't mean to sabotage you."

Tony smiled. "I'm the one who asked for snacks." He threw an empty chip bag at Vida. "Touch the stash, woman, and you will find a few fingers missing."

Vida caught the bag and crumpled it. "That is what all addicts say. We'll let it go this time, stress and emergency situation and all that. Also, I've been bribed with chocolate." She took a bite of the candy bar.

Georgette might have brought up her wonderful idea for a documentary again. She had intended to do just that before Vida joined the party. But Vida had joined the party and now Georgette felt like a third wheel. If she were being honest with herself, something she found herself being more and more these days, she would have admitted the only reason she would work to put together a documentary was for Tony. Listening to the easy banter between Tony and Vida reminded her Tony wasn't available.

"Maybe I should try to get some sleep," Georgette said.

"Really? All hopped up on caffeine and sugar?" He was kidding, but there seemed to be a hint of disappointment in his voice. No, she was just imagining it. He was being nice. Being nice was what he did.

"It's been a very long day." With that, she lay down and turned her back to Vida and Tony. The caffeine and sugar were doing a tarantella in her brain and it was hard to settle in. Tony and Vida talked quietly for a few more minutes—something about going back to the city and hoping the roads would be okay. Georgette was relieved that the banter was done and was even more relieved when, a few minutes later, the conversation stopped all together.

When Tony woke up the next morning, the cot where Georgette had slept was empty. The blanket was smoothed down over the sheets and her bag was missing. It was as though she had never been there at all.

Snack wrappers were littered around the cot, the remnants of a party that had never gotten off the ground. He began sorting the trash from the leftover snack packs into two piles in his lap.

"Breakfast?" Vida was sitting on her bed, watching him.

"I smell coffee." Tony held up a toffee bar. "Toffee and coffee, a rhyming combination."

"Yum." Vida glanced over at the empty bed and raised her eyebrows.

Tony felt obligated to answer her unasked question. "She said something last night about wanting to make sure the beach house hadn't floated out to sea."

Vida seemed satisfied with his explanation, though Tony found he wasn't. "Maybe we should stop at the beach house on the way home?" he asked.

He hoped Vida wouldn't ask him just how desperate he was to see Georgette again. She didn't. "Sure, why not?" she said and then got up and began packing her things together.

The roads were all reopened, including the beach road. The house looked the same as it had yesterday, not a shingle or clapboard out of place. Harvey was loading a suitcase into a Mercedes, which was the only car in the driveway.

Vida pulled in beside the parked car and Tony rolled down the window. "Looks like you and the house both weathered the storm."

Harvey trotted over to Tony's opened window. "Never a question that it wouldn't. You could have stayed here and spared yourself a night at the discomfort inn."

"We had a fabulous time. Didn't Georgette tell you?"

"I haven't seen her. Knowing Georgie, I figured she'd still be fast asleep. Then again, she isn't used to less than five-star conditions."

Tony didn't like Harvey's assessment of Georgette. "She made it fun, actually. She must have headed back to the city." Tony wondered, though not aloud, how she could have left without saying goodbye.

The apartment had been repainted in the same buttery colors as before. The furniture had been shampooed and the draperies dry cleaned and re-hung on the windows. Georgette breathed in the freshness as though it were a remedy for the long and arduous weekend.

"I'm going to take a nap," she told Richard and Poppy. "I didn't sleep well last night." They didn't argue. Georgette knew they had spent a sleepless night as well. Richard had woken her at six o'clock and asked if she were ready to go home. Since they had the only available car—Harvey had dropped her off at the high school the night before with another warning about how awful it would be—she had little choice in the matter. She gathered her things and did a hasty wash up in the rest room. She had wanted to leave Tony a note, but Richard grabbed her bag as soon as she came out of the restroom.

Now, laying in the comfort of her bed, with the

Egyptian cotton sheets and the silk duvet cover, the curtains closed to turn the room a lovely shade of gray, Georgette still couldn't drift off to sleep. Bone tired, she closed her eyes. Her body ached and begged her to succumb, but her brain raced and hummed over the events of the last day and night, resting again and again on Tony: Tony showing up unexpected at the beach house, Tony in the cot grinning at her silly offering of snacks from the vending machine. The pictures in her head made her warm all over and would have been perfect but for one thing—they were always amended by Vida. This wasn't, after all, a soap opera, where one lover could be dumped unceremoniously off a cliff to make room for a new love.

Chapter Ten

When the phone rang on Monday morning, Georgette harbored a fleeting hope it was Tony calling. It wasn't Tony but Harvey, who had gone into his office bright and early and set up a meeting with the ColorCare Hair people. "We're all set for Thursday morning. You can thank me later."

Georgette put the phone down for a moment so she wouldn't do something foolish, like throw it across the room. Once she composed herself, she picked it back up. Harvey hadn't hung up. "I can't do Thursday, you know that."

"No, I don't know that."

Georgette put the phone down a second time, took a deep breath and picked up again. "I'm shooting the public announcement spot for Helping Hands on Thursday."

"Oh for the love of God, Georgie, you can't be serious about turning down a national TV spot for some voluntary local yokel thing."

"I can and I will. Either you change the meeting or you can count me out."

"You don't want to blow your chance with these people." Harvey sounded slightly desperate.

Desperation could only mean one thing—there was something in it for him because Harvey did nothing out of the goodness of his own heart. "Well, if they can't change a silly little meeting, then I don't think I want to work with them anyway." With that, Georgette hung up. She hoped she was right about Harvey, because she needed the commercial spot.

She wouldn't have needed it quite so much if it weren't for Richard. On the ride home from the Hamptons, Richard told her he had no money in his bank account.

She figured he had misspent it on this crazy venture of his. Money was something one could make more of. "But you have a good job." Georgette was going to add "trading bonds" but, quite honestly, she wasn't exactly sure what it was Richard did in London.

Richard had pretended to watch the road signs, though they were still miles from the city and until then all he had to do was stay on the highway. "I don't work there anymore."

"You lost your job?" The idea sent a jolt through Georgette. Electra's murder made her sensitive to these issues.

"It lost me." Richard's eyes went to the rear view. Poppy had climbed into the back seat when they'd left the shelter and fallen asleep by the time they got on the L.I.E.

Something else occurred to Georgette. "You haven't told Poppy, have you?"

"It wasn't supposed to go like this." Richard sounded like he had at eight, when he'd broken Georgette's favorite vase by throwing it off the apartment roof. He had told her he thought crystal was shatter proof.

"How was it supposed to be?" Georgette felt like she ought to give Richard a time out.

"It was... I was supposed to be an entrepreneur. I was going to be the next Steve Jobs."

"You were peddling vacuum cleaners, not founding Microsoft."

"That was Bill Gates."

"Bill. Steve. I don't much care. How do you plan to support yourself?"

Richard looked hurt. "I thought I could stay with you for a while. There are plenty of jobs in New York. I'm sure I can find one."

"What about Hillcrest? You were very excited about being an earl."

"Father is hale and healthy. And I told you, he may sell the estate."

Georgette thought through the conversation. In her estimation, Nigel would just as soon sell his liver as sell his ancestral estate. After she hung up on Harvey, the phone rang again and this phone call proved that her opinion of Nigel was spot on.

"I hear he's crawled back to Mumsy," her ex-husband said by way of greeting. Not auspicious since Georgette hadn't spoken to him in months.

"How are you, Nigel?" she asked as sweetly as she could manage. She was sure he heard the sarcasm laced through the syrup.

Nigel cleared his throat. There was a moment of silence. Georgette hoped he was clearing his anger away. Quite honestly, it wasn't like Nigel to be rude. In the better times between them, she had teased that he was lord of the manners. He must have been beside himself about Richard and the money he'd lost.

"In answer to your question," she said, though Nigel hadn't asked a question. Not yet, at any rate. "Richard told me about your financial troubles. I'm sorry about Hillcrest."

"What about Hillcrest?" There was another moment's silence in which Georgette made ready to further explain, though it was hardly necessary, and she would have done just that had not Nigel let out a large gaffaw. "You haven't bought into his scheme, have you?" Nigel sounded almost, but not quite, concerned. Then, as though remembering what she'd said, he asked again, "What about Hillcrest?"

"Richard says you may need to sell."

There was a cough and another barking laugh at the other end of the line. "Sell? Have you gone mad?"

"Richard told me you invested rather heavily in his vacuum cleaner enterprise. Though, quite honestly, I can't imagine you'd do such a thing."

"That may be, my dear Georgette, because I would never do such a thing."

It was her turn to take a pause. "Why would Richard lie?"

"Surely you can figure it out. You are not as lame brained as all that." When she didn't answer, he did it for her. "He wants your shelter and your money. He needs to reestablish himself with that girl of his. No matter the little hussy nearly ruined him with this foolish scheme."

Georgette couldn't help smiling at "little hussy." She also couldn't help needling Nigel. "I rather like the little hussy."

"You would. The two of you are peas in a pod."

"Peas in a pod?" Georgette let out a laugh and contained an urge to tell her ex where he could take his opinion.

"She could learn a thing or two about gold digging from you. You are the master."

"What?" The indignation she felt was palpable. Consider the source, she told herself. Revisionist history was Nigel's specialty. Of course he'd revised the reasons for the breakup of their marriage. He'd had twenty years to fashion a new story. Then something else occurred to her. "You didn't cut him off, did you? Because of Poppy? Tell me you are not that petty."

"He wants to marry the girl. I don't want him to make the same mistakes I made."

"I can't believe you."

"He tried to bilk me out of money. Though that was all the girl's doing. He's besotted. It's simple, really. He gets rid of the girl and he gets Hillcrest. He needs to make a choice."

"I am glad I divorced you," she said before hanging up the phone.

Georgette wanted to give Richard a piece of her

mind. She hated being lied to and hated being made part of some scheme. Richard, though, was her son and he had inherited more from her that his good looks; he had inherited a sense of romance. It was terribly romantic to choose the girl over his father's ancestral estate. Terribly stupid, too, and Richard might well come to regret his decision, but Georgette had to admire him for it. Even if Poppy was a twit.

Well, twits could be remade. She pledged again to take Richard's girlfriend under her wing. She would reshape Poppy. Into what, she wasn't quite sure.

On Tuesday, Peggy came by to revise the script. It was a perfect time to begin the reshape-Poppy program. The girl was amazingly good at creating advertising copy and, by the time they had finished, the spot was so good that Georgette could not imagine anyone who wouldn't pick up the phone and make a donation to Helping Hands after seeing it.

Peggy, too, seemed astonished it was as good as it was. "Straight forward, to the point and very poignant," she said grinning at Poppy. "How do they say in England? Well done, you!"

Poppy blushed at the compliment. "I liked doing it. Better than trying to sell vacuums, isn't it?"

Georgette began to understand how Richard could have been taken in by a vacuum scheme. Poppy could sell water to fish. Only one hard sell remained. "What about Mollie?" Mollie had decided, at the last minute, that she would not involve herself in what she termed "the butchering of my script." Peggy waved her hand in the air. "Leave her to me. There is no way she could not love this spot."

Georgette could think of several ways, but she was more than happy to leave the convincing to Peggy. "Then we should be all set for Thursday."

"What about the director?" Peggy asked.

Georgette had been trying to call him since she got

home. She got his voice mail each time and he hadn't called back. "If I don't hear from him by tomorrow, I'll go over and see him personally."

"That would be fabulous!" said Peggy. And Georgette almost liked her enthusiasm.

In a small corner of her brain, Georgette worried that Kent had come to a grievous end. He hadn't answered her phone calls and he *was* an old man. Besides which, he hung around with radicals who wanted to free wild animals from zoos. She didn't want to be the one to discover him lying helpless, or worse, not breathing, in a puddle of blood on his bathroom floor and, not wanting to face disaster alone, she decided to continue the Poppy make-over program by bringing the girl along with her.

Her worries were laid to rest when Kent buzzed them into his apartment and greeted them at the door looking spry in a tiger-striped polo shirt and matching tiger-striped sweat pants.

"I called you several times. You didn't answer your phone." Now that her fears had been allayed, Georgette was not above being annoyed with the old man.

Kent leaned in close, his crepe paper cheek touching hers and whispered "I think my phone is bugged."

"Bugged?" The only thing bugged, as far as she could see, was Kent Markham's brain.

"Shh." Kent, finger to his lips, looked like a cartoon character. He motioned them into the living room and shut the door. "I knew you'd come by. You have good instincts." He nodded to Poppy. "And you brought reinforcements." He picked up a large coil of rope that lay on the floor next to a tool box, a ladder, and a roll of duct tape.

"What's all this?" Poppy looked more amused than horrified.

"Georgette hasn't given you the details?"

"You didn't give us any details." Georgette, thankful her years as an actress could match her rising distress, kept her voice even.

"We meet outside the penguin enclosure right before the zoo closes. Then we liberate them!"

Georgette thought it best to let the old man talk on about his fantasy. "Who are we? Are there others?"

The old man sat down. "You don't need to know." He nodded again to Poppy who was staring at him open-mouthed and twinkle-eyed. "It's better you don't know, less chance for snafus. The plan is simple—we climb into the enclosure and hand them out and put them into cat carriers. Then we bring them to Central Park and let them fly free."

Poppy's twinkle-eyed look had become a stare. "Release them in the park? Poor little blighters will get run over, won't they?"

Together, they could guide Kent back toward reason. Georgette was glad she'd thought to bring Poppy along.

Kent considered. "You might have a point."

"I mean, you have to bring them home, don't you? To Antarctica?"

Georgette would need to get her hearing checked. Had the girl just suggested stealing penguins and sending them to Antarctica?

Even Kent's smile faded at the suggestion. "Air travel is expensive."

"Maybe you should raise some money first, then? Before you release them?" The girl was crazy like a fox.

Georgette's faith in her returned. She offered up reinforcement. "Raising money is a wonderful idea."

"But we're all set to release them tonight."

"They can wait just a little longer, don't you think? We have the PA spot filming scheduled for tomorrow morning. Why don't we work on that and then we can figure out how to raise money for the penguins?" Distraction seemed a good way to go.

Kent took the paper with the studio's address on it.

Poppy furrowed her brow. "Why do you want to free them anyway? The penguins?'

They had finally gotten Kent's attention away from his lunatic cause and here Poppy was, bringing it front and center again. Kent began pacing. He lectured for quite some time on sentient beings, animal rights, and unlawful imprisonment. And just when Georgette thought the lunacy was winding down, Poppy said, "I'd never considered it quite that way. It's unfair, isn't it?"

Georgette saw it would be up to her to contain it. She went over to the old man and patted his arm. "Kent, you must put the breakout on hold. You do not want to endanger the poor creatures. Central Park is full of danger."

Kent sat down, his agitation drained away and replaced by despair. He put his head in his hands. "How will we ever get them home?"

Poppy sat down next to him and took his hand. "I'll help you find a way."

She would what? Comforting the poor old coot was one thing. Aiding and abetting was quite another.

Chapter Eleven

Tony wasn't thrilled about being stuffed into Mollie Hammerstein's car on Thursday morning to be driven— or as Tony thought of it, escorted—through the early morning Manhattan streets to the Hot Times Studio in Paterson, New Jersey.

Mollie had taken on the role of conquistadora, ready to reign over her spoils, which in this case was a day at the studio she'd acquired to do the PA spot. She did have a right to be proud—everything seemed to be going along marvelously for the spot—they had a place, the new script was quite good, and Peggy had told them that both Georgette and her director would be available all day.

The studio was in an old warehouse, a nondescript brick building and nothing like what Tony imagined when he pictured a "movie studio." Mollie parked alongside several other cars. "Oh good, the others are here." How she could possibly know if the cars belonged to the crew or a group of longshoremen was beyond him. She retrieved a box of donuts she'd gotten before picking him up and got out Tony's chair. Tony had gotten pretty good at maneuvering himself in and out of the chair, though proving this to Mollie seemed impossible and she insisted on "helping him" by clasping onto his arms with a vise-like grip and lifting in a way that made it harder for him to transfer. He did manage and even managed to thank Mollie, who meant it well at any rate.

The directory in the lobby said the Hot Times studio was on the first floor. They went down a deserted hallway to double doors with a plaque that announced they'd found the place. Music flowed out from behind the doors along with some soft moaning.

"We are not using that soundtrack for the commercial," Mollie said. Tony didn't think they would, but was glad to hear Mollie wasn't fond of the music either, which sounded like the kind of thing you'd hear while waiting to have your teeth drilled at the dentist's office.

"Oooh yeah, baby," a women's voice sang out as Mollie opened one of the doors. She dropped the donut box and stood blocking the doorway as though she'd been turned into a pillar of salt.

"Mollie?" Tony's calling of her name seemed to animate her again. Though, instead of holding the door, she stepped forward, stepping on the donuts and allowing the door to swing into Tony's footrest all in one fell swoop. He wheeled forward and bulldozed his way through, ready to give Mollie a large chunk of his mind. He would have done that if it weren't for the tableau in front of him. On the far side of the room was the largest bed Tony had ever laid eyes on. A pair of handcuffs swung from a bedpost. A man and two women were scrambling from the bed. Stark naked, they quickly slipped into robes that had been discarded to one side.

A balding man of indeterminable age was standing behind a large studio mounted camera and next to him stood Mollie with her finger wagging. Tony couldn't hear what she was saying, the music was still turned up loud, but by the looks of things, the man was getting quite a tongue lashing.

One of the people from the bed, a woman with platinum hair and very large breasts, went over to the sound system and switched it off in time for them all to hear. "My lawyers" emerging from Mollie's mouth.

The camera man matched Mollie hand gesture for hand gesture. "You got one helluva nerve. I was doing you a favor." He would have gone on to argue his point had Tony not wheeled over. Instead, he stopped, pointed the accusatory finger he'd been pointing at Mollie in Tony's direction, and folded his eyebrows. "Who the hell are you?"

"This," Mollie pointed her own finger at Tony, "is the director of Helping Hands. I think you owe him an apology."

"Apology? For what? You busting into my studio and disrupting my film?"

"Film? Is that what you call this...this smut?"

The three people on the bed had all come over to the camera. "Problem, Howard?" asked the second woman, a petite red head.

"Not now, Bambi."

Tony quelled the impulse to smirk.

"Are we doing this thing or not?" This came from the trio's sole male, a tall hunk of a guy who looked as though he divided his time between the gym and the tattoo parlor.

"Not. Go get dressed. All of youse."

The blonde shot the camera man a killer stare. "Tell me I did not drive over from Teaneck for nothing. You better be compensating me. All a us."

"Not now. Get yourself dressed."

The tattooed man stood looming over the camera guy. "Full compensation."

"Okay already. I'll figure something out. For now I need you to make like a tree and leave. Got it?"

With much grumbling, the trio went out a door labeled "dressing rooms" the belt of the blonde's robe dragging behind her like a tail.

Once they had disappeared, Mollie turned the full volume of her fury on the camera man. "What do you think you're about?'

"I'm about making money, honey. Something your old man tells me you are good at spending."

Mollie stomped her foot. "Does Saul know about these...films?"

"Of course Saul knows. How the hell do you think he paid for that Mercedes you're parading around in?"

Mollie snapped the air like a fish out of water. "I don't believe you."

"You believe whatever you want, sweetheart."

Tony eyed the paraphernalia left littered on the bed—a pair of pink fuzzy handcuffs, a pink blindfold and what looked like a tube of cream. He knew he shouldn't, but the whole deal made him want to laugh. He could imagine telling Vida later. She would laugh for sure. Then he imagined Georgette. Would she find the humor in this? He loved the idea of the two of them in a café, a wobbly table between them. He could imagine her saying "Do you remember that time we shot the PA spot in New Jersey?" And he would answer, "How could I forget? It's what brought us together."

The camera man, Howard, and Mollie were still arguing, though Tony had tuned them out. He tuned back in see Howard throw his hands into the air. "I gotta see to my actors." And storm off to join them in the dressing rooms.

Mollie watched him go and then walked over to the abandoned donut box and picked it up off the floor. She put the box on the table and began to do triage, sorting the salvageable from those that were annihilated. "Got the dates wrong, Hah! Grief. That's all I ever get. I try to do a good thing." When she glanced at Tony, he noticed the tears in her eyes. She *had* worked hard at making the PA spot a success. She *had* found them a studio. It might have been a studio where they shot porn movies, but a studio none-the-less.

"You've done a wonderful job, Mollie."

Mollie dried her eyes with a Dunkin Donuts napkin. "That's nice of you to say."

"Sometimes I don't voice my appreciation. And I should. I'm grateful to you. Thank you."

Mollie smiled at him and then her smile fell flat as Howard came back into the room. At nearly the same time, Georgette, Peggy and an ancient man dressed in yellow from head to toe walked in through the double doors.

Howard took in the trio, his face lit up as though someone had brought him a birthday cake. "Holy cow, you didn't tell me you had TV stars on this project of yours. My dear Jesus, Georgette Alden. In my studio. What kind of good have I been, huh?"

Georgette took Howard's proffered hand. He bent to kiss her hand and she seemed to take this in stride. She did light up a room. And clearly, Howard was as caught in Georgette's orbit as Tony. How did she make the room spin?

Howard took a scrap of paper form his pocket. "Could I trouble you for an autograph?"

Georgette found a pen in her purse, signed her name to the scrap, and handed it back to Howard. He folded it carefully and put it back into his pocket.

"So this is the studio." Tony had all but forgotten the old man in yellow. He had broken free of the pack and was wandering around the room's parameter. He stopped at the bed and picked up the tube. "What kind of a PA spot are we making here?" He raised the evidence and his eyebrows at the same time.

Peggy's jaw dropped open. Georgette looked at Tony—she had the most wonderful sparkle in her dark brown eyes—with a hint of question and a Mona Lisa smile on her lips.

"Seems Mr.—uhm—Howard got his days mixed up."

Mollie snapped the lid of the donut box shut. "It's more than a mix up. It's an insult. We will take our PA spot elsewhere."

"Where else you gonna go?" Howard began waving his arms again. "You got another studio lined up already?"

"No. But I will find one that isn't tainted by degradation and degeneracy."

"Are you calling me a degenerate?"

"If the condom fits."

This got a gasp from Peggy. Tony was astounded himself. He never would have imagined those words coming out of Mollie's mouth. Georgette, who must have been equally astounded, let out a snort. Mollie, who had been sticking her finger into the airspace between her and Howard, marched over to Georgette and stuck her finger into the airspace there. "I do not find this the least bit funny."

Georgette took the pointing hand into her own. "That's because you have no sense of humor."

Mollie pulled her hand away as though Georgette had burned her and waved the hand at all of them and then at the ceiling. "This thing has been a disaster ever since we invited her to be our spokesperson. Go ahead, make the spot with a washed up floozie in a porn studio. Ha! We'll see who gets the last laugh."

"Who do you think you are? I have three daytime Emmys." Georgette's voice was ice.

"Daytime Emmys. Hah!" Mollie retrieved her box of donuts and marched from the studio.

"How many have you won?' Georgette shouted at her retreating back. Then, once the door had swung shut again, she took a deep breath. "I'm sorry. I shouldn't have let her goad me like that." The flush on her cheeks made her all the more appealing.

"Nonsense." The man in yellow came over to her and patted her on the shoulder. "You are a passionate woman, Georgette. It's what makes you a great actress."

Georgette ran her hand through her hair. "Yes, well." She glanced at Tony. "Let's shoot a PA spot, shall we?"

"Oh. We can't possibly now." These were the first words Peggy had uttered.

"Why not?" asked the man in yellow.

"Mollie did a great deal of work on the project. A great deal! It wouldn't be right for us to leave her out of it now."

"As I see it, she left us." Georgette crossed her arms and the flame in her eyes matched the flame lipstick she wore.

Tony would have agreed with her. Unfortunately, it was still his job to keep Mollie happy. "I'm afraid Peggy's right. We can't do this without Mollie."

"I blew off a morning's work here." Howard wasn't happy, either. "You know how much this is going to cost?"

"We've all given our time," Tony said. "I'm sorry, but we have to reschedule."

Howard looked at him as though he'd just stepped in dog crap. "You can reschedule all you want, buddy. You can find someplace else to do your business. I'm done with all of youse." With this he marched to the door and held it open. "Everybody out. Now. And none of you is welcome here. Except Georgette. You ever think about doing adult movies, sweetheart? "

If looks could shoot flames, Howard would have been on fire from the one Georgette shot him now. She shook her head and breezed out of the studio without saying another word. Tony wanted to applaud. Instead, he frowned at Howard. "Thanks for your time." And hoped the sarcasm in his voice was equal to Georgette's exit.

They all trundled out to the parking lot. Even Peggy looked perturbed and perturbed was not a good look for Peggy.

"Well then, we might as well go home." Peggy fished the keys to the only remaining car in the parking lot from her purse.

One glance at the car, a Volt, spelled out the next bit of trouble. "I'll take the train," Tony said.

"Whatever for?" Peggy unlocked the door with a click, then lowered the keys. "Oh dear. There's no way to get you in and out of the car, is there?"

The wheelchair was so much a part of Tony's life that he didn't think on it much. He should have been gratified that Peggy, too, needed to be reminded. But with Georgette standing there looking concerned, he felt so self-conscious he would have liked to disappear. "The train station is just around the corner," he reiterated. "I saw it coming in."

"Can you ride the train? Is it safe?"

Was it safe? What was he, ten years old? "Of course it's safe, Peggy. I use public transit all the time. How do you think I get to work?"

"Well yes, but this is New Jersey."

"I'll go with you," Georgette said. Then, turning to Peggy, "Could you give Kent a ride home?"

Peggy sputtered for a moment and then said, "Certainly." Though it was clear she didn't feel certain about this at all. Tony, who would ordinarily have protested that he could handle the train by himself, was thrilled with the turn of events.

There were so many things Georgette had never considered. The escalators, for one; she had ridden them, up and down, all her life and never once thought how impossible this would be if one were wheelchair bound. The sidewalks, for another; the two blocks to the station had sidewalks with concrete slabs that were uneven and riding over cracks with a wheelchair was difficult and seemed fraught with danger. There was a gap between the platform and the train. The times she'd taken public transportation—which hadn't been often in recent years, true enough—she would never have noted the small crevice that ran between the concrete and the train's interior. Tony had to call the conductor, who put down a bridge plate, a temporary sort of ramp, because a wheel could easily get stuck in the seam.

The front seat of the train was collapsible, and there was just enough space for Tony to maneuver his chair into as though backing into a tight parking spot. He set the brakes just as the train jogged forward and began rocking.

All of this made her acutely aware of Tony in the chair. Not that she hadn't considered it, of course she had. But before the chair had been an adjunct, almost an accessory or a prop, the sort of thing actors used until the scene was shot then blithely rose out of and walked away from. Tony would not, could not, walk away. She had known that but now the concept hit her on a visceral level.

Enough so that Tony, who had been joking with the conductor, stopped to ask if something was wrong. Should she tell him what she was thinking? Was it something she could even voice, this feeling in her gut? "I was just—"

Her confession was interrupted by a stranger. The woman stood over her, her hands tucked nervously around her purse. "Excuse me, but aren't you Electra Holmes?"

"I used to be," Georgette said, "before she was killed." She meant it lightly, as a kind of joke, but maybe because she was thinking about Tony and the chair and...At any rate, the stranger felt like an intrusion and so Georgette's voice had an edge to it.

The woman caught the edge and seemed to dangle on it for a moment. It gave Georgette time to compose herself. Long ago, she'd made a vow to be polite to fans. She liked it when they walked away, satisfied just to have met her. Sometimes, she would overhear them as they returned to the group they'd broken away from to venture forth to meet her. "She's really much nicer in person." Electra, after all, would never have been accused of being nice. "I am Georgette Alden," she said to the woman now.

The woman seemed to relax. "Oh, I knew it. I knew it. I've been watching *Our Time Tomorrow* forever! I love the show. I wanted to tell you. That's all."

The woman stood there, looking awkward and unsure of where to take her declaration. Georgette took pen and paper from her purse and signed her name to the paper and handed it back to the woman.

"It must be hard sometimes," Tony said, once the woman had walked away with her inscribed treasure and sat down in a seat the next car over. She wondered again how he could think that anything about her life was hard.

"Sometimes. Though, really, they mean no harm. And it doesn't happen that often. It's not as though I'm Angelina Jolie."

Tony appraised her as though she were a fine art painting. "You are much more beautiful than Angelina Jolie," he said. From another man, she might have taken this to be a pick up line. God knew, men would say most anything to get her to do what they wanted, which usually involved sweaty bed sheets and a cab afterwards. But Tony seemed so serious when he said it, as though it was a statement of fact. She didn't trust her voice to answer.

In Penn Station, the conductor put down the bridge piece once more and helped to steer Tony from the train before pointing out where the elevators were. They found their way to the street, between a sign that said "taxi stand" and another that pointed the way to the Empire State Building. "I've never been in the Empire State Building," she said.

Tony turned his chair to face her. "Never?"

"Nope. Never."

"We should go."

"It's awfully high up."

Tony laughed a deep throated laugh that warmed Georgette to her toes. People parted around them on the street as though they were traffic barriers, some aiming curious glances at the chair and then at her before going along their way.

"Well, we're here. And it's right there. Let's do it."

"Now?" Tony looked up at the towering building and then back to Georgette. "Okay." They negotiated around some pedestrians to get to the curb cut. He turned to her. "This chair is a pain. I wish I had my racer."

"You have more than one?"

"Three actually—standard issue that I use at work, a racer for marathons and the park and this one, which

126

folds. But it's tougher to maneuver." He seemed so matter of fact about it, as though he were talking about bicycles or skateboards. Well of course he would be. It was so much a part of his life, wasn't it?

"Would you like me to steer you?" she asked, wondering if it was a question she could or should ask. It felt too intimate a question, as though she were asking if he wanted her to unbutton his shirt or unzip his trousers.

"That might be a good idea," he said. And soon she was pushing him over the concrete, circumventing fast walking New Yorkers, looking for curb cuts. They had to enter through the handicapped door, another thing she hadn't considered.

The building was busy, but not overly so. It was a Thursday and a bit overcast besides, so tickets to the observatory were available, though pricey, and the line to wait for the elevator wasn't out the door. The elevator was fast moving and her stomach heaved as it raced to the top of the building. It was a feeling she wasn't particularly fond of, but this time she didn't mind. She could have ridden up and down all day long, standing behind Tony and studying, unobserved, the whirl of chestnut hair at the crown of his head and the hard broad muscles of his shoulders under the cloth of his shirt.

When the elevator opened, Tony took the wheel and steered himself out to the observation deck. Whether this was out of habit or because he had intuited her ogling him, she couldn't be sure. They made their way past a school group to the windows. "What a fabulous view," she said.

"Not too high?"

"I could get to like it," she said. "Being a tourist is kind of fun. We should do all the sites—the Statue of Liberty, the Bronx Zoo."

"Times Square, Rock Center," Tony added.

"I could give you a personal tour of Rock Center."

"Do you miss it?" he asked more seriously.

"I haven't had time to miss it," she answered with equal seriousness. "There was this big hole in my life and it got filled in. At least it has been so far."

"I know what you mean. Sometimes you lose something and it makes room for something else."

"Yes, exactly. I hadn't expected it to be this way. It's not so bad, is it?"

"No, it's not."

They stopped by one of the massive windows to admire the view. The city spread before them in miniature as though it was a plaything and Georgette could imagine a child's hand reaching down through the clouds to rearrange the buildings and the bug-sized yellow cabs.

"I haven't been up here in twenty years," Tony said. He studied the scene before them. "My wife and I came here on our second date. She was from this tiny town in western Pennsylvania and I was using Manhattan to impress the hell out of her." He glanced down and Georgette wasn't sure if she was pleased he'd shared something so personal. He had mentioned wife and that word twisted her feelings.

"Your wife? You mean Vida."

Tony looked at her as though she'd said something both fascinating and appalling. "Vida? You thought Vida was—"

"You and she went to Hampton for the weekend."

Tony laughed. "Oh God. She's my therapist and my trainer and she'd probably be more interested in you than in me. Though I warn you, she has a girlfriend. It's serious, they're talking marriage."

"Oh." Chagrined and relieved, she tried to figure out the mystery wife. He wore no ring. He hadn't brought the wife to Hampton. "Ex-wife?" she ventured.

"I'm a widower."

The word widower hit her like an electric shock. "I'm sorry."

"It's okay. It was a long time ago. Ten years."

"She died young." Georgette imagined a tragic

heroine. Electra had been at death's door more than once before her final demise. Sad and beautifully dramatic.

"In a car accident. The reason I'm sitting." He brushed a hand over his thigh. "I'm the one who ought to be sorry, dragging you down my maudlin memories. You're surprisingly easy to talk to."

"Why is that surprising?"

"Because your—you seemed larger than life when I first met you."

"And now you've figured out I'm just a Jersey girl who got lucky."

Tony appraised her again. "It's more than luck. You're talented and beautiful."

It was the second time he'd called her beautiful. Was he flirting? Georgette decided to take a leap of faith. "Have dinner with me."

Tony's mouth opened into an oh of surprise and she quickly added, "No vending machines, I promise. Unless you have a hankering for barbeque chips."

His surprise melted into a smile, complete with crinkles around the eyes. "Okay, dinner. When?"

"Tonight?"

He raised an eyebrow. "Tonight it is. I know a great little place in my neighborhood. Do you like Italian?"

She felt as though she could swoop over the rooftops. Of course she liked Italian. She would like anything he'd picked. "Sounds great. Eight o'clock?"

Chapter Twelve

Tony sat in front of the open door of his closet looking at the contents as though there would be a clothes test later on and he wanted to ace it. He took out a suit still in the dry cleaning bag, began removing the bag, then put it down and called Vida. "Does wearing a suit on a date make it seem like I'm desperate?" he asked when she picked up.

"How would I know? Wait a minute—did you say date? As in going out with the object of your affection?"

Tony was glad that Vida wasn't on Skype; otherwise she would have seen the heat rise in his face. "Dinner, tonight at Alfredo's."

"Alfredo's. Good choice, cozy, not too expensive but not cheap. No suit. Alfredo's is casual. No tie. You could go no shirt, so she could get a load of your well-developed pecs, but Alfredo might not allow it."

"Why did I call you again?"

"Sorry. I couldn't resist. You do have nice pecs. Seriously, dressy casual. You know the drill. Think about what you usually wear when you go there."

Tony was a regular at Alfredo's, his go-to because it was close to home and easily accessible with a wheelchair. He liked that the wait staff knew him well enough not to make a fuss. "I'm over-thinking this, right?"

"Just a bit. She agreed to dinner with you. That means she must be at least a little interested, right?"

He didn't tell Vida Georgette had been the one to ask. "Thanks for the pep talk."

"Anytime. Go get her, tiger."

Hanging up, he realized it wasn't his wardrobe he was nervous about. He rolled over to the picture he kept on his nightstand and picked it up. In it, he and Sophia were standing on a beach in Key West at sunset. He had his arm around her waist, the two of them barefoot and smiling. He ran his hand over the photo, tracing his fingers over Sophia's lacy beach cover up. It didn't seem that long ago—Sophia handing the camera to another tourist. The man who had taken the picture seemed old at the time. He had been obliging, had he seen what Tony saw in the photo now? Two kids, young and in love and so very, very naïve. Mostly, what Tony remembered was the love—he'd been head over heels crazy about Sophia from the day she walked into freshman English and took the seat next to his. But the memory was mitigated by what came after: years of wanting kids and not having any, seeing each other at their best and their worst, the awful time in the hospital after the car overturned on the Deegan. Those grinning youngsters in the picture couldn't see how it ended. Tony knew, he had the chair to remind him.

He knew how love could end so abruptly on an icy highway. And so he guarded his heart, he kept himself to himself. He never let anyone except Vida get close. Then along came Georgette with her junk food and her adventures and her electricity. Vida was wrong if she thought dating Georgette was just the fulfillment of an adolescent fantasy. There was more to it than that. There was the way Georgette made him feel as if he were forever riding the elevator to the top floor. He liked feeling as though he'd soon be on top of the world.

Had she been asked a year ago, Georgette would have said she preferred men who were so sure of themselves they had no thought of not winning her over.

It had been that way with Nigel, years ago. He'd swept her off her heels and the romance had been so wonderful it made her smile even now to think of it. Of course, the memory came packaged with what happened later and what happened later could also be tied to Nigel's self-confidence. Later, Georgette would name it arrogance. He had been so sure of what she'd wanted that when she told him in no uncertain terms what he wanted for her wasn't what she wanted, he'd been sure she was mistaken. Even now, he changed the story to make himself the hero, sure that she had married him for some other reason besides love.

Harvey, too, was sure of himself. He was sure he could read her every thought, though he seldom knew what she was thinking. When she made it clear what she wanted was to get Electra back, he was sure she was being petty and childish in wanting something he wasn't willing to provide.

Tony, though. Tony was different. It wasn't that he wasn't self-assured, but that he was quiet in his assurance. He seemed a man who wanted nothing from her—and that both intrigued Georgette and distressed her.

He'd seemed surprised when she asked him to dinner. Then he'd said yes. He had even pointed out the restaurant on the cab ride they'd shared. She had helped fold his wheelchair and unfold it again and he'd watched her, giving instructions on what to do and looking so pained about the whole affair she felt pained, too. He'd leaned into her shoulder getting in and out of the taxi and she might have reeled from the closeness, the heat of his skin against hers, the smell of a masculine kind of soap she couldn't name off hand, but she'd felt the tension in his arms, the way they seemed to indicate he wished she weren't here to witness this. And yet, when the cab had driven off, he had waved from the sidewalk and she'd told the cabbie to go to Sak's instead of her apartment. If Tony wasn't entirely sure, she'd do her damndest to win him over. She'd start by buying a new dress.

She bought a red one, not too dressy, the color a perfect complement to her dark hair, the length perfect for showing off her still well-toned legs. Then she bought a pair of red shoes to go with the dress. She came home with her purchases tucked under her arm to find Richard in boxers and T-shirt lying on the couch. He was pale and for a moment she considered that he might have contracted the flu.

"What are you doing?" she asked. Though it was obvious—he was wallowing on the couch with one sock on and one off, a half-packed suitcase at his feet.

"She left me." Georgette hadn't thought Richard capable of wailing, but there it was—a keening sort of wail that made her wonder if "left" was a euphemism for "died".

"Poppy left you?"

"She's on her way to the airport. She's going back to London."

"Why?" The moment the question was out of her mouth, Georgette realized there was no point in asking it.

"I told her we were moving to New York. I was going to look for a job here."

Georgette counted to ten. Richard was her son and Poppy was—well—Poppy. But this sort of boorishness was just what she'd decided was the worst in men. "You told her that the two of you were moving? Did you think to ask her how she felt about it?"

Richard looked at her as though she'd taken his favorite toy truck away. "She claimed to love me, to want what I want. I guess she was lying."

Georgette picked up the stray sock and handed it to her son. "She wasn't lying, Richard. Love is a two-way street."

"I knew you'd say that. Father always said you were selfish. You'd still be married if you hadn't been so selfish."

She restrained herself from throwing Richard out

of the apartment. She'd feel terrible about it later and besides, he outweighed her. "You have no idea what you're talking about."

"You didn't divorce Father because you refused to move to England?"

"Your father and I divorced because he expected me to give up my life for him. Ask him how willing he would have been to—" Georgette waved the rest of the sentence away. What was she doing, bringing up her ancient history with Richard? "You can't just tell Poppy she's going to move. How can you be so callous?"

Now Richard looked as though she'd pulled the wheels from his favorite toy truck. "You don't understand. I love her."

"If you love her you'll value her opinion. You wouldn't tell her the two of you are coming to New York on vacation and then suddenly say 'oh by the way, we're moving here. Go find us an apartment.'"

Richard considered without arguing back. Georgette continued. "Did you tell her about your father's ultimatum?"

"You know about that?"

"Of course I know about that. Your father's being a horse's ass, by the way."

She had just given Richard his toy truck back. "Quite. Poppy's brilliant. She's bright and cheerful and great in—she's bright and cheerful."

"And you are letting her go back to London by herself." She glanced at the half packed suitcase. "Unless you've decided to follow her. Which, by the by, is a wonderful idea."

"I don't think I can go back to London, Mumsy. Even if Poppy will have me, I have nothing to go back to."

"We'll see about that." Georgette was already planning the long conversation she'd have with her ex-husband the Brit. If she could talk sense into him, she was sure there was a nice London solicitor somewhere who could. She picked up her phone.

Richard took it from her. "Who were you going to call?" His voice had gone up several notches. "Not Father, certainly. It's the middle of the night."

Georgette tugged the phone from her son's hand. "While it would give me the greatest pleasure to rouse your father from his dreamy sleep, I'm calling the airport."

"The flight leaves at eight. I already checked."

"Then I'm calling you a town car. You have plenty of time to get to the airport and either stop her or get on the plane with her."

"Will you come with me?"

"For heaven's sake, Richard."

Richard grabbed her hand and clung to it. "She likes you. She'll listen to you. I'm not sure she'll listen to me."

Georgette put both hands around Richard's. "You need to fight your own battles, sweetheart. Go to her. Tell her you care about her. You do care about her?"

"I love her!"

"Well, tell her. Be prepared to get on the plane with her. Don't let her go."

She helped him pack up the rest of his things, before handing him a clean towel and telling him he needed to freshen up. Once he had on clean clothes, she gave him the once over, told him he looked fine and escorted him out to the elevator. "Go get her," she said as the elevator doors opened and he stepped into the car.

The elevator doors shut. Georgette breathed a sigh of relief. One love crisis nearly solved. Now she had her own love life to think about. She had planned on taking a hot bath in lavender salts. She might still have time for a soak if she hurried. She wanted to look great this evening—she thought about sitting across a candle lit table from Tony and her heart skipped a beat. Yes, she'd spend time to make sure her hair and makeup were perfect. She would have done just that if Peggy hadn't cornered her in the hall.

Peggy sprung out of her apartment just as Georgette was about to re-enter her own. "Oh good! You're here!"

Well, where else would she be? She gave Peggy a quick nod, said, "How are you?" and made ready to shut the door.

Peggy grabbed her arm. "That Kent Markham is a marvel, Georgette. An absolute marvel! And I have you to thank for introducing us."

Peggy and Kent made for an interesting match. Well, why not? "You're welcome." Georgette wanted to shut the door again, but Peggy was still hanging on to her arm.

"He's so very smart and charming and so involved in his project. He told me you and Poppy were also involved in Free the Fenguins."

"Involved might be a bit of an exaggeration."

"Nonsense! Kent told me you were raising money for plane tickets." Plane tickets? For goodness sakes, Poppy had just been trying to placate the old coot. Georgette didn't say the words out loud, but Peggy must have read them on her face, because her smile fell. "Oh dear. You weren't serious about the tickets, were you?"

"Peggy." Georgette considered how best to handle this. Gently, she decided. She would tell Peggy gently that "Kent is a sweet man, very charming, but he's—"

"Off his rocker?" Peggy finished.

Georgette signed in agreement. "That's a good way to put it."

Peggy's arm-clutch tightened. "The thing is, I like him. I really do. I drove him home this morning and he offered to buy me lunch and we went to this wonderful vegan restaurant—Kent's a vegan, you know. And he told me all about his wonderful project. It sounded a little crazy, sure, but he was so sincere and so I went along and...oh, dear."

A horrible feeling about what "oh, dear" meant

crept up Georgette's spine. "Peggy, is there a problem?"

Peggy tugged on the arm she was still clasping, nearly dragging Georgette down the hall into her own apartment. The layout was a mirror image of Georgette's, but the two couldn't have been more different. Peggy's walls were colored in bright pastels and lined with shelves full of knickknacks. Peggy pulled her down the hall to the bathroom. She opened the door quickly, to allow a peek inside and then shut it firmly again. "Did you see it?"

Georgette wished she hadn't. On the vanity sink had been a spray of tulips. Next to the tulips sat a penguin.

"It's a rockhopper." Peggy planted herself against the closed door as though the penguin might jump from the sink and throw it open.

Georgette asked the obvious question. "Why is there a penguin in your bathroom?"

"A rockhopper."

"Why is there a rockhopper in your bathroom?"

"Funny story." Peggy didn't look like she'd break out in laughter any more than she'd move away from the door anytime soon.

"Let me guess. Save the penguins?" Georgette resisted the urge to roll her eyes, though she did cross her arms. Peggy might be a little overenthusiastic, but she couldn't possibly be as crazy as Kent Markham. Then again, the people pictured on the Wild Things website looked normal, too.

"He's such a nice man. So charming."

"You've covered that."

"He started talking about his cause over lunch. It seemed such a noble thing. You know, I'd never given a second thought to animal incarceration. It was eye opening." Peggy widened her eyes as though to illustrate.

"So you agreed to help Kent with his cause."

"He said you were on board. He said Poppy had begun a campaign to raise money to send the penguins back to Antarctica."

"Poppy was..." Georgette searched for the right phrase, 'buttering Kent up on my behalf' didn't seem the right thing to say, "humoring him."

"Of course she was! I understand that now. And anyway, rockhoppers live in the Falklands, not Antarctica." Peggy tried to smile and failed. Georgette didn't have the heart to ask her what penguin habitat had to do with anything. "Anyhow," Peggy continued. "Kent told me all about his cause and then he asked for a teensy favor. And then he winked at me."

"He winked at you?"

"He's very charming. And he's so passionate about his cause. I figured he'd be very passionate—" Peggy clapped her lips shut, her face gone beat red.

"And the next thing you know, there's a penguin in your bathroom," Georgette finished for her.

"Rockhopper."

"Where is Kent?"

"He went home. I think he had another shipment coming in. Of rockhoppers. He said he'd come back with instructions. That was a few hours ago." Peggy glanced uneasily over her shoulder, as though the bird could see through doors. "I don't know what the rockhopper will do if he gets hungry."

Georgette had a mind to tell Peggy that the very hungry rockhopper wasn't her problem. She wasn't the one who'd agreed to harbor smuggled birds in her bathroom because Kent had winked at her. But the wild-eyed woman standing guard at the bathroom door aroused an annoying pang of sympathy. She pulled out her cell phone and called Kent. No one answered.

"He never answers his phone," Peggy said after the fact. "One of us is going to have to go talk to him."

"One of us?"

"I can't leave the rockhopper here alone." Peggy whispered, presumably not to arouse the rockhopper's suspicion.

Kent's apartment was not far from her own.

Georgette walked over as quickly as she could, her phone in one hand as she dug for the paper on which she'd written Tony's cell phone number. She'd call and say she might be a few minutes late. He'd understand, she was sure, and, besides, she'd have a funny story to tell him. She pulled out the paper and walked into another pedestrian in the same instant. Startled, she dropped her purse, her phone and the paper fluttered away. She chased it as the man who'd bumped her lectured her on watching where she was going. She watched, instead, the paper flutter into a nearby storm drain. She retrieved her purse. The man handed her the cell phone, "You need to watch where you're going," he repeated. As if she hadn't heard him the first time.

Georgette snatched the phone. "Thanks for the advice," she said before sauntering off. She didn't add "thanks for ruining my evening" because, in truth, the pedestrian she'd bulldozed wasn't the reason her evening plans were under threat. No. The reason for that lived in the building she now stood in front of. Well, she'd deal with crazy Kent. Then she'd run home, zip into her new red dress and hope she could still make dinner.

She found Kent in the hallway, staring at the door to his apartment. He took note of her as she came off the elevator and turned to stare at the door some more. "I think I might have made a mistake in bringing the rockhoppers home."

"Rockhoppers? As in more than one?" This was worse than she'd thought.

"As in three. A trio of rockhoppers in my apartment." To hear Kent say it, it sounded like the birds came in a taxi and were now squatting in Kent's apartment out of spite.

She thought to ask how he'd managed to steal four penguins from the zoo, but then thought better of it. How didn't really matter anymore than why. The only question that had any relevance at all was "what are you going to do now?" Georgette did not get to ask that question, because Kent said, "I don't know what to do."

"Return them?" Georgette figured she might as well try the reasonable answer. Kent shook his head back and forth with a vehemence she hadn't known he possessed.

"I can't. I can't do that. People are counting on penguin release."

"What people? You mean Wild Things people?"

Kent's vehement head shake turned into a head nod. "They've gone out of their way for phase one. I suggested it might be better to wait until we could take them to Antarctica."

"That sounds reasonable." The whole endeavor was so screwy that transporting them to Antarctica *had* started to sound reasonable.

"They laughed at me. The kid who runs the show, Bernard, said that rockhoppers weren't even from Antarctica and I needed to get my facts straight."

It was clear, from the way Kent spit out the name "Bernard" that the old man didn't have much use for the kid. "What does this Bernard know anyway? He reads an article that rockhoppers live in the Falklands and suddenly he's an expert?"

Kent looked at her with new found admiration. "Exactly. And now, because of his audacity, I have three rockhoppers in my apartment and one staying with that lovely neighbor of yours. I think I scared her and that's too bad, because she's a cutie. I have no idea what to do with them." Kent started pacing in front of the door. "I fear I've angered them."

"The Wild Things people are angry with you?"

"Not them. The birds."

"The penguins are angry?"

"The rockhoppers. Of course they are. You would be angry too if someone locked you into an apartment with no food."

"At least they have cable."

Kent stopped pacing and stared at her as though she were a rockhopper who had eaten his lunch. This was going to be harder than Georgette thought. She put a hand to Kent's arm and, gently as she could, asked, "Did you ever consider that they might be happier in the zoo?"

Kent tore his arm away. "Happier?"

"Well." Georgette took the arm again. "They have all their family and friends there. What if the zoo is not so much a prison and more a gated community?"

Kent scratched through his thinning hair. "I've never considered it that way."

"Of course you're right; they are sentient beings who deserve the best. But the Falklands? I hear the weather is awful. What chance does a poor defenseless penguin used to being served three meals a day have there?" Georgette bit her lip, wondering if she'd gone too far.

"I never considered it that way," Kent repeated

"Well, consider this. Those poor birds are in your apartment without food or water, torn away from their loved ones. It's unjust. And need I mention the poor lonely fellow at Peggy's?"

"Oh, what have I done?" Kent put his head in his hands and slid down the wall. Georgette slid down beside him.

She patted his arm. "You might have done a bad thing. But you did it for a good reason."

Kent nodded into his hands. "What will I do?"

"You have to give them back."

"I can't."

It was a good thing Georgette had unrelenting determination. "We'll call the animal rescue people. You don't have to tell them how the penguins got into your apartment. You can say you came home and found them there."

"How can I not tell them? It will be all over the news that the rockhoppers are missing."

"All over the news" gave Georgette another idea. "What if you used the publicity to further your cause?" She got out her cell phone and held it to her chest. "Are you prepared to go to jail for your beliefs? Like those protesters back in—back when whatever they were protesting?"

Kent leaned away from her as though the cell phone were poisonous and capable of biting him. "Jail? I have a record! They'll throw the book at me and I can kiss the rest of my life goodbye."

"Okay, then we'll have to make it look like you had nothing to do with the penguin heist. Who dropped them off at your apartment?"

"It wasn't—it was a group effort."

"Come on, Kent. Do you want to do anything at all?"

"Fine. It was that Bernard guy who spearheaded this thing. Bernard Sternhope. He's the one in charge."

Georgette handed the phone to Kent. "Call him."

"I don't have his number."

"Yes, you do. I know you do." She didn't know any such thing, but she had been an actress for a long time and she knew how she'd act if she were trying to hide something—she'd be twitchy, just like Kent was right now.

"Fine." He dialed the number and she took the phone from him.

"Is this Bernard?" she asked when a man answered. When he told her yes, she said. "Listen up. I know about the penguins and this is how it's going to be."

"Who is this?"

Georgette ignored the question. "You're going to turn yourself in to the authorities."

There was a pause. "Why would I do that?"

"The way I see it, you can turn yourself in and get a lot of free publicity for your cause, or you can be the reason four rockhoppers died needlessly."

"Died?" Bernard's voice shot up an octave. "You'd kill them?"

"Don't test me."

"And if I turn myself in?"

"Lots of TV news coverage. People love a good penguin story."

"Will it make the national news?"

How would she know? "No question." She held her breath. Then, when he didn't respond, she added. "I'm going to call the news station. They'll find the birds. Whether they find them dead or alive is up to you."

"Okay, okay. I'll be there to pick them up in an hour."

"Forty-five minutes."

"Okay. Just don't—"

She hung up before he could finish and noticed Kent was looking at her as if she were Jack the Ripper. "You would kill my rockhoppers."

"I would not, don't be stupid. I will call the news station though." She reported the incident to channel five in an anonymous news tip and told Kent goodbye.

"You're not leaving?"

"I've got other problems to solve." She raised a hand as the elevator doors opened and stepped inside without turning. No need to say goodbye twice.

~❧~

Alfredo's was two blocks up the avenue from his apartment. Tony took his 'work' chair—though bulky, the most comfortable of his wheels—because it was easy to maneuver through the bike lane. The night had warmed. Lovers walked by holding hands and Tony felt a ping of regret. No. He would not let himself be maudlin over what couldn't be when there was so much that could be. Vida had told him long ago self-pity was a waste of time. He'd since learned what she'd said was true. He had a date with the most beautiful woman in the whole damn city. There was nothing to be maudlin about.

The restaurant was lit in festive white twinkle lights, which gave it a fairy-tale romantic feel. Tony wheeled through the vestibule to the front of the dining area where Franco, the maitre-d, ruled from behind a podium. Franco looked up from his list. "Tony! Usual table?"

"Yes. For two tonight." It embarrassed him, how much it pleased him to say those words.

Franco looked pleased on his behalf. "Very good." *Yes*, Tony wanted to say. *It was.*

The table was near the front in a small alcove, the space big enough for Tony to maneuver into without knocking into nearby dinners. As usual, it was covered in a white cloth, a small candle in cut glass flickering at the center. Franco handed him a menu and left a second at the place setting across from him. Tony didn't really need a menu; he knew the choices by heart. "Maria will be over in a few minutes."

The waitress, Maria, had worked at Alfredo's since Tony had begun frequenting it a few years ago. She showed up a moment later with a basket of breadsticks. "Company tonight?"

"Yes." Again, Tony felt a swell of pride that must have been readable, because Maria teased him.

"Hot date?"

"Matter of fact."

"Good for you. Something to drink while you wait?"

Tony wasn't a big drinker. Most of the time, when he dined out, he had Pellegrino water, joking that he had to drive home. "A glass of Sangiovese."

Maria brought him the wine. Tony sipped it and nibbled at the bread. When he finished the wine and the bread, he checked his messages. Maria came back over and he ordered a second glass. She said nothing, which was worse than any quip she might have made. He drank the wine. Still no sign of Georgette. He checked his cell phone again. No messages. There was nothing for it but to pay for the wine and go home.

Maria brought his change along with a paper bag. "Pasta fagioli. On the house."

On the house felt like charity he didn't want. Still, he couldn't be rude and so he took the bag and left an extra five with the tip. Bag on lap, he rolled out the door and into the still busy street.

Dinner! She was already twenty minutes late. Forget the new dress. Forget the hair and nails. Why, oh why did everyone else's life have to interfere with her own? She caught a cab near the corner and gave the cabbie the name of the restaurant and added "hurry." He didn't. It took what seemed like forever to get through Central Park. When they finally pulled up to Alfredo's, she threw twenty dollars at him and flew from the car as though it had caught fire.

There were a few patrons waiting for tables. Georgette elbowed her way through them to the maitre' d. She grabbed his arm to get his attention. "I'm looking for Tony Rodriguez."

The maitre' d glared at her with heartfelt distain. "Mr. Rodriguez is not available."

"Not available? He was to meet me here."

"Well, you are a little late, aren't you?"

"Did he leave? Where did he go?"

"How should I know? I imagine he went home." The man turned his back to her and addressed two other people. "If you'll follow me, please."

"Which direction?" Georgette asked his retreating back.

He turned looking as if he wanted to chase her from the premises while swatting her with the menus he carried. She wasn't above pleading. "Please. I need to find him." She took the man's hand. "Please."

For a moment, Georgette thought he really would throw her out. But then he sighed and gave her Tony's address. "Three blocks to the left."

"Thank you." She kissed his cheek and waltzed back past the waiting patrons.

One of them caught her arm. "Aren't you Electra Holmes?"

"Yes," she said, peeling herself free. "Yes, I am."

Then she ran out the door before any more time could
be wasted.

Tony heard his name being called. He stopped and
heard "Tony" a second time as he turned the chair to see
Georgette weaving through pedestrians to reach him.
She had one hand clutched around her purse and
another around her shoes. Why was she carrying her
shoes? Tony watched, fascinated.

She was wearing the same pants and blouse she'd
been wearing earlier, a look of sheer determination on
her face, her hair coming undone and her forehead
shiny. The sight of her—looking so frazzled—almost
made him forget his anger and humiliation at being
stood up. Almost. Georgette Alden was just too high
maintenance for him was what he'd been thinking
before he'd heard her call his name. He decided that her
running towards him changed nothing and he turned
back and started again for his building. He was under
the awning when she caught up to him, breathless and
red-faced.

"I'm so sorry," she said as she caught her breath.
She followed this with "Why didn't you wait?" Tony
studied her, dark eyes, long neck, raven hair, was she
always this difficult? He could imagine her always
needing to apologize for one thing or another. He pushed
a button to open the door and slid inside. She followed
him into the apartment lobby. "You could let me explain.
It's been quite the evening. I bought this new dress and
Poppy left Richard and Peggy had a rockhopper in her
bathroom."

He had been rolling towards the elevator about to
push the next button. "A rockhopper?"

"It's a kind of penguin. They live in the Falklands,
among other places. I knew the rockhopper was Kent's
doing, so I went over to where he lives and lo and
behold, he has three more birds in his apartment. Only
he's in the hall because he's afraid of the penguins. I

called the news station and the Wild Things guy, who is what my ex-husband would call a nutter. I hope it's settled. I didn't stay to find out because..." Georgette threw up her hands, purse in one, shoes still attached to the other.

Tony nodded to the shoes. "Why aren't you wearing them?"

She raised an eyebrow. "Have you ever tried to run in heels?"

He couldn't help grinning. "I can't say I have."

She leaned on his wheelchair, slipping on one shoe, then the other. "I wouldn't advise it."

He knew that he ought to get into the elevator and leave her standing there; she would no doubt have one crisis after another and he didn't want to be in the center of all that drama.

Or did he? Right now, his pulse was racing and he couldn't say he didn't like the feeling. The elevator opened and shut again. He lifted the paper bag in his lap. "Do you like pasta fagioli? I'm willing to share."

"I love it. And I'm famished."

He pushed the elevator button again and waited until she stepped inside.

Chapter Thirteen

The apartment, thought Georgette as she stood in the living room, was exactly like the man. Books crammed into a bookshelf, a scarred end table next to a comfortable-looking leather couch with a throw blanket tossed over the back. She wanted to sit there, take off her shoes again, and curl her feet underneath her. There wasn't much furniture in the room and still it gave off an air of relaxed clutter.

"Kitchen's in through there." He wheeled effortlessly thorough the living room to an airy space with low counters. She put the paper bag down on one of them and examined the neatly stacked bowls and utensils. "I like to cook," he said, watching her.

"Do you? I never learned."

He leaned back in his chair as though she'd just confessed to having a third eye in her navel. It made her laugh. "I just—I've always worked. It's easy to send out in New York, isn't it?"

He cocked his head. "Cooking is relaxing and it can be rewarding. I could teach you."

"I'd be terrible, I'm afraid. But I'd be game to give it a try."

His mouth slid it into a sly smile. "Really?"

"Yes, really."

"Okay, we'll make scrambled eggs to start."

"What, right now?"

He put the bag on the counter and unpacked a

small container. "If we share the pasta fagioli we'll get about three tablespoons each. Not that it won't be delicious, but Alfredo meant it as an appetizer for one."

She feigned horror at the thought and was glad to get a grin. She could spend her life making him grin.

"Okay then." Tony wheeled over to the refrigerator. "Our choices are limited."

Georgette couldn't believe he'd think this, he had the best stocked refrigerator she had ever seen. She told him so. "You really don't live on vending machine food, do you?" she said, surveying fresh fruit and yogurt and milk.

"I have a stash of barbeque chips under the sink," he whispered.

"Ooh, a closet junk food junkie. My kind of guy."

His face went slightly flushed. Then he cleared his throat and took the eggs out and handed them to her. "Eggs are easy."

"Maybe we should start with water boiling. I can make coffee."

"So you are not a complete novice."

"I learned recently. I'm not so bad at it, either."

"Excellent." He handed her a bowl. "Soon you'll be making scrambled eggs a la Tony."

"A la Tony? You have an egg dish named for you? Impressive."

He flushed again. "It changes depending on what's available." He took out a hunk of parmesan and some basil and a tomato.

"Even more impressive."

"Let's break some eggs."

"I like breaking things." She opened the carton, lifted out an egg and smashed it against the side of the bowl. The shell caved, pieces spattering over the counter top, into the bowl. "Part of the yoke made it in."

He picked a piece of shell from her finger. "You may need to work on your technique." He rinsed the bowl and put it back on the counter. "Practice," he said taking another egg from the carton and holding it up, "makes perfect."

"I may wreck the whole carton," she said as he handed the egg to her.

"It's all in the wrist." He took her hand in his. "Gently but firmly." Together they struck the shell on the counter. There were still a few fragments. "Not bad, I think it's a keeper."

She picked the fragments out as he took another egg and handed it to her. She examined the egg. "I don't think I'm ready to go solo."

Tony took her hand again. Together, they broke half a dozen eggs into the bowl. Georgette took one more, cracked it into the bowl without adding any shell to the mix. "You're a quick study," he said.

"Helps to have a good teacher."

"I'll chop the tomatoes. You whisk the eggs. All you've got to do is stir them up."

"I like stirring things up." She took the whisk he handed her and whipped it through the eggs. She was going to like cooking. She was going to like cooking a great deal.

He heated the pan. "The secret is not to cook them too long."

While he cooked, she found two plates in the cupboard and some forks in a drawer near the sink. He divided the eggs onto the plates, heated the pasta fagioli and split it into two bowls. She took them to the small table in the corner of the kitchen. "Perfect," she said assessing the arrangement. It wasn't much, really—some eggs and some soup, a fork and a spoon, on the bare tile table. She wouldn't have traded it for crystal and silver.

Tony studied the table. "Something's missing." He pulled a utility candle in a holder from the drawer, put it on the middle of the table, and lit it. "Better." Then he added, "Damn."

"What?"

"I forgot the drinks. And I haven't got any wine."

"I saw some sparkling water in your fridge. Do you

have wine glasses?" She got the water and he got the glasses and poured. She raised her glass. "To wonderful meals." She clinked her glass against his.

The eggs were fabulous and she told Tony so, although really, it was the company that made them fabulous.

As they ate, she told him about the penguins, doing an impression of the rockhopper sitting on Peggy's vanity. "Poor guy, he looked like someone who had gotten drunk and woke up in a strange place." She loved his laugh, a deep baritone that warmed her like a cup of coffee on a cold day.

They talked until long after the plates were empty and the wine glasses had been refilled and refilled again. When they ran out of water, she hunted down a second bottle while Tony got out his stash of barbeque chips. "Dessert," he said, ripping the bag open.

They passed the bag between them, Georgette moving her chair next to Tony's so they could share. A spot of orange dotted Tony's lip. She took her fingers, ran them over the orange spot and put the fingers to her mouth. "Good," she said, "but messy."

He caught her hand, his own hand—big and warm—and kissed her palm. She kissed him then, firmly on the lips, taking in the taste of barbeque and the smell of soap and the warmth of skin. She hadn't been spun around by something as simple as a kiss in a long time. Yet here she was, feeling like a teenager, like Tony was the first boy who had ever kissed her and all the men between that time and this fell away and were forgotten.

When the kiss ended he ran his hand through her hair. "You are so damned beautiful" His voice, deep to begin with, took on a husky tone. She undid the top button of his shirt and he put his hand on hers.

He gazed into her eyes with a question. "What about Harvey?" Naming Harvey was like throwing a bucket of cold water over her as she was having a wonderful daydream.

She pulled her hand back. "What about him?"

"He won't mind?"

"I don't care what he thinks." She leaned over and kissed him again, wanting desperately to regain the wonderful feeling that had moments ago left her flying.

Tony broke off the kiss and took her by the shoulders. "You don't care?" His chocolate eyes on her, it hit her. He was jealous. Tony Rodriquez was jealous of Harvey Bristol. It was ridiculous, but the thought of it was so delicious it made her smile.

"Harvey and I are friends. He was my producer. That's as far as it goes."

"Really?"

Well, that wasn't quite true. Though she didn't have strong feelings for Harvey. Kissing Harvey had never had the impact of kissing Tony. "Really."

She kissed Tony again, but the kiss was tentative and drained of all the passion and promise the other kiss had carried. She wanted the first kiss back. She wanted another and another like the first. "Don't let Harvey get in the way," she said softly.

Tony pulled his chair back. "It's getting late. Maybe we should call it a night."

How could he kiss her so soundly and then dismiss her? Jealousy was one thing, but this went way past jealousy. "I like you, Tony. I like you a lot."

He nodded. "I like you, too," he said. His eyes looked sad. "We'll talk soon, okay? Your idea of doing the commercial at Helping Hands is a great one."

"The commercial?" Here she was, ready to be swept off her feet, and he was talking about a PA spot? She'd been ready to give up her heart. Well, she would just snatch it back. At least she could hang on to her pride. "Fine." She put on her shoes and sauntered to the door. If she had to exit, she would do it with flair.

"Georgette," Tony wheeled out after her. "I just—"

"You just what? Invite me to dinner and lead me on?" When he didn't answer, she hurried out the door. So much for a perfect exit.

Tony pushed himself hard in his workout the next morning, wheeling twelve miles to Vida's three. He hoped to dispel the stormy thoughts that had robbed him of sleep. It didn't. He couldn't out wheel the feelings. Worse, he couldn't keep them from Vida. Over coffee and a shared bagel, she asked what was wrong.

He could have said nothing, but Vida wouldn't have bought it. And besides, he needed someone to tell him he wasn't a fool for sending Georgette home.

Vida wasn't reassuring. "So you kicked her out?"

"I didn't kick her out. It was late."

"You kicked her out because you're chicken."

Vida, as usual, struck the very nerve he'd been working to leave unexposed. He wheeled from the table with such force that he overturned the half empty coffee cup.

"Hey." Vida put her hands to his armrests and stood in front of him before he could leave the Starbucks. "I'm sorry."

"I don't think you are. I tried. It didn't work out."

"Honey," Vida said softly. "You won't let it work out." He wanted to leave again, though the only way forward was to run her over. "Do you still like her?"

He didn't want to admit that kissing Georgette had turned him inside out. And that Vida was right, it scared the hell out of him. He wheeled forward, forcing her out of the way. "I've got to get to work," he said, leaving Vida and his half-finished coffee behind.

Chapter Fourteen

The devil himself, in the form of one Harvey Bristol, whose uninvited presence in Tony Rodriquez's brain had caused him to shut down faster than an engine without gasoline, called Georgette the next morning. "I moved heaven and earth for you. You can thank me later. We meet with the ColorCare people next Tuesday. Lunch. Be there."

His tone could be annoying and today, since he'd been the cause of her romantic derailment, it was downright infuriating. She would have hung up on him if she hadn't wanted the job.

Instead, she was sweet as she could manage, assured Harvey she'd be there and thanked him profusely to massage his overblown ego. When she finally did hang up, thinking she should go back to bed—and maybe try to make up for a sleepless night spent tossing around while reconstructing her dinner with Tony and trying to figure out what had made it all turn sideways and how she could reassure Tony that Harvey was not a threat—the doorbell rang. There stood Peggy Lemon-Lime looking like she hadn't gotten much sleep, either. "They carted poor Kent off to the hoosegow."

"The what?"

Peggy threw up her hands. "Jail! They've jailed him for penguin kidnap."

Why, oh why did these crazy people keep accosting

her? "I take it the rockhopper problem is solved, then."

Peggy looked at her as though she were a runaway rockhopper come to roost in the bathroom. "It is not solved! The rockhoppers are right back where they started! And now poor Kent is in jail!"

"Kent knew he was taking a risk when he took those birds."

"Honestly, Georgette, did you not hear me? He's in jail! We have to get him out!"

Georgette felt a pain in her temples. Yes, perfect. She would have a monstrous headache if she had to spend the morning with Peggy, pleading with some precinct cop to let her people go.

"Where were you last night?" Peggy asked as they squeezed into her Volt. "You called channel 5 and then you just up and left."

Georgette was not at all fond of accusatory Peggy. Accusatory Peggy was much more annoying than enthusiastic Peggy. "I did what I could."

"By just leaving? Even you can do better."

Enough was enough. Georgette tried not to raise her voice. "Look, I've had a tough night. Penguin kidnapping was not my idea. In fact, I tried to talk Kent out of it. And now, I'm helping you to mop it up out of the goodness of my heart and—"

"Goodness? Ha!"

Well, that tore it. Wasn't it bad enough she was squished into Peggy's tin can of a car, sitting in traffic on the way to tour the local jail? Nobody went to jail on purpose. Georgette had never in her life even been to a jailhouse, discounting of course the several brushes with the law Electra had had in *Our Time Tomorrow*. Going to jail wasn't exactly like going shopping at Sak's, was it? And here was Peggy, judging her. "You can let me off right here."

Georgette gave Peggy a hard look, to let her know she meant it. Those weren't tears, were they? Ah, but they were. There sat Peggy behind the wheel shedding big silent tears and gasping for breath like a tuna on the deck of a fishing boat. "I can't pull over in traffic."

"For God's sake, Peggy. It isn't as though he's been sent to prison."

"Yet. Not yet. It's that Bernard person. He wants to turn this into some big media circus. That's all this is to him, some silly stunt."

Peggy sniffed in deeply as they stopped at the light. Georgette thought about jumping out of the car. Unlikely she'd be run over, though with the cabs in this town you never could tell. And then there it was again—a pang of sympathy. Why, oh why, did she have to feel sorry for Peggy Twiddle-Dee?

"Do you know what he said, Georgette? He said 'Wait for me, Peggy.' Can you imagine? It nearly broke my heart in two."

Georgette understood heartache as well as anyone. Why, her own heart was close to breaking, wasn't it? "You really care for him, don't you?"

"Of course I do. He's a dear, dear man. Oh, I know he's old—anyone can see that. And maybe he's a little nutty. Okay, maybe he's a lot nutty. But I'm not exactly a great catch. I'm not like you."

True enough, Peggy wasn't like her. But she had a lot of redeeming qualities. She was loyal and she knew how to cook and she was cheerful and, well, there must be other things to add to the list. Georgette was about to praise Peggy on her cooking skills, when Peggy said. "I'm a frumpy old woman without a cause, that's what."

"You have causes." Georgette foraged through her purse and came up with a tissue—clean if crumpled—and handed it to Peggy. "You work at Helping Hands. You are a very helpful person."

Peggy blew her nose. "I wish I were a very beautiful person. Like you."

As much as Georgette wanted to bask in the glow of Peggy's compliment, she couldn't. "Do you know why they killed Electra? Because she wasn't young and sexy anymore."

"Really?"

Admitting what had happened felt more liberating than she would have imagined. "Yes, really."

"But you're Georgette Alden. You're glamorous. Everyone thinks so." The light changed and the taxi behind them beeped. Peggy pulled over and waved him around. "Mollie doesn't care for you and I'm pretty sure it's because she's jealous. I was, too. Because Tony, well not that he ever, but he never looked at anyone the way he looked at you."

Yesterday, she would have agreed with Peggy. She would have sworn Tony was into her. Then, after she'd kissed him, he had treated her like a plate of cold mashed potatoes. Peggy pulled out into traffic and Georgette was tempted to confide in her about the date. But Peggy had a crush on Tony that bordered on hero worship. Best to quit while she was ahead. "Don't worry about Kent, we'll figure it out."

The Police Department was in a building Georgette had passed hundreds of times. She hadn't paid much notice—it was a brownstone, four floors high, which blended in with the others in the neighborhood. She wouldn't have noted it now, except for the dozen or so protesters out front, walking in a circle. They held signs that said, "Free the Penguin 8" and "Penguins have Feelings, too." A channel 5 news van was double parked and the camera man was getting out as they skirted around it. Peggy, against all odds, managed to squeeze her tiny car into a tiny parking space a block up the street.

By the time they'd walked back, a blonde reporter, who had a striking resemblance to a Barbie doll, stood on the street near the protesters. As they approached her, reporter Barbie looked up from hooking her mic. "Excuse me, aren't you Electra Holmes?"

Peggy looked pale, the sooner they got Kent out of this mess, the better. "Yes, I am." Georgette took Peggy's arm to guide her past the hoopla, when Peggy did the unexpected. The next thing Georgette knew, Peggy had shoved—yes, shoved was the right word—her in front of

Barbie's camera. "She's Georgette Alden and yes, she used to play Electra, until they killed her because she wasn't young and sexy. Like these other good people, she's here to protest the unjust incarceration of Kent Markham, the champion of penguins and all sentient beings."

Georgette gaped at Peggy, and took a moment to compose herself. She was an actress, wasn't she? She could make something out of Peggy's impromptu speech. She put on her brightest smile and said, "What can we do for you?" to Barbie, who looked like she'd just unwrapped a tennis bracelet.

"Would you be willing to speak on camera about the protest?"

"Of course." Georgette was already digging lipstick and a compact from her purse. She reapplied as the camera man set up. "Are we ready?"

The camera man held up three fingers to count down and Georgette felt like she was back at the studio—or no, filming on location with *Our Time Tomorrow*. Only this time, she had to improvise the script, something about Electra championing a kindly old man. Yes, that would work.

"I've known Kent Markham for ages. He was a director, you know? Before he ran into trouble." She leaned down and whispered at Barbie and the camera. "Went to jail for a crime of passion." Then she straightened and blinked away imaginary tears. "This could be terrible for him. He doesn't deserve to go to prison. He's practically begged me to do a documentary with him, gratis of course."

"A documentary about penguins?" Barbie asked.

Could the woman ask a more inane question? Georgette shook her head. "No. A documentary about a group of homeless shelters here in New York, Helping Hands. They do so much good work and we've been working hard, too, to raise public awareness and solicit some much needed funding." She took Peggy's arm and pulled her into the frame. "This is my dear friend

Peggy—" what a time to forget Peggy's last name. Georgette scanned her brain and hoped for help from Peggy herself, but Peggy was standing statue still and looking at the camera as though it were an oncoming train and she was tied to the track. Miracle of miracle, the scanning worked "Bowles-Smythe is on the board." Georgette continued.

"Smythe-Bowles" Peggy said, smiling like a loon.

"Well, Ms. Smythe-Bowles," said Barbie. She was good at smoothing over awkward, Georgette had to give her credit. "Tell us about Helping Hands."

Peggy stared at the camera. "They serve soup. Chicken noodle on—"

Georgette grabbed the mic. "They run a soup kitchen, but that's just the beginning. Did you know that ColorCare Hair is sponsoring a documentary which will feature Helping Hands and shed some light on the plight of the homeless? I myself am ColorCare's new spokeswoman and I'm producing the film."

"ColorCare covers the grey?"

Barbie's credit was revoked. "We're not here to discuss me, are we? We're here for the shelters." She smiled her brightest smile. The camera still loved her. "And to help Kent Markham, who is an integral part of this campaign. His is such a wonderful story—soaring success and then losing it all in a moment of passion and then redeeming himself with good works. We simply can't let his story end with his being sent back to prison. It would be wrong. There are no other words for it. Just plain wrong."

"In so many ways," said Peggy as though she were a backup singer.

"So, in your opinion, Mr. Markham had gotten himself entangled in—" Barbie gave her a questioning look.

"He's passionate about the downtrodden and the defenseless and that's why we're standing here today."

She handed the mic back to reporter Barbie and took Peggy by the arm. "Let's go save us a director," she said, ready to storm the Bastille.

Bastille might have been an overstatement. The inside of the precinct house was nearly as nondescript as the outside. A reception room held a desk where a harried looking policeman was typing into a computer. The linoleum reminded Georgette of the elementary school where she'd attended first grade, the walls were painted an industrial green—leading her to think the city bought up paint by the vat at cut rate prices. There were hard benches along the corridor, many of them occupied by people who looked like they'd come from the Helping Hands shelter to this place and were spending the day sitting before they could go back to the shelter to slurp soup.

Peggy still had the look of a zombie about her. She stared straight ahead and said, for about the fifth time, that she didn't like being here at all. They went up to the desk, behind an ashen faced woman who was asking the policeman a question. The policeman told the woman to go sit down and wait her turn. Georgette pulled Peggy aside. "Did you notice a Starbucks across the street?"

Peggy looked at her as though she'd said aliens instead of Starbucks. "Near where we parked?" Georgette added to clarify.

"I don't remember."

"There must be a Starbucks on this block somewhere. We're in New York—a Starbucks on every corner is in the city charter. I think there was one where we parked."

"Starbucks." Peggy nodded as though trying to remember what, exactly, a Starbucks was.

"You need to run down there and get a large coffee, no, make that a latte. And something from the bake case, nothing too exotic. A muffin might do the trick."

"You want a snack? Now?"

"I'd go myself but I don't want to attract any more media attention."

"You want a snack?" Peggy repeated as though she couldn't quite grasp the idea.

"Not for me." Georgette tipped her head to the precinct desk. "That poor police officer looks like he could use a pick me up."

"He wants a snack?"

Peggy could be a little thick. Georgette raised her eyebrows. "Just do it. Please."

Peggy sighed and walked out the door. Georgette sat on one of the benches. How in the world anyone could sit here for hours on end was beyond her. By the time Peggy came back with a sack and a cup some fifteen minutes later, Georgette's butt had already fallen into a deep sleep.

"Mortimer's bakery, not Starbucks." Peggy handed over the bag. "I hope that's okay. And it's a corn muffin. I wasn't sure what kind, you didn't say what kind."

"Perfect."

"Now what?"

Georgette winked at her and sauntered over to the desk. The police officer, whose nametag read Sergeant Connor, was still busy typing. She leaned over the desk and said, "Pardon me?"

"Yeah, what?" The sergeant didn't bother to look up. Georgette pulled the muffin out of the bag, put it onto a napkin and slid it across the desk.

"You look hungry." She pulled the top off the latte and slid that over next to the muffin. "And thirsty."

The sergeant looked up at her and then at her offering. Georgette watched his expression change from confusion to delight to confusion again. "What are you trying to pull?"

Georgette leaned over the desk. "I'm bribing you," she whispered.

"Excuse me?"

She flashed him her Electra-on-the-prowl look. "It's an urrr-gent matter." She growled out the r in urgent."

"Urrr-gent?" The sergeant's growl sounded like a black bear's. Maybe Electra-on-the-prowl didn't work on desk sergeants. Maybe it was true; Electra was no longer young and sexy enough to get her own way. Then his look changed. "Say, aren't you Electra Holmes?"

"Yes, I am." Georgette leaned over further.

"What are you doing here?"

"I need to see the captain right away." She winked at him. Let his imagination run wild as to why she needed to see the captain.

"It's urgent?"

"Oh yes. Very urgent."

The sergeant's face colored as he picked up the phone. "I'll see if she's available."

She? This was going to be harder than Georgette thought.

The sergeant stared at her as he spoke into the phone. "Captain Lange? Electra Holmes is here to see you."

She didn't bother to correct him. Electra, after all, had gotten herself out of a few jails in her time. Why, once she had been jailed inside a deserted freight train. Georgette couldn't recall the details of why, but the handsome young cop, Raymond Tisdale, had freed her. This was a cake walk by comparison.

Tony wheeled home through the park, hoping the extra exertion would alter his gloomy mood. It didn't. Neither did taking a shower or changing for work. He was still feeling out of sorts when he wheeled into his office. It didn't help to have Mollie Hammerstein waiting for him there, either.

"A documentary?" she asked by way of greeting.

"Hello, Mollie. And how are you this fine morning?" The sarcasm was thick, but it would have to be thicker than a brick to deter Mollie on a mission.

"Why wasn't I told?" Mollie plunked herself into a chair like a petulant teenager. "First, you have to bring that woman into it and now she's taken over."

Tony wheeled behind the desk and opened his

laptop. "I've got work to do. Are you here to complain or is there some real reason you're in my office?"

Mollie popped up out of the seat, stalked over to his desk, put both hands on it and leaned forward. "That woman has been nothing but trouble. Did you know she's tied to a group of crazies? They think tigers should roam free, or some such nonsense. Yesterday, they took penguins from the zoo. Can you even imagine such a stunt? And she's in the middle of it and she's got Peggy involved. We can't be associated with this. We have a reputation to uphold."

Tony didn't like Mollie leaning on his desk and he certainly didn't like her poking at him where the tender subject of Georgette Alden was concerned. "Our reputation? You were the one who booked a porn studio for the shoot."

Mollie stood tall and straightened her blouse. "Saul will hear about this."

Tony glared at her. "You go right ahead and tell Saul. I'm sure he'd love to hear how Georgette wants to make a documentary on our behalf. The audacity! She wants to increase awareness. Which, by the way, were what the PA spots were supposed to do."

Mollie pointed her forefinger at him. "You are infatuated with that woman. I see the way you look at her, you practically salivate in her presence."

Tony had always prided himself on being able to keep his calm. Mollie was like a match set to paper and he clenched his fists and counted to ten to contain the flare up of his anger. "Get out of my office, please. Before I say something I'll regret."

She opened her mouth to say more and he glared at her and slammed his fist onto the desk hard enough to make the pencils rattle. "Out now."

Mollie closed her mouth and turned on her heels. She stopped and turned back at the door. "You haven't heard the last of this." With that she stepped over the threshold and slammed the door shut.

"I'm sure I haven't," Tony said to the empty space.

Chapter Fifteen

Captain Isobel Lange was pencil thin. Georgette imagined she painted the no-nonsense look on her face and took it off with face cream every night. "Your friend is about to be arraigned," she said, not bothering to answer the "lovely to meet you" Georgette had thrown at her upon walking through her office door. Clearly, Electra Holmes could do little to impress this woman.

Peggy, upon hearing the word "arraignment" sat down in the nearest chair and sobbed out an, "Oh, dear."

Maybe it was Peggy's paleness, which suggested she might pass out any minute, or maybe it was the way she'd plopped into the chair as if she'd suddenly become boneless, but something in Peggy's demeanor served to soften the captain. "Can I get you some water?"

Peggy shook her head and said, "Oh, dear" again.

Georgette put a hand to Peggy's shoulder. "Don't worry. We'll get him out. We must."

Captain Lange frowned at her as though she'd just suggested breaking Kent out from the zoo. "You do understand he's a convicted felon?"

Georgette blinked away imaginary tears. "A felon who had served his time. He's an old man." She walked over to the captain and gave a nod toward Peggy and then a nod at the door. "Can we speak?"

"Of course." The captain led the way out into the hall.

Georgette pointed back at Peggy, who was still sitting in the chair holding her head forlornly in both hands. "As you can plainly see, my dear friend Peggy is very upset. She's a gentle soul. If Kent Markham is sent back to prison it will break her heart. Worse, it will break her spirit."

Captain Lange shook her head. "I'm sure you mean well, but I'm afraid it's out of my hands. Mr. Markham is being transported to the courtroom as we speak."

Peggy raised her head, making it clear she could still hear the conversation in the hall. "The courtroom," she repeated, sounding like the most miserable member of a Greek chorus.

Georgette walked back to Peggy and put both hands to her shoulders. "Well then, we'll have to go speak with the judge. Who is he?"

Captain Lange looked as though she'd asked for the CIA's most classified secrets. "You want to—?"

"I'm sure the judge will listen to us." Georgette swiped a hand through the air. "He's a judge. I'm sure that means he has good judgment. We can shed some light that can help him make the right decision and show some mercy to a kindly old man."

"Mercy." Peggy stared intently at the captain. Georgette couldn't have scripted it better if she'd tried.

The captain bit her lip and looked out the window. "Well, okay," she said after a moment. She scribbled some information on a post-it note. "Judge Eaton. You'll have to hurry if you want to get down there before court is in session."

Georgette pocketed the scrap of paper as Peggy said, "Thank you. Thank you so much. We are so very grateful. Thank you." Until Georgette grabbed her by the shoulders and marched her out the door.

No sooner had Mollie exited Tony's office, slamming the door in her wake, than the phone rang. Tony, whose mood had gone from bad to worse, considered throwing the annoying contraption across the room. "Get a grip," he told himself firmly. He took a deep breath, counted to ten, and picked up.

"What the hell do you think you're doing?" The man on the other end of the line had apparently not bothered with counting.

"Yes and you are?" Tony didn't attempt to mask his irritation.

"Harvey Bristol. What is this nonsense about ColorCare Hair sponsoring some absurd documentary about your homeless people?"

"My homeless? I thought we were done with slavery." Tony should have, but couldn't resist the jab. He had a picture of smooth talking handsome Harvey in his head that he wanted to smash to smithereens. Then he thought about the rest of what the man had said— something about sponsorship? "I have no idea what you're on about," he added.

Harvey laughed, and not in a pleasant way. "Right. You know nothing about it. It's all over the friggin' news. That idiot Kent has gotten himself into hot water and now Georgette has created a media circus and you're the reason. Tell me again you had no inkling and I'll sell you a bridge in Brooklyn."

Tony, honestly, had no clue. He could have told Harvey that. He also could have told the guy he was a horse's ass. But Tony did neither of those things. He hung up without saying anything else at all.

"The judge is in chambers," said a sober young woman whose badge said "bailiff" when Georgette and Peggy raced into the courtroom.

"Well, where are his chambers?" Georgette asked as Peggy took her arm and clung to it like a barnacle.

"Down the corridor, but you can't go down there. It's not allowed."

Georgette had quite enough of allowances or the lack thereof. "Why not?"

"It's not allowed," the bailiff replied, her big dark eyes round as saucers.

"That's not an explanation. I need you to allow it."

"I don't have the authority."

Georgette looked the young bailiff in her big owly eyes. "My dear young lady, we have a situation on our hands. Are you aware that all three major New York news networks have reporters parked outside this courtroom?"

Peggy had to take this opportunity to pipe up. "Three? I thought it was only—"

"Three," Georgette said again, shifting her stare to Peggy.

"Okay, three," Peggy mumbled.

"All the major networks. Do you know why they are out there?"

"No," said the bailiff, "I don't."

"No," said Georgette to Peggy, "she doesn't." She turned back to the bailiff. "It is because a great injustice could happen in this courtroom today. Judge Eaton is the only one who can stop it."

"Yes," Peggy repeated, " a great injustice."

"If my friend and if I don't intercede, an innocent old man will go to jail and Judge Eaton and everyone else involved in the hearing of that man's case will be roasted up and served for dinner by the press. We wouldn't want that, now would we?"

"No," said the bailiff. " We wouldn't want that."

"So we need to see the judge immediately."

"It's not allowed," said the bailiff. Georgette resisted the urge to take the young woman by her shoulders and shake some sense into her. Really, Electra had never had this much difficulty in convincing anyone.

"This is awful, just awful," Peggy sniffed and took a tissue from her pocket and blew her nose, "because now we have to break the rules."

Was Peggy really suggesting they break the rules?

Georgette nearly asked her to repeat what she had said, but then figured it was better to roll with it. She linked her arm through her friend's. "Then let's do it."

The two of them marched past the bailiff who, after staring after them open-mouthed, hobbled after them. "Hey, wait a minute. What do you think you're doing? I'll have to arrest you."

Judge Eaton's door was marked with a plaque and stood partially opened to reveal a pudgy, slightly balding man studying a computer screen from behind a desk. It was, luckily, the first door along the long corridor. Lucky, because the bailiff hadn't quite caught up to them yet, which may have led to their arrest. Of course, chances were still pretty good they'd get arrested. Well, no matter. If Peggy could throw caution to the wind, who was Georgette to stop her? The two of them marched arm-in-arm over the threshold. The judge looked up. Peggy stopped short nearly throwing Georgette over. "Stan?"

"Peggy?" Judge Eaton got up from behind his desk.

"Stan Eaton. Funny, I never made the connection. So you're a judge. How nice for you."

"Yes." The judge's eyebrows, bushy enough to be combed backwards into a toupee, ran together and he looked like he was getting ready to formulate a question when the bailiff came barreling through the door. "You are both under arrest. You have the right to remain—"

"Joanie, what are you doing?" asked Judge Eaton—Stan.

"The rules say no one but court personal is allowed back here. These two crashed the gate."

The judge grinned. "Gate crashers, eh? Leave 'em to me, Joanie." The bailiff stared at him open mouthed. "Well, go on. Back to your post."

"Say," he added, once the bailiff had left, "aren't you on that soap? What's it called? *Our Day Comes Tomorrow?* My aunt Mimi watches it religiously."

"*Our Time Tomorrow.* And yes, I am. Was." Georgette stuck out her hand. "Electra Holmes."

"They killed her off," said Peggy.

"Well, that ought to be against the law." He shook Georgette's hand and then took Peggy's hand in both of his. "What's it been? Thirty years?"

"I guess. About that," said Peggy.

"I still haven't forgiven you." Peggy's face had gone tomato red. Either she was blushing, or she was having the mother of all hot flashes. "This lovely lady broke my heart. She went to the prom with another guy."

"Well, he asked first and I didn't know." Peggy mumbled as though this had happened yesterday.

"Ah, it's okay. Anyhow, it's good to see you again. Now, why am I seeing you again?"

"We've come to ask a favor," Georgette said.

"Not a favor," Peggy interjected. "You're the only one who can stop a grave injustice from happening."

"I am?"

"Yes," Georgette said. "You see, we are all set to make a documentary for Helping Hands. They have homeless shelters all over the city. Peggy's on the board."

"We serve soup."

"Yes, and we need to raise awareness."

"Well, that sounds nice. Are you looking for donations?" Stan dug out his wallet.

"Always," said Peggy.

"Well, actually," said Georgette, "we have a problem. Our director was arrested. He's a brilliant director, but it seems he's gotten himself mixed up with a radical animal rights group. There was an incident."

"You mean the crazy old coot who stole the penguins?" Stan asked.

"He's not crazy," said Peggy, "just passionate. Well, all right, he's a little crazy. But he's a good man. He can't go back to jail."

"*Back* to jail?" Stan asked.

"Yes, you see." Peggy's eyes filled. If she'd been a puppy in a pound, Georgette would have adopted her.

She told the whole story to Stan, who listened with great care. " I'm sorry I turned you down when you asked me to prom," she added at the end. "I hope it doesn't affect your decision."

As it turned out, Peggy's old jilt didn't affect Judge Stan Eaton's decision. Neither did her impassioned plea. The zoo, after hearing the protests on the news, decided that, since the penguins had been returned, charging an ancient man with a crime wouldn't help publicity in the least. They dropped the charges and Kent was released before ever getting arraigned. The message came just as the judge was about to leave for court.

"Well, it seems you came down here needlessly," he said. "Although maybe not. It's a little late for prom, but perhaps we could have dinner some time?"

"Well, I..." Peggy sighed.

"Don't tell me. There's someone else. Of course there is."

"I'm sorry, Stan."

"Ah, don't be. I gave it my best shot."

They met Kent back at the station and Peggy flew into his arms, nearly knocking the old man over. "Oh my dear, you look emaciated."

"Oh for goodness sakes, he was in jail overnight, not in prison camp."

"I could use a nice lunch," Kent said. "My treat."

"Good. We can talk about the documentary," said Georgette.

"What documentary?"

Georgette frowned at him. "The one for Helping Hands that Peggy and I are making and you are directing."

"I thought it was a one-minute public announcement spot."

"It's grown into a documentary. It's going to be

wonderful. I wouldn't be surprised if it got an Oscar nomination." Up until that moment, Georgette hadn't allowed herself to dream big. But now she could imagine herself sitting next to Tony at the premier, the two of them dressed to the nines. He might not be interested in her, but he would love this project. Yes, it would be magnificent. Electra was dead, but Georgette, most assuredly, was not. She would put her passion into this work and Tony and Harvey and even Mollie what's-her-name would be so stupefied at its brilliance they would have to wear sunglasses.

It was sweet; the way Kent drew his chair close to Peggy's, the way Peggy took his hand under the table as if Georgette wouldn't notice. She had noticed, well of course she had, and it made her feel a pang of something she couldn't quite identify, a kind of longing mixed with a hint of envy. She shook the feeling away. It wasn't as though she wanted the old coot for herself and it was lovely, wasn't it, Peggy had found someone who found her endearing. Yes, she would celebrate them. She only wished they wouldn't remind her of Tony.

Because it was Tony she thought about all through the eggplant and fennel casserole. God knew, she'd made mistakes with men before, so many of them she should write one of those tell-all memoirs that were so popular these days. Maybe after the documentary was finished she'd do just that. It would fill the time nicely for a few months. She could impart some wisdom while she was at it—there was no such thing as no-strings-attached sex, she would tell her readers, the women of the world. Maybe Electra Holmes could pull it off, but in real life, sex always had a price. Her relationship with Harvey was a case in point—it had cost her any hope of having a relationship with Tony. Well, the relationship with Harvey was over, no matter what else might happen. So what if she lost the ColorCare deal, there would be other deals. So what if they decided not to get on board with the documentary. She'd gotten the publicity she wanted and someone somewhere would step up to offer funding. She was sure of it.

Kent took Peggy's hand when they left the restaurant. "What a sparkler of a day."

She put her other hand on his arm. "I imagine it must seem so much brighter, after having been locked up."

Georgette bit her cheek so she wouldn't again remind Peggy he'd been in jail less than twenty-four hours. Let Peggy do tea and sympathy, it seemed to work for her.

"You know what would be fun?" Kent said as they strolled down Fifty-ninth Street, "Going to Central Park and riding the carousel."

"What a wonderful idea! I haven't been on a carousel since I was a girl!" Peggy's eyes lit up.

Georgette felt more the third wheel than ever before. "You kids go on. I'm feeling a little tired. I think I'm going to go home and take a nap."

There was a momentary look of compassion in Peggy's eyes that was quickly replaced by something Georgette would have sworn was relief. "Are you sure?"

Georgette patted Peggy's hand. "I'm sure. You go on ahead. You deserve to have some fun, Peggy. You work so hard for everyone else. Take a little time and enjoy the wonderful day."

How was it that so small a compliment could light up Peggy's face? Lit up Peggy was almost pretty. She'd have to compliment her again. Later, because Kent and Peggy were already strolling towards the park arm in arm. Maybe she would take Peggy shopping, a new dress from Saks and some decent shoes, she would knock Kent over. Then again, Peggy seemed to have knocked Kent over without any help from her at all. She was the one who ought to go to Saks, though she had the feeling all the dresses in the world wouldn't make a hill of difference where Tony was concerned.

The man was a puzzle. She'd been so sure when

she kissed him that he felt the same. Why in the world had he turned her down? It hurt too much to think about it, so all the way home, she tried thinking about the documentary. She could almost imagine it as a finished project, though there was so much to do. First off, she'd need someone to write a script. The thought of Mollie's script, which she'd secretly dubbed "Chicken Soup on Tuesday," made her shudder. Thank goodness for Poppy, who had managed to turn a sow's ear into a silk purse. She'd call Poppy in London first thing when she got home. The girl might be a little flighty, but she could write them a wonderful script.

Harold stood waiting at the door. Georgette remembered his name without even thinking about it twice. Harold, he was the one with the pleasant smile, who always had chocolates at the ready and would offer them, even though she always said no. Maybe today she wouldn't say no. "Hello, Harold. Beautiful day, isn't it?"

Harold looked at her, surprised. "Yes, isn't it? I've got some wonderful Godiva, what do you say, Ms. A?"

"I say delicious."

Again, a wide-eyed shocked look crossed Harold's face before he covered it with a broad smile. "Well, wonderful." He took a wrapped truffle from his pocket and presented it to her.

"Thank you, Harold. You are a good doorman." Georgette walked off before he could give her the wide-eyed surprised look a third time.

Chapter Sixteen

She sat down on her couch and unwrapped the candy. It had been a long time since she'd allowed herself to eat chocolate and just then it seemed the right thing to do. She would let the truffle melt on her tongue and forget all about silly old men who stole penguins from the zoo and men in wheelchairs who could kiss you like there's no tomorrow and then kick you to the curb. She'd forget all about Harvey, who would no doubt be furious at finding out about her TV interview, and the ColorCare people, who might well decide to find someone else to be their spokesperson.

She closed her eyes and let the truffle do its magic. It would have if the phone hadn't rung. It was probably Harvey, who was the last person she wanted to talk to, much less be yelled at by. She swallowed quickly, cursed a few times and answered.

It wasn't Harvey, but a cheery sounding woman. No doubt one of those time share people, they called at least once a week. "Ms. Alden?"

"Yes. I don't need time share, thank you." Georgette hung up. She'd run a bath with lavender bubbles and sit in it until she was boneless. No sooner had she turned the bath faucets than the phone rang again. The annoying cheery woman was on the phone, sounding a bit more desperate this time. "Ms. Alden, please don't hang up. I'm Janet Bane, from ColorCare?"

"You're not trying to sell me a time share in

Toledo?" Georgette felt a little chagrined but, honestly, the woman should have introduced herself in the first place.

Janet Bane chuckled. "I would never try to sell anyone a time share in Toledo. Or even Cleveland, for that matter." Then she turned more serious. "I'm calling about the documentary you mentioned on the news?"

Georgette braced herself. Here it comes, they wouldn't hire her as spokesperson, she would make no money, Harvey would be furious, the Brit would demand the apartment back and she'd have to live on soup at Helping Hands. "Yes, I was hoping maybe we could meet. Discuss things. It's a wonderful project, wonderful PR for your company." She wasn't going to go down without a fight.

"You must have ESP." Janet Bane chuckled again. "I was hoping the same thing. Could we meet for an early dinner? If you're not busy this evening?"

"Let me check my schedule." Georgette put down the phone and counted to fifty. The only thing on her schedule was a bath and a nap, but she knew from experience it was best not to let Ms. Bane know that.

Georgette took her time dressing for dinner. She decided, after much deliberation, on a pair of black tailored slacks with a cinnamon silk blouse. She had a jacket to match the slacks and, though the colors were a bit too somber to suit her taste, it did make her look the part of sophisticated business women, which was precisely the look she was trying for. She did add a gold scarf, as a bit of panache was always a good thing, business meeting or no.

She was putting the finishing touches on her makeup, carefully applying a red lipstick, when the phone rang. She thought it might be Janet Bane, so she picked up. She was sorry she had the minute she heard Harvey's voice on the other end of the line.

"What the hell, Georgie?" he said in a voice that

could only be described as huffy.

Georgette didn't appreciate huffy. "What the hell what?"

"Did you purposely set out to destroy my career as well as your own, or am I just collateral damage? "

Georgette considered hanging up. She had no reason to talk to him. Except, of course, that she had him to thank for the ColorCare position. If there still was a position. "I have no idea what you're on about." This was an out-and-out lie, she knew exactly why he was calling. It was the same reason she'd dressed so carefully for dinner.

"You've put me in an untenable position; I know damn well ColorCare didn't offer up sponsorship of some silly documentary."

"How do you know what they offered?" She wasn't going to let Harvey get the best of her.

"It's because of that wheelchair guy, isn't it? Dear God, Georgette, he's in a wheelchair. I do not understand why you feel the dire need to impress anyone with a penis."

Georgette reminded herself not to let Harvey get to her. "It's none of your business, Harvey. And you are not in a position—you know what, never mind." With that, she hung up the phone. As she suspected it might, the phone began ringing again a few minutes later. Georgette grabbed her black purse and headed out the door.

Janet Bane had suggested a bistro on Lexington, a cozy little place that served Asian fusion. There weren't many tables and, if Georgette was worried she wouldn't find Ms. Bane, she needn't of. A small black woman, impeccably dressed in an ivory jacket and slacks that looked as though she'd had the same thoughts as Georgette as to how to dress for a casual dinner, stood the minute she walked into the dining room. She held out a hand, her nails looking salon-fresh with a coat of shell pink polish. "Ms. Alden, I'm so pleased to meet you."

"Call me Georgette." She was already warming to the ColorCare woman.

"And you can call me Janet, and I promise not to sell you a timeshare."

Georgette laughed. "I am sorry about that, those people have been incessant. They are so sure I need one." The waiter came over and they ordered two glasses of Pinot. "May I ask something?" she asked when he walked away. "Don't business executives usually travel in packs?"

It was Janet's turn to laugh. "No, not this time. Just me. I hope that's all right. I've been authorized to discuss the ad account with you. I hope you're still interested?"

"Yes, of course."

"Well, then, let me come right out and say it. We want you for our spokeswoman. You were and remain our first choice."

"Why do I sense something wrong? Usually when someone starts with that sort of compliment, it doesn't end well." Georgette figured honesty was best; she would put her cards on the table. "It's about the documentary, isn't it? Helping Hands is a wonderful cause, but I do understand I might have been a bit hasty in naming you."

"Helping Hands is a non-profit, right? We have no problem at all with sponsorship. It's good public relations for us to support community causes."

"Well, that's wonderful! Honestly, it's a relief."

"Though next time, run it by me first, okay?" The waiter delivered the wine and handed them menus.

"Well, then, I'm ready to sign on the dotted line."

Janet picked up her glass. "There's no problem with our sponsorship of Helping Hands, but there is a problem with the other sponsorship."

"What other? You mean Harvey Bristol's movie?"

"Yes. After seeing the script, we've decided it isn't something we'd like to have the ColorCare name associated with.. It's...well, it's tawdry. There's no other word for it. We simply can't put our product behind it. We have a reputation to consider."

Georgette nodded, trying to take in the words. The only reason the ColorCare people wanted her was because of Harvey's movie. That's what he'd told her anyway. "I don't understand, you don't want to sponsor Harvey's movie, but you want me as spokeswoman and you'll sponsor the documentary?"

"I know you've insisted we sponsor the movie or the deal was off. I was hoping I might change your mind. Maybe if we agreed to sponsor the documentary, you might be persuaded? Helping Hands is a bit of stretch for us commercially, but as I've said, community projects are good PR—the women in our demographic love the idea that we help out where we can."

Georgette wondered if she'd heard right. "You said my taking the job was contingent on Harvey's movie?"

"Well, yes. Mr. Bristol said you wouldn't work with us otherwise."

"Did he?" Georgette picked up her wine glass. "I think there has been a terrible misunderstanding. You see, I really don't care if you do Harvey's movie or not."

"You don't?"

"No, I don't." She clinked her glass to Janet's. "Here's to the start of a wonderful relationship."

All the way back to her uptown apartment she berated Harvey in her head, calling him out as the dishonest weasel he was, which was just the tip of the iceberg where her complaint with the man began.

She was ready to call him up right then and there, but when the taxi dropped her off in front of her building, she stood looking at the attractive awning decorating the front of the tall and attractive apartment house she'd lived in for the last thirty years and thought about how the place was one she could count on, it was always comforting to go home. If only the men in her life could be like that, life would be about perfect.

The men in her life were far from perfect, though. Harvey had thrown away the character she'd given her heart and soul to like yesterday's trash and then tried to make it like he was giving her charity. Maybe, she thought, she wouldn't call him after all. She was done with him and she felt no small measure of satisfaction at the thought of cutting him loose. She never should have taken up with him in the first place. In her defense, he was good looking and what they had seemed so harmless at first—there was even a name for it— friends with benefits. Only friends looked out for one another and the only one Harvey had ever looked out for was himself.

Not ready to go upstairs yet, she began walking around the block. It was a lovely summer's evening, the sun only now beginning to go down. A couple strolled by hand-in-hand and then a group of women dressed for a night on the town walked by chatting happily together. The forlorn feeling she'd had in the taxi hit her again.

What in the world was the matter with her? She'd found work on a series of commercials that would more than pay her bills and she had funding for a documentary which would, with any luck, enrich her life. She had a lot to be happy about. And yet, here she was all alone in a city of eight million souls without a single soul to share her happiness with.

Tony flashed into her mind, more specifically, the feel of his lips, warm and soft on hers. She'd felt that kiss all the way down to her toes. And then he'd turned her away. It made no sense.

It made no sense! She stopped walking, nearly causing a collision with a couple who walked up behind her. "It makes no sense," she said aloud like a crazy woman responding to the voices in her head. "It makes no sense at all."

Georgette may not have been a Rhodes Scholar, she may not have finished community college, but she knew a lot about men and what she knew about men was that they were as predictable as the sunrise. She knew she was attractive and she knew when a man was truly interested in her or when, as in Harvey's case, they were opportunistic and interested in a good time and not much more. She would have bet money Tony was truly interested. All the signals were there, they'd been loud and strong when she brought him junk food and they'd grown stronger when the two of them had stood on the top floor of the Empire State Building surveying the city at their feet. He was interested, so why had he turned her away? She had no idea, but damned if she wasn't going to find out. She hailed a taxi and gave the cabbie Tony's address.

A few minutes later she was ringing his bell. He didn't answer. It was nearly eight o'clock, so he should have been home from work hours ago. He had to be home. She rang again and the determination she'd felt on the cross-town cab ride began to drop away; she wouldn't have been surprised to find it in a puddle on the sidewalk at her feet.

Just as she was trying to figure out what to do next, she caught sight of him wheeling up the street, his powerful arms making her heart spin faster than the wheels of his chair.

He didn't see her until he was nearly at the door , then he stopped, and the two of them stared at each other as if they might have a high noon style shoot out right in the middle of the street. Georgette took a deep breath. If the pulsing in her neck didn't let up, she was going to be too tongue-tied to talk. So she spit it out. "Why?"

The question didn't make any more sense than her standing on the sidewalk in front of his apartment building with her face flush, her hair blowing in the light breeze, and her dark eyes shiny. "Why?" Tony repeated.

She threw her hands up in the air. "Why did you throw me out yesterday?"

He wanted to take those hands, kiss each of the

fingers. "I threw you out?" What she said, or asked, hit him like a sack of bricks. Did she really think he'd thrown her out?

"We were having a wonderful time. At least I thought we were."

Tony looked down at his hands, not sure he could answer her. Wonderful didn't begin to describe it. He hadn't felt this way about a woman since before his accident. He had really messed it up, he thought. Then another thought came up, in a voice that sounded strangely like Vida's: "So fix it, you big lug."

He looked into her eyes, so beautiful and hurt and angry and sad. Had he done that? "You want to come in?"

She seemed to think this over, pursing her lips and he was afraid she'd tell him he'd blown his chance and that he'd have to watch her walk away. He held up the Starbuck's bag on his lap. "I bought some fresh ground beans. I was going to make coffee."

She followed him into the elevator and waited while he fumbled with his key. If she decided to run off, he would grab her arm to stop her. Once he'd shut the apartment door behind them, she stood in front of him, blocking his way to the kitchen, with her arms crossed. "Okay then, why?"

"Should I go make coffee?"

"No." She didn't move and he stared at her.

"Are you always this dramatic?"

"You have not begun to see me be dramatic."

God, he wanted to kiss her, though judging by the way her lips were pursed, she would probably slap him if he tried. "I—" How the hell was he supposed to explain something he wasn't ready to explain to himself. "I wasn't ready."

Her lips opened into a surprised "Oh."

"Maybe you should sit?" he suggested.

"Yes, maybe I should." They went into the living room where she sat on the couch, and stared at him some more. She looked nothing like Electra, her hair was a mess, her face was flushed and her beautiful eyes were full of questions. He owed her more of an explanation, and so he put down the bag and wheeled over next to her. "It's not you, Georgette. You are gorgeous and sexy."

"Then what?"

He glanced at his arm rests, not sure how to begin. She began for him. "The chair?"

Why was this so hard? He nodded. "I haven't been with a woman, romantically, in a long time. Since before."

He couldn't look at her, but then he felt her hand on his and her face so close he could feel the heat of it. "I don't care about that. Not even a little bit." She kissed his cheek and he turned and took her face in his hands and kissed her hard on the lips.

He pulled his hands through her hair, his tongue exploring her lips, daring himself to let go, just this once, let go. He chased away the fear and the annoying voice in his head that told him to wait a minute. And he let go.

Finally, though, they both had to come up for air. He ran his fingers over her cheek, flushed and hot, and looked into her eyes, alive and bright and dark and, dear God, he was falling hard and fast. He was falling and he didn't care if he landed with a thud. Because those eyes of hers—they told him she felt it too, the electric current that crackled between them. She was falling, too.

He kissed her again and again, and would have, could have done it all night, but the fear and doubt that had kept him company for so long came back and found a seat in his brain and he stopped. "We need to talk."

She nuzzled his neck. "I don't want to talk." Her breath on his ear was oh so enticing, but not enough to still the voices which grew louder with each kiss.

He pulled her back and took her face in both his hands. "I could make some coffee."

"I don't want coffee," she said. Though she caught the look in his eye, he could only imagine what it broadcast. "You really... Okay." She got up and took the bag he'd gotten from Starbucks. "We'll make coffee. And we'll talk."

"Okay."

"Okay." She took the bag into the kitchen, he watched her go; he could watch those shapely legs all night. He wanted her, God, did he want her. But she was a hurricane and as much as he wanted her, another part of him was afraid of being battered by the very force of her.

"Where do you keep the French press?" she asked once he'd followed her into the kitchen.

"I have a coffee maker." He pointed to Mr. Coffee on his counter.

"I don't know if I can work one of these." She shrugged at him, carafe in one hand. "I know, I'm hopeless."

He took the carafe from her. "Not hopeless. Astonishing. Do you always have this much energy?"

"Only when I make out with a really handsome man like I'm still a teenager." She smiled at him and wet her lips with her tongue. He wished she wouldn't flirt, but maybe she was trying too hard, maybe they both were.

He filled the carafe and measured out the coffee. "Hey, that looks easy," she quipped. "More time for kissing and such." He didn't answer her and she sat down and said nothing while he got mugs and cream and sugar. "I don't know what you're thinking. It scares me a little."

The thought that beautiful vivacious Georgette, the woman who made him feel like a tongue-tied schoolboy was anything but self-assured made him smile. "I'm not hard to figure out."

The coffee maker beeped. She got up and poured them each a cup. "All the men I've ever known are easy to read, they really want just—well, the obvious. And when they're done, they want you to disappear until they want or need the obvious again. But you—when you sent me away yesterday, I didn't know what to think. I kept hearing Harvey tell me my sexy has disappeared along with my young."

Tony hadn't liked Harvey in the first place and he liked him a whole lot less now. "He is an ass of monumental proportions."

This got a smile. "I really don't want to talk about him."

"But we are talking—and maybe you need to tell me about what's going on between the two of you."

"There is nothing going on between us. Not anymore." She sighed, then went on to tell him about the commercial she'd just landed and about Harvey's hand in almost blowing it for her. "So you're right, he's an ass of monumental proportions." She took his hand "You are worth a thousand of him. But I feel off balance around you."

"I'm not that different from other guys. Except I wouldn't want you to go home after."

She ran her fingers over the pad of his thumb. "You have wonderful hands. I know, or think, you're a little worried, about the chair. This is new ground for me too."

Coming from anyone else, Vida, for example, he might have protested. He might have told her to leave and kept hold of his pride, but she was causing the most wonderful sensation by running her fingers over his palm and she sounded so sincere.

"You are so damned good," she said. Then shook her head and laughed a little. "No, that sounds terrible. It's just that you're the first man in a long time who doesn't expect anything of me. I'm saying this all wrong."

"No, you're not. And I do want you. You are the most extraordinary woman I've ever met. I can't believe you're sitting at my dinette."

"Believe it. Underneath this exterior, I'm just another girl from Jersey."

He laughed at her assessment and put his hand to

her beautiful cheek. "Here I thought you were raised by nannies and went to finishing school in Switzerland."

"High School in Camden is more like it. We don't do finishing; I had to learn the rest on my own."

"You learned well." He leaned in and kissed her again.

"I'm okay with it if we take things slow. I don't think I've ever done slow before. It would make for a nice change."

He wanted to tell her slow wasn't what he wanted. That maybe slow was all he could give her. He hoped it was enough, he worried it wasn't.

She unbuttoned the cuff of his shirt and ran her hand underneath, along his forearm. "So, you'll have to tell me when to stop, because I'm not so good at figuring that out."

Stop wasn't even close to what he wanted. Take the next step, he told himself, go for it. "Maybe we could lie down."

She smiled and closed her eyes. "Yes, maybe we should."

He wheeled to the bedroom, the bed, thankfully made and his clothes, thankfully, not in a discordant heap on the floor. "This is nice," she said, eying the triangle strung from the ceiling.

"It helps me to get in and out."

She nodded again and lay down on her side and waited for him. He'd done the transfer thousands of times, and yet he was nervous he'd falter. He didn't. "You are incredibly graceful," she said.

"I don't think anyone's ever called me graceful." He lay on the wedge, as he always did, thankful that it kept him propped up so he could watch her. "We, I might need some medication to, um, proceed. I don't have any on hand."

She ran her fingers up his arms. "I'd like it if you'd hold me. I haven't been just held in a long time." When she smiled, tears welled in her eyes and he got a sense of something that hit him hard—she was lonely. And, maybe, just maybe, she needed him. She put her head on his shoulder and he put his arms around her. And she nuzzled into his neck. "Okay if I spend the night? I promise not to snore."

"I would like that. I would like that a lot."

Chapter Seventeen

Georgette woke up early. There she was, still dressed, Tony's strong arms encircling her and she'd never been as happy or content with a man. She wanted to tell him, but he was fast asleep, and so she cuddled into the heat of him again and closed her eyes and felt his chest rise and fall under her ear. He stirred a few minutes later and she watched as he opened his eyes and then as he smiled when he looked into her own eyes. "Hey there," he said.

"You're good at your word, not sending me home." She said.

"I think I like waking up next to you."

"I like it too."

Then his smile was erased and he looked pained again. "I want to give you more. I do."

She kissed him. "You will. There's no rush." There was time, oodles of it. If she could stay in Tony's embrace forever that might just be enough.

They spent the day together, in the park, where he showed her the route he wheeled to train for the marathon. They talked for hours about nothing and everything, the particulars of their lives. Tony told her about growing up in the Bronx, his mother had been a teacher and a single mom. She told him about New Jersey, the little bungalow where her mother had kept house and her father had been away for days at a time hauling goods from one city to the next in his truck.

They had similar taste in music, preferring classical, and similar taste in food—though he was no fan of sushi, a favorite of hers.

The day was over far too soon. She invited him up when it was done, and they kissed for a long time before he left; the taste of him lingered on her lips long after she watched him go down the elevator.

There was time and it amazed her that a day and night with Tony, withcut sex, had been so wonderful. She could wait. It would be perfect, she knew. Even if it wasn't, it would be a far better thing than anything she'd ever had with Harvey, because sex with Harvey had been about as much fun as getting her eyebrows plucked and had left her feeling a lot less pretty when they were done. No, this time she'd found something wonderful and she could hardly believe her luck.

She was ready to take on the world, with the kind of enthusiasm she hadn't felt in ages and ages. She would begin work on the documentary project. Tony had promised to tell his board about it when they met the following day. Meanwhile, she would do some planning. She went to Alahandro's with pen and legal pad, ordered a large latte and a scone and had at it.

The plan came easily and she jotted as she went. She would call Poppy in London to write a script, the girl could do it and it would be the perfect thing for her. She would get Kent to direct and— The coffee shop door opened and in walked Peggy. Georgette looked up and waved. "Just the woman I wanted to see. Come sit with me."

Peggy stood opened mouthed at the invitation, as flustered as if Georgette had just thrown gold bullion at her feet rather than offering her a seat at the table.

Once Peggy was settled, Georgette told her the good news. "The ColorCare people are sponsoring the documentary, so we're a go."

"We are? Well, that's wonderful!"

"Yes, it is wonderful. It's going to be brilliant."

Peggy's smile faded. "Are you sure we can do this?

We had such trouble with the public announcement and that was a one minute spot."

Now Georgette opened her mouth in surprise. Peggy was a glass-half-full kind of woman. What in the world had happened to her optimism? "Of course we can do this! I've been in the acting business for a long time, we've got sponsorship. I'm going to get Poppy to write us a script—and anyway, we'll mostly talk about the problem of homelessness in the city. Tony can address that." Tony's name caused her to flush, just a little. Peggy didn't seem to notice. "We'll get Kent to direct it. I'm hoping you'll join me as executive producer. You are a wiz at organizing."

"Executive producer?" Peggy began to brighten.

"Yes, you'll be fabulous." Georgette was sure she would be. "Your first job will be to hire Kent."

Peggy's smile fell like an undercooked soufflé yet again. "There may be a conflict."

"What conflict?" Kent wasn't working, and he would be more than happy to spend his time in Peggy's company. She was sure of it.

"He's become a friend of the zoo."

Well, that was unexpected. "A friend? I thought he despised the zoo."

"Actually, we went there yesterday. I told him he ought to see it firsthand. They've been so nice, after all the fuss with the rockhoppers. Kent had a complete change of heart. It was nothing like prison at all, he said. Anyhow, he's got a membership and he wants to do volunteer work on their behalf."

Peggy seemed to glow at the very thought of Kent.

"Maybe he can do both. If he directs the documentary, you and he will be spending a lot of time together.'

Peggy's glow got positively luminescent. "I hadn't thought of that. I suppose he could do both. He has such energy!"

Georgette dressed carefully for the board meeting the next day. Although she'd spent the evening before with Tony, she still felt flush at the thought of seeing him again. He'd agreed to let her come in and talk about the project to the other members of the board. There were twelve of them, Tony and a woman named Victoria Homera, who ran the kitchens in the shelters, Peggy, the Hammersteins, and a handful of other community movers and shakers, one a city selectman who didn't usually show up for the meetings.

The boardroom was small and windowless with a large scarred wooden table crammed into the middle of it and wooden chairs scattered around. Tony, though, seemed proud to have her there and the room felt a lot larger as she stood in front of the gathering with the notes she'd sweated over the previous day. Getting up in front of groups bothered her not in the least and she thought she made a great show of it, explaining how ColorCare would pay for the documentary, which would run about an hour in length, and what a great thing it would be to raise awareness about the homeless in the city.

Tony beamed at her and Peggy looked ready to roll up her sleeves and dive in. Even Victoria seemed anxious to include a segment about the challenges of running the kitchen. It would have gone spectacularly if not for Mollie Hammerstein.

Mollie stood up after Georgette's impassioned presentation and gave a speech of her own. "I, for one, do not want to be used commercially to sell hair dye."

The woman might as well have taken a steak knife and driven it through Georgette's heart. She blinked away her ire and said, as evenly as she could. "I don't understand your concern, Mollie. It's wonderful exposure and we want to shed a light on the problem. Wasn't that the whole point of the public announcement spots? And weren't they your idea?"

"They were a good idea, too, until you came in and blew everything all out of proportion. You turned a simple idea into a nightmare tangle. The very idea of you, an actress on a two-bit soap opera, making a documentary as though you're Ken Burns is laughable. I, for one, will not be party to it."

The steak knife in her heart twisted and tears welled in her eyes. How dare Mollie suggest she couldn't do this, who was she to decide? She was an actress; she knew more about films and television than Mollie could ever dream of knowing. She also had her pride and, using her best acting skills; she swallowed her emotions and straightened her spine.

"I'll leave it to the board, then. Let me know what you decide." And she strode out the door.

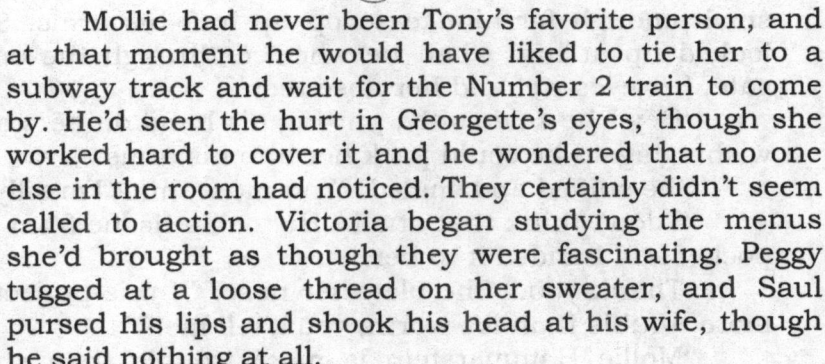

Mollie had never been Tony's favorite person, and at that moment he would have liked to tie her to a subway track and wait for the Number 2 train to come by. He'd seen the hurt in Georgette's eyes, though she worked hard to cover it and he wondered that no one else in the room had noticed. They certainly didn't seem called to action. Victoria began studying the menus she'd brought as though they were fascinating. Peggy tugged at a loose thread on her sweater, and Saul pursed his lips and shook his head at his wife, though he said nothing at all.

Tony cast his own stare at Mollie. "I hope you're proud of your display. This documentary might be the best thing that's ever happened to the shelters and you managed to blow our chances sky high."

"It's not a good thing, or are you too caught up in that actress's net to notice?"

"I think you ought to look in the mirror, Mollie, because you're the one who's letting her personal agenda get in the way what's right for the shelters."

"My ego? Dear God, it's surprising Georgette Alden can get her big head through the door."

He formed his hands into fists, resisting the urge to pound them on the table. Instead, he pointed a finger at

Mollie. "We are doing this documentary. If you can't live with that, then maybe you ought to find some other charity to bother with your miserable attitude." And he wheeled out of the room.

He hoped to find Georgette, but she'd left the building. Then he remembered she was going to ride home with Peggy, so he went out to the street, thinking she wanted fresh air. He knew he did.

There was a green space between the shelter and the apartment building next door to it. It wasn't much, a small garden enclosed by a wrought iron fence, some grass and a scrawny maple with a bench under it. He found her sitting on the bench. She had always been such a presence that he forgot she wasn't really very large and now, as she sat hunched forward, she looked small enough for him to scoop up into his arms. She looked up at him when he wheeled through the open gate, her eyes wet and her nose red.

"Hey," he said softly, putting his hand on hers and wishing again he could pack her into his arms.

She sniffed and smiled. "You must think I'm silly."

"I don't think that at all." He took a tissue from his pocket and handed it to her.

"Thank you." She blew her nose. "If this project is more trouble than it's worth, you'll tell me?"

"Mollie Hammerstein is more trouble than she's worth. You were right about everything you said in there."

"I don't understand why she hates me so. She doesn't even know me."

"I think she's jealous. I would be, if I were her. You are glorious and beautiful and talented—and Mollie sees green when she sees all that."

"That's very sweet of you to say."

"Besides, it doesn't matter what she thinks." He reached out and brushed a last tear from her face. "I like you. I like you a lot." Then he came in and kissed her, right there in the park.

Kissing Tony had a medicinal effect and her emotions shifted. She'd been shifting like the sands in the Sahara since she'd met him—and she didn't mind it in the least.

"Dinner tonight?" he asked.

"Are you cooking?"

"No, I'm buying. I thought we'd try Alfredo's again. Maybe we can get it right this time."

"Or maybe Alfredo will kick me to the curb. He likes me about as much as Mollie does."

"He's going to love you once he gets to know you. Probably give you extra pasta."

The sun peeked out from behind the clouds and she basked in the stream of sunlight, or maybe it was just Tony's warm eyes. "What time?"

"Oh shoot, it has to be later. I forgot, I have a training session with Vida at four. How about eight?"

She nodded. "Eight's good. So you're really going to do the marathon?"

"Yup. I'm hoping for some sponsorship, too. I'm wheeling on behalf of Helping Hands."

"No kidding?" An idea hit her as the sun had a few moments earlier. "Hey, we should include that in the documentary."

Tony frowned, but just a little. "You want scenes of me wheeling around?"

"Hell, yes. Your muscles will make women for miles around swoon. And then they'll give freely to your cause."

He laughed. "I don't know about that."

"I do." She leaned in to kiss him again. For a moment the world was a perfect place, but then she looked up and caught sight of Peggy standing by the fence like an orphan wanting to come into the garden.

Tony glanced up and saw her too and broke the kiss. "I'd better go back inside and do some damage control." He nodded to Peggy as he wheeled past her.

"Well," said Peggy once they were settled into her tiny car.

"Go ahead, Peggy, say it. Yes, Tony and I are dating. We are both single and I don't see a problem, do you?"

Peggy studied the key as she turned it. "It explains why you are so all-out interested in doing this documentary."

"Believe it or not, my interest in Tony has nothing to do with the documentary." She hadn't realized it was true until she said it. She would have done the documentary regardless, it gave her a new direction— something she needed badly—and that was its own reward.

"Ha," said Peggy.

She could have gotten angry, but decided maybe, just maybe, Peggy had reason to doubt her motives. "It's true. I'm really not that shallow."

"I hope it's true." Peggy stopped talking as she pulled into traffic. "Because Tony isn't shallow. He's deep and complex and wonderful."

"I know." Georgette smiled at the thought of him.

"So don't you go hurting him."

"I don't plan on hurting him, Peggy."

"Good." And they said nothing more.

"You want to get coffee? I'm not sure what to do with this change in schedule, I'm all discombobulated," said Vida once they'd finished the afternoon workout.

"We'll go back to mornings the day after tomorrow. I can't get coffee; I've got to get home. I have a date." Vida had been walking beside him, but stopped dead in front of him, both hands on his chair. "You trying to get me to run you over so you don't have to run in the marathon?"

"What's this about a date?"

"Jesus, Vida. Is it that hard to believe I could go out with someone?"

"Someone like the beautiful Ms. Alden?"

He felt his face flush at the mention of her name. "Matter of fact. Yes."

"That explains your increased vitality. Well, good on you. Don't blow it this time."

"What makes you think I'll blow it?"

Vida raised her eyebrows. "History?"

"I'm working on it."

"Want me to come coach you?"

"I think I can manage, thanks anyway. We're not there yet at any rate."

"You'll do fine. You just have to relax."

"Right. Relax."

"True, you are dating your teenage crush. So there's that."

Vida was right; relaxing would help, though Georgette didn't inspire quietude. Then again, when she'd fallen asleep in his arms, he felt more contented than he had in a very long time; he could have spent the whole night just watching her breathe.

He knew she would want more. Hell, he wanted more. And for all her talk about taking it slow, he thought about taking the next step. Give it time, he told himself. A day, a week, it wouldn't matter. The more he got to know Georgette, the more he liked her. She wasn't Electra Holmes, not really, she was an honest to God flesh and blood woman and that was a far better thing.

Chapter Eighteen

The fall weather charged the city, or so it seemed to Georgette. The trees in Central Park burst in an array of red and gold, the brisk wind was refreshing and people walked around with an extra spring in their step, as though the cooler weather had revitalized them. Then again, it could just be that she was falling in love, because that's what the lightness of her own steps suggested.

It seemed, too, as though her life were divided into two segments—before and after Tony. The before life was a distant and shallow thing, she'd spent her days fighting with her own aging, trying to stay pretty, filming her show and going home tired at the end of the day with a new set of lines to memorize. She'd dated men who couldn't see past her carefully made up face and her carefully dressed figure. They wanted what they saw on television, a woman they could point to as though she were a prize they'd won. Even Harvey, whom she'd thought was a friend, hadn't called her since she'd had dinner with Janet Bane. Apparently, once she couldn't be of use to him—either for a romp in bed or a ticket to furthering his career—his interest in her vanished.

Tony, though. Tony was different. She saw him every day as the documentary began to take shape. Wonderful, attractive, warm-hearted Tony, she hadn't known how bereft her life had been before he came into it. Two weeks flew by, then three, and she was as content as she'd ever been. Or nearly so—because there was a tiny if only—if only she didn't feel a deep sense of longing and of wanting more with him. When she'd told him that she wanted to take it slow, she'd meant it. She was tired of men who waltzed her into bed and then forgot about her. Tony wouldn't do that and, when things finally did get to the point of sex, she knew it would be different. She hoped it would be a good thing, a perfect thing, but there was a little niggling of doubt. What if it didn't happen? Or what if it did and went all wrong?

She had begun attending all of the board meetings at Helping Hands, along with Kent, although she wasn't officially a board member. Mollie had been absent since her strident speech against the documentary, which didn't trouble Georgette in the least. If anything, it made her life easier.

Then one Tuesday, three weeks after the blow up with Mollie, she sat watching Tony wheel into the room, her focus on his powerful forearms and her thoughts again turned towards the longing she was having trouble containing. So lost in those thoughts was she, she missed the concern in his eyes when he looked up and announced to the meeting. "The Hammersteins are pulling their funding for Helping Hands." He looked at his hands and Georgette had the urge to take his head and cradle it against her chest. She went from worried lust to guilt, and she didn't think either train of thought was much worth entertaining.

"Oh dear," Peggy, usually optimistic, frowned deeply, and Kent put his hand over hers.

"So what?" he asked. "There are many people funding the shelter, right? It's a good cause."

Tony sighed. "Not to the extent that Mollie and Saul did. They have deep pockets and we were their favorite charity."

"We'll raise the money." Georgette wasn't about to let herself get defeated by Mollie. "The documentary will raise awareness. I can talk to ColorCare. If we do a fund drive, I'm sure they'll match donations."

"It's still small potatoes, compared to what we need."

"I'll give generously, so will Kent." Kent nodded at Georgette's statement.

"No offense, but you two can't match what the Hammersteins gave. We're talking a million a year."

Kent whistled. "That's a lot of dough-re-mi."

Georgette sat back in her chair, feeling as though a million in gold coins had hit her on the head. Then she sat up again as something else hit her. "A fund raiser! We could do a fund raiser!"

Tony shook his head. "We've done that, we do that. We had a block party and street fair last year. We already count on that money. Same goes for wheeling in the marathon. Folks will support us, but we need more. The Hammersteins provided the more, and now they've pulled the plug."

"They're wealthy," Georgette said and everyone, Tony included, looked at her as though she'd just stated the sky was blue. "What I mean to say is, they are wealthy, so we need to raise funds where the money is."

"In Cos Cob?" asked Peggy.

"In New York—we have a lot of wealth in our apartment building alone, Peggy."

"True, but—"

"You and I and Kent, we know wealthy people. We'll have a fund raiser for them. A charity dinner with auctions and entertainment. The whole nine yards." Another thought hit her. "We could do it when we premier the documentary."

"That will be a while, won't it?" Tony asked.

"We could finish it by spring, I think." Georgette looked to Kent who nodded.

"That may not be soon enough," Peggy said. "The budget is tight to begin with."

Georgette looked around at all the worried faces in the room. "You people need to start thinking positively. If we can't do it for the premier, we'll do it sooner. We'll do a second one for the premier and a third one on the one year anniversary and a fourth—"

Tony held up his hand, but he was smiling now. "Whoa, there. I love your enthusiasm, but let's not get ahead of ourselves. Are we all in favor of a fund raiser?"

"Sure," came a lukewarm response from the board.

"You're going to need to do better." Georgette stood up. "Let me hear you—are we gonna do this thing?"

"Sure," this time a little brighter, but Georgette knew it would take a lot of work to get up to anything that sounded enthusiastic.

She pointed at them one after another. "We need to be all in. If you care about Helping Hands, you will care about this. Now, are we all in?"

"Yes," Peggy stood up and took Georgette's hand and one by one, all the members joined hands as Georgette and Peggy chanted, "all in."

Tony was beaming, which was most gratifying, and after the rally settled, he said. "Okay then, next question. Where do we hold this extravaganza?"

"The Bronx Zoo!" shouted Kent, throwing a damp rug on what could have turned into a blaze of enthusiasm.

"The zoo?" Even Peggy, who had become well acquainted with Kent's eccentricities, seemed baffled.

"Yes! Yes! The white rhinos are magnificent!" Kent was practically jumping up and down. He began whirling his hands in big circles as he went on about how wonderful the zoo was, how they were doing so much for conservation and helping with extinction and conservation education.

He was, despite this exhibition, a sweet man and, as it turned out, a brilliant director, which was the only reason Georgette didn't stop him right away, though she watched as the other board members, Tony included, sat in mortified fascination. When their eyes began to glaze over, she knew she'd have to step in and stop the madness.

"It's an interesting idea, Kent." Georgette put a

hand to the old man's arm. "Tell you what? Why don't you and I go over to the zoo tomorrow and scout out the prospects?" She had no interest in going to the zoo, but it did get Kent to stand down.

Once a promise is made it needs to be kept, and it seemed Kent was going to make sure she kept hers. He was at her door at nine the next morning, wearing a safari hat and cargo shorts, a pair of hiking boots at the end of his skinny legs. She wanted to ask him if he thought they were going on safari in the Bronx, but it would do no good to rile him.

She hadn't been sure what to wear to a zoo outing and had chosen a pair of black slacks complimented by a light blue cashmere sweater. Kent inspected her and frowned when he got to her shoes. "You don't intend to traipse about in those, do you?"

Georgette pulled off one black pump and examined it. She liked these shoes, she'd found them at a little boutique on Fifth Avenue not a month ago and they matched her outfit perfectly. "What's wrong with them?"

"You can't wear heels to the zoo. There is walking involved. A lot of walking." He pointed to his boots with the walking stick he carried. "You have to dress for contingencies."

She sighed and resisted the urge to roll her eyes. "What do you suggest?"

"Boots or sneakers."

"Sneakers?" He had to be kidding. Sneakers were for workouts, not outings. She might have argued the point, but she'd been working with Kent for a few weeks and she'd learned an argument could last into the later part of the day. She didn't have the energy.

"Fine," She went back to her bedroom, found her sneakers and put them on. Then she frowned at herself in the mirror, the horrid things sticking out from under her tailored slacks would never do. She changed into jeans and, although things matched, she was far from happy with the ensemble, it was one "I love New York" T-shirt away from a masquerade as a tourist from upstate.

She strode back into the living room, ready to get the ordeal over with, and picked up her phone.

"What are you doing?" Kent asked.

"Calling a town car."

He took the phone from her. "We need to learn to conserve, my dear. Town cars make a huge footprint on the environment. You ought to think about these things, particularly when going to the zoo."

She was about to ask him if he planned they hike to the zoo when he pulled two Metro Cards from his pocket and handed her one. She nearly threw him out.

"The subway?" She wanted to ask if he was out of his mind, but the answer to that was obvious. "You can't be serious." She had long stopped careening through long hot rat-infested tunnels in the dark with the unwashed masses.

Kent frowned. "We are doing it for the homeless. To show solidarity."

"No."

"Do the homeless get to say no? You need to change your attitude or you'll have to find someone else to direct your project."

She nearly told him fine, she'd find another director. But Peggy would never forgive her if she fired him. She took the card. "Anyone ever told you you're a pain?"

He smiled. "You have—at least once a week." He pointed his walking stick at the door. "Onward!"

The subway was every bit as bad as she remembered. It was dark and smelled of garbage and was hotter than Hades. In fact, she wondered if hell might not be a subway platform. The train car was crowded and they had to stand all the way into the Bronx. To make matters worse, an unkempt man got on board at 166th Street and began begging for handouts. Kent waved him over, gave him a dollar and introduced him to Georgette as "the woman who could help you with your plight." He went on for some time about Helping Hands and the wonder of homeless shelters. The beggar clearly wasn't interested—and tried to excuse himself several times.

Luckily, their stop came up and Georgette practically dragged Kent from the train, as he was telling the guy all about the gala and how he should think about attending.

The zoo was a pleasant surprise—with all the trees it reminded her a little of Central Park. They walked to a picnic area near some old buildings she remembered from childhood and she could nearly picture a gala here, under the stars, with sea lions barking in the background.

The zoo's offices were housed in one of the buildings and Kent explained he'd called the PR director, a woman named May Hurley, and that she was very excited to be meeting with them.

Ms. Hurley smiled patiently, if a bit nervously, at Kent and then raised her brows at Georgette. Kent wasted no time in explaining, in detail and hand gestures, his ideas of what he hoped would be the greatest gala ever held at the zoo or anywhere else on earth. "We could include the animals. They would have a wonderful time."

Ms. Hurley, to her credit, didn't seem horrified by Kent. She took his arm. "Speaking of animals, we have a new baby giraffe. Would you like to go take a look?"

"Wonderful! Come along, Georgette. You are going to love this."

Ms. Hurley then took Georgette's arm. "Maybe I could borrow Ms. Alden for a few minutes. I have... I wanted to talk to her." The awkward excuse passed unnoticed by Kent who was already halfway out the door. When he'd gone, Ms. Hurley sat down with a sigh.

"He's a bit eccentric," Georgette offered, realizing she might have to defend her director.

"Honey, he's nuttier than a Christmas cookie. But, honestly? I kinda like the old guy. Maybe I've spent too much time with monkeys."

"I kinda like the old guy, too. And, believe it or not, he's a brilliant director—and his heart is in the right place."

"That's good to know. Since the debacle with the penguins, he can't seem to do enough for us. His enthusiasm is catching, even if it is a bit over the top." She pulled her brows together, "Can he really direct?"

"Yes, he really can. He's worked harder than anyone on my Helping Hands project. We do need funds and the gala was my idea. I realize having it in the gorilla enclosure might not be in the best interest of our guests."

Ms. Hurley laughed. "The gorillas wouldn't like it much, either. Do you have other venues in mind?"

"It's a new idea, so I haven't thought it through." *If I had, I wouldn't be here*, Georgette didn't add.

"Actually, having it at the zoo is not a terrible idea." She retrieved a folder from behind her desk. "We have our gala at the Central Park zoo—it's smaller and more intimate. And we actually did have the sea lions included. They like parties."

Georgette wasn't sure if the woman was kidding or not. "Central Park is a wonderful idea. We wouldn't have to do it in the zoo."

"No, I imagine you might just find a small part of the park—maybe near the museums or Tavern on the Green."

"Tavern on the Green, what a great idea. Thank you, you've made my sojourn out to the Bronx well worthwhile."

"Glad to be of service. Now, I do have a favor to ask you. Kent has mentioned the documentary he wants to do on behalf of the zoo?"

"He's mentioned it, yes."

"I'm a little wary—you can understand why. But if you were to produce the project, well, then I think we might be interested. I understand you'd have to finish your current documentary first."

"I'd love to. But, you do know that I'm new to making documentaries? I know my way around a studio and a camera, and I'm versed about shooting scenes, but there is an awful lot I don't know. Sometimes I wonder what I've gotten myself into, I have no idea how it will all turn out." Georgette surprised herself in admitting any of this, and to a stranger who wanted to hire her, no less.

"I admire your honesty. Let's keep the idea open, okay? Besides, I don't think anyone else can work with Kent." She smiled.

"Speaking of Kent, you don't think he's trying to free your giraffes, do you?'

"He's given his word. Though maybe we should go check on him, just in case."

Chapter Nineteen

Tony invited her to dinner at his place and, as Georgette came through the door, the smell was heavenly. "Shrimp in rum sauce," he said. "My Cuban grandmother's recipe."

As they ate his family specialty, she told him all about her zoo outing with Kent. It was quite a story, from the subway to Ms. Hurley to Tavern on the Green. "Kent is crazier than—I can't even come up with a comparison."

Tony, who hadn't said much during the meal, picked at his food and nodded. "Is something wrong?" she asked.

"I went to see my doctor today."

Panic rose in Georgette's chest. "Is everything okay? Are you sick?"

He smiled at her. "No, nothing like that." He rolled away to the bathroom and came back with a prescription bottle and set it down on the table in front of her.

She picked it up. "Viagra." It dawned on her, what he was telling her. "Oh."

"I'm not sure it will work, Georgette."

"We won't know until we try." She handed the cylinder back to him and kept her hand on his. He hoped she wouldn't notice the tremor in them. Then again, judging by the way she was absently biting her lip, maybe she was nervous, too.

"Okay then." He went to the kitchen and got a glass of water and took one of the pills. "Here goes nothing."

"Now we wait?" she asked.

"Now we wait."

"Okay."

"Maybe we could wait in the bedroom?"

"Yes. Good idea."

He transferred himself into the bed, using the triangle that hung from the ceiling. She watched wordlessly and he was glad she didn't say anything. But damn, why did this have to be so hard? Bad enough he couldn't sweep her off her feet and carry her to bed. She lay down next to him and began kissing him—his forehead, his eyes, his cheek, his neck, his shoulder and he took her face into his hands and put his lips to hers.

They kissed for a long time and then she lay with her head on his shoulder, he buried his face in her hair, which smelled of ripe peaches and she traced the line of his shirt buttons with her fingers. It was pleasant, more than that—it was wonderful and warm, but—underneath was a feeling of impending doom. What if it didn't happen? What if he couldn't make it happen?

She sat up and, not taking her eyes from his, began to slowly unbutton her blouse. She wore a shear bra in a shade of baby blue and her breasts rose and fell with each breath. She pulled off the blouse and reached around and unhooked the bra. He managed to catch her arms as she began to pull it off and he took his fingers and ran them over the straps and then pulled the bra away.

She leaned into him again, cradling his head in her hands as he kissed the space between her breasts, her skin warm and soft against his lips, and he felt a tightening in his stomach and, sweet relief, felt his erection start to grow. "Yes," he said.

She leaned back to look at him and then unzipped

him and stroked her hand over his hardness. "Well, will you look at that?" she said.

Slowly, and a little awkwardly, she helped him out of his clothes and then stripped off what was left of hers. "You'll have to be on top." His voice had gone husky and he reminded himself to breathe as she climbed astride him.

Tony looked into her beautiful face as they came together, so determined and flushed, he knew he had to kiss it, and he pulled her closer and stroked the skin of her back as their lips met. Her hands were everywhere at once, on his shoulders, his arms, his chest, her lips following her hands as they traced over him, mapping his skin, until he was totally lost in sensation and didn't ever want to be found again.

She hadn't known what to expect and had told herself not to expect much. But this? It was so real and so whole, she wondered what the other men in her life had been doing. That was sex, but this was making love and for the first time in her experience, she understood the difference. He made love with such tenderness, and his hands felt so good on her burning skin, stroking her back. She was full of sensations, building and building until they exploded, or rather imploded.

She climbed from him, her legs gone to jelly. "Wow."

"Yeah? You're not just—"

She stopped the rest of his question with her lips on his. "Wow," she said again and this time he smiled.

"Want to do it again? There are twenty pills in the bottle."

"You trying to kill me?"

He pulled her in close and kissed her head. "No, I wouldn't want to do that."

"I definitely plan on coming back for more. If you were wondering." She stretched out alongside of him like a contented cat. "Okay if I stay the night?"

His arm tightened around her. "You really don't think I'm going to let you out of this bed anytime soon, do you?"

She sighed. "That's good. I don't want to go anywhere. I'm not sure I could."

"Good." He pulled a strand of hair from her face. "What do you want for breakfast?"

He woke up to find Georgette, still gloriously naked, asleep with her head on the pillow next to his. If he could wake up like this for the next fifty years or so he would be one happy man. He lay there for a minute more, watching as she breathed in and out and decided he'd make scrambled eggs. Then another thought hit, it was Saturday and he was supposed to do a workout with Vida in, he looked at the clock, exactly twenty minutes. He found the shorts he usually wore to bed in the nightstand drawer . It was a chore to get them on, though he'd become pretty good at it after ten years, and he was afraid his rolling around would wake Georgette. She was, he discovered, a sound sleeper and even when he transferred back into his wheelchair it did little more than cause her to sigh and turn.

He grabbed his cell phone and wheeled into the kitchen and called Vida. "I can't make it today. Sorry for the late notice."

"You feeling okay?"

"Yes. I'm great."

He might have known Vida wouldn't let him off the hook quite so easily. "So why aren't you here? I'm at the park waiting on you and if I were doing my job, I'd come haul you out of bed myself."

"I've got a pretty good excuse. Named Georgette."

"Really?" There was a pause. "Really?" This time, the word was followed by a tiny cheer.

"So, let's just say I'm busy."

"Okay, lover boy. That is a pretty good excuse. You better not be lying, either."

He wondered himself if he had fantasized the whole thing, but then Georgette walked into the kitchen, still naked except for his unbuttoned shirt. "I've got to go," he told Vida.

"Who was that?" asked Georgette.

"Vida. I forgot to cancel my workout with her."

"You don't have to cancel on my account."

"Woman, you're standing in my kitchen wearing nothing but my shirt. Wild horses couldn't drag me away."

She pulled the shirt off her shoulders. "I could be standing here naked."

"You better leave that on if you want me to fix you breakfast."

She pulled it back on and, sadly, buttoned the buttons. "Um, breakfast. I'm starving."

"If I make you eggs, you have to promise to take off the shirt and come back to bed afterwards."

"You've got yourself a deal, mister."

Chapter Twenty

Georgette couldn't remember a time when she'd been as happy, not even the heady first days of her marriage. Tony was the most considerate man she'd ever known, both in bed and out of it. They were together much of the time and when they weren't she was busy with the documentary. The work of putting it together and producing it seemed endless —a challenge like she'd never known before, but she loved doing it. It was as though she was made to be a documentary film maker and everything before had been leading to this. She was almost glad they had killed Electra Holmes, because in killing off the character she had made room for a new life, a better life.

There were also the ColorCare commercials. She had done commercials all through her career and the work reminded her of her old life—spending time in the makeup chair, memorizing lines, rehearsals, several takes to get it right. It wasn't something she was particularly interested in doing anymore, but it paid the bills and the work came easily.

They finished the first commercial in half a day and she sat in the chair with a jar of cold cream, removing the heavy makeup, her head already on the afternoon, when she and the crew would film some exterior shots of the Harlem shelter, which was also an excuse to go see Tony, not that she needed an excuse. She was thinking about bringing him coffee, maybe getting donuts for the crew and was so lost in these thoughts she didn't notice Harvey until he was standing next to the chair.

"Congratulations, Georgie."

She knew he was fishing for gratitude. To his mind, warped though it might be, he was the reason she was doing the commercials. She thought about giving him a piece of her mind. The old Georgette would have done just that, and maybe have thrown her hair brush at his head for good measure. She really hadn't the energy or inclination. "Thank you."

"Long time no see. We should get together. Dinner?"

Again, she wanted to tell him he could take his overpriced meal and what he expected in return and stuff it where the sun didn't shine. She got off the chair, kissed his cheek. "I've moved on, Harvey. I suggest you do the same." She put her purse over her shoulder. "See you around." And whistled as she left him standing open mouthed.

She went home to shower and change into jeans. She found, much to her surprise, that she liked wearing jeans or, more to the point, she liked the way Tony eyed her when she was wearing jeans.

She walked over to Peggy's apartment to see if they could leave a few minutes early so they could stop at Alahandros and get coffee for the crew. She would get some for Tony, too. Maybe a cinnamon bun, because they were his favorite. Peggy answered after her first knock, her face flushed and motioned Georgette through the door. "I see you got my messages." Georgette was going to ask which messages and explain that her phone battery had died on the way home, but Peggy grabbed her by the arm before she could. "Please. Come in." And then she nearly dragged her through the vestibule to the living room.

There on the couch, amid a flurry of tissues, a

suitcase at her feet sat— "Poppy?" Georgette had an urge to rub her eyes. Richard had, in her last conversation with him not a week ago, told his mother he was ready to propose to the girl. Then again, Richard had a history of being less than honest.

Poppy looked up from the tissue she was wiping her eyes with. "You're here. Brill. I knocked up the neighbor when no one answered your door. She's a wonder, your Peggy. Very kind." With this Poppy's voice caught in another sob.

"She's been here all morning," Peggy said. "I'm going to have to go the store for more tissues."

"Why are you here?" Georgette thought it best to ask the obvious.

"I've left him." Another sob and wail came from the girl.

Peggy sat down next to her and patted her arm. "Now, now." She looked uneasily to Georgette, who wanted to ask what was expected of her, but didn't. "Remember what we talked about. Deep breaths."

"You left Richard?" Georgette had to ask.

Poppy gulped and nodded. "I came here because you said I might write for your documentary."

She *had* asked, and Poppy had been enthusiastic, but—"You didn't need to come all the way to New York. I meant to give you a job where you could stay in London. Maybe I wasn't clear... You left Richard?"

The girl nodded again. "Because I love him." She blew her nose.

"Because you love him?" Georgette's head was spinning.

"He asked me to marry him." This elicited another sob.

"He asked you to marry him. You love him. So you left him. Poppy dear, that makes absolutely no sense," Georgette said as gently as she could manage.

"I can't allow him to throw away Hillcrest. His father has threatened to disinherit him if he marries me."

Georgette sighed and sat on the couch. "Listen to me. I was married to Nigel, so I know him pretty well. He might threaten to disinherit Richard, but he won't do it."

Poppy looked at Georgette as though she'd told her Christmas wouldn't be cancelled after all. "He won't? Are you sure?"

Georgette was not at all sure. "Richard is his only child. Who in the world is going to take care of that drafty old house if Nigel disinherits him? He's not likely to leave it to the butler or even his sheep dog, though he does love that dog more than he ought." Georgette shook her head at the thought of stuffy old Nigel trying to throw his weight about and interfering with their boy's happiness. She would see to it that it didn't happen— and the first step was not to let him have his way. "Have you talked to Richard?"

"I left him a note. I said I was leaving."

"Poppy, did you tell him why?"

"Of course not! He'd choose me, wouldn't he? And then he'd think his whole life he could have been a posh earl instead of a lowly banker."

"You need to tell him. It's his decision to make, not yours." Poppy didn't look convinced. "At least call to tell him where you've gone. You owe the poor boy that much."

Peggy led Poppy to the bedroom, so she could have some privacy to make her call. "Do you think she'll tell him?"

"I certainly hope so. If she doesn't, I will. And then I'm going to call Nigel and give him a large piece of my mind."

"Is that a good idea?"

"I am not about to allow that man to destroy my son. Richard loves Hillcrest. It is his birthright."

"Maybe it would be best to let them settle it." Peggy frowned uneasily. "Without your intercession."

"He's my son, Peggy. Of course I will intercede."

"Don't take this the wrong way, but sometimes, well; things get more complicated when you get in the middle of them. You create, um, drama."

Georgette stood up. "Maybe drama is what is needed. It can be good to stir things up once in a while."

Peggy didn't look convinced.

Well, at least they had talked Poppy into calling Richard. She'd calmed after coming from the bedroom and Georgette had taken up her suitcase and settled the girl into her spare room. Poppy lay on the bed and stared up at the ceiling—not a good sign. "You could come along, since you're to be part of this project," Georgette offered.

Poppy smiled sadly. "Thank you, but I'm tired. If you don't mind, I'll have a bit of a lie down."

Georgette closed the door, hoping Poppy would be okay.

Her phone rang as Peggy found a parking spot up the block from Helping Hands. "Hello, Mumsy?"

"Richard." She raised her brows at Peggy who nodded and left her in the car to her conversation.

"I'm beside myself, I'm afraid." There was a choke in his voice. "Poppy's gone. I've rung everywhere and—well, I thought I should ring you as well. Though why—"

He sounded so lost and confused she wished she could crawl through the phone and hug him. "She didn't call you?"

"No. She left a note and—"

The poor boy sounded as though he'd swallowed glass. "She's here. In New York. She said she'd called you."

"In New York? " He brightened, though just a little. "But why?"

"I think she should explain to you. Can you come here? I can send plane fare if—" There was an uncomfortable silence on the other end of the line, which prompted her to say "Richard?" in case he'd passed out.

"Oh yes, well. I'll speak to her later, Mumsy. Take

good care of my girl, will you?" With that the line went dead.

Georgette considered calling back but then remembered Peggy's warning—maybe it was best to let them settle it. She wouldn't call. For now.

"Dinner?" Tony asked as she popped her head into his office to say they'd finished up with shooting exteriors for the day. Was babysitting Poppy more important than a romantic evening with Tony? He had promised to make pizza—and she was looking forward to it.

She sighed. "How hard is it to make a pizza?" she said half to herself.

"We can have something else." He looked so taken aback that she had to laugh. She leaned in to kiss him lightly.

"No. I'm really asking. I have a visitor. Poppy is having a lie-in in my apartment as we speak." She went on to explain about Poppy and Richard and her ex-husband. She liked the way he listened to her concerns and she talked on and on, something she never would have thought to do with the men in her life before. "I'm sorry," she said when she had finished "I've talked your ear off."

Tony reached up and touched the side of his face. "Nope. It's still there. So what's this about pizza? To answer your question, it's pretty easy to make."

"Good." She took a pen from her purse and handed it to him. "Write down everything we need to make it. Remember I'm hopeless at cooking."

He raised his eyebrows. "Yeah, but you make up for it in other ways. You plan on making pizza?"

"See, I've already taken you for granted." She shook her head. "If you would like to come over this evening, I would like to attempt to make you a pizza. I might need help." She knew it was easier to meet at his place, where everything was wheelchair accessible, but there were extenuating circumstances.

"You're on."

"You're sure? I mean I know it's easier—"

"I'll put up with just about anything for you, sweetheart. Now what do you like on your pie?"

The Food Emporium was much bigger than she remembered and she feared she would get lost before finding all the ingredients on the list. She could scarcely imagine how suburbanites dealt with those warehouse style supermarkets. A sign that read groceries pointed down an escalator and she rode down to wander around the narrow aisles and hope she didn't need to drop breadcrumbs to find her way out again.

It took much longer than it should have, the ready-made crusts Tony had suggested weren't in aisle three next to the jarred sauces, and the pizza tins were against the wall in aisle eight. She finally gathered all the ingredients on the list and was rung up by a young woman dressed in black, who absently put the items into a paper sack. "You need to reconfigure the store," said Georgette as she handed the girl her card.

"Cash or charge?' asked the girl, ignoring Georgette's comment completely, and Georgette considered asking her if she had a hearing problem and then decided she had enough troubles without taking on management of the local market. Besides, she had gathered up everything on the list, which gave her no small measure of satisfaction.

The apartment was quiet as a church sanctuary. "Poppy? I'm home," she shouted as she shut the door with her foot while hanging on to the three shopping bags she had hauled half a block up the street and up the elevator. Getting no answer, she figured the girl was still asleep and so went to the kitchen and unpacked her treasures. She lined them on the counter top—pizza tins, two readymade crusts, a jar of sauce, a ball of mozzarella, a bit of pepperoni, which Tony professed to love. Thoughts of Tony made her feel warm all over, and she stood there lost in a daydream for a minute before coming back to herself and thinking that things were too quiet and she should go and check on Poppy.

She abandoned the food stuffs, walked down the hall, and cracked the door to the guest room a sliver. The room was dark and smelled vaguely of body odor. Had the girl really slept the afternoon away? It would be good for her to get up. "Poppy?" she said softly, opening the door another notch.

The lump in the bed that Georgette had identified as Poppy didn't move an iota. She opened the door and stepped inside. "Poppy?" she said again, not quite as softly this time. She walked over to the window, ready to pull the curtains aside and let some sun into the darkened room when she noticed the open prescription bottle tipped on its side on the night stand.

She picked it up and examined it. The fine print was unreadable, but the word "Vicodin" along with a warning not to take more than one was printed clearly enough to see without the help of glasses. Georgette felt a tightening in her throat. Poppy wouldn't do something so stupid, would she? Then again, Georgette herself had tried to set up an attempted suicide not all that long ago.

It struck her like a ton of bricks—had she really been so self-indulgent as to consider a suicide attempt a good way to get attention? If she could go back in time, she would have taken herself by the shoulders and shaken some sense into the silly woman who thought life was a soap opera. She couldn't go back in time and so she took Poppy by the shoulders instead and began to shake her hard enough to jiggle the bed.

"Poppy, you need to wake up!" She slapped the girl on the cheek and finally, Poppy opened her eyes.

The girl put her hand to her cheek and looked at Georgette as though she were a mugger. "Whaa?"

"Wake up," Georgette said with all the force she could muster. She got off the bed, went to the window and tore the curtains asunder. Sunlight assaulted the room and the girl sat up, blinking at the bright light.

"What the hell?" she said.

"What the hell," Georgette repeated, grabbing the cylinder and thrusting in the girl's face, "is this?"

The girl just sat there blinking. Georgette was in no mood for blinking. "How many of these did you take?"

"I dunno. Two or three?"

It wasn't the whole bottle, though Georgette wasn't quite ready to let it go. "Two or three? Then how come the bottle is empty?"

"Cause they're all gone?" Poppy had stopped blinking. She sat up in bed and rubbed her eyes. "What are you on about anyway? Everyone takes aspirin for headaches, don't they?"

"Aspirin? It says Vicodin."

"Yeah, well, I didn't want to take the economy size in my purse, did I? I put a few in there. For storage." She scratched her head. "You thought they were Vicodin?" She began to giggle. "Three Vicodin and I'd be out for a week. One was enough to make Richie all goofy after he'd had the root canal."

Georgette sighed and shook her head. "I'm going to make pizza for dinner."

"You're going to use the oven. That's awful brave of you, isn't it?"

Tony came bearing a bottle of Chianti as she was setting the table. "It goes well with pizza," he said, handing it to her and surveying the dining room. "Looks like you've got everything under control."

"Looks can be deceiving." She had spent the last twenty minutes hunting down stove directions on the Internet. She'd found them and they'd done nothing for her self-esteem; if she'd known how simple it was, she might not have nearly burned down her apartment the last time through. She said as much to Tony. "I did get it going, though. It's preheating. I think. And I got all the ingredients." She sighed. "I may have to leave cookery to you from here on in."

Tony wheeled to the kitchen door and stopped. Georgette hadn't realized how narrow her galley kitchen was, or how high her counters were. "You can't maneuver in here, can you? And you should take note of the fire exits. Just in case."

He smiled and grabbed her hand. "I'll talk you through it. First, you need to uncork the wine."

"Now there's something I know how to do." She found the corkscrew, uncorked and poured them each a glass and handed Tony one. "I suppose we'll have to share with Poppy. She's still in the shower."

"How is she?" He seemed genuinely concerned and this touched Georgette in a way that surprised her. Maybe she cared about the girl more than she wanted to admit.

"She'd be better if she would talk to Richard." She took a sip of her drink. "We'll all feel better if we eat. You sure we shouldn't send out?"

"You are a very accomplished woman. Pizza is easy."

"Okay then." Georgette made a show of rolling up her sleeves and flexing her fingers. "Let's get to it."

Pizza making was easy, especially with Tony coaching her. She finished putting together two pizzas, one with pepperoni and one plain cheese, as the oven dinged. "Oven's ready," Tony said.

"It tells you? Will wonders never cease." She opened the door to a gush of hot air and pushed both tins in. "Ten minutes, right? What will we do to pass the time?"

"We could make out." Tony put his wine glass down on the table and held out his arms.

"I like how you think." She bent down and gave him a long and languid kiss. "I don't think ten minutes will be enough time."

"We'll make do." He reached up and pulled her in again.

"Ahem." She stood up to see Poppy in jeans and T-shirt, her hair wrapped in a towel, staring at them. Georgette's face went hot as the oven.

"Poppy, you remember Tony?"

"Sure, yeah. From up at the beach, wasn't it?" The girl's head bobbed from Georgette to Tony, her eyebrows bent together. "So you two are—?"

"Dating," Georgette said. She liked the sound of it and the way it made Tony smile.

"I thought you were with that Harvey bloke."

Tony's smile fell and Georgette took his hand. "Are you kidding? Why would I want Harvey when I can date this guy?" She raised her eyebrows, hoping the mood had lightened. Tony squeezed her hand. The oven timer dinged and Poppy started to sob.

"I'm sorry," she said, grabbing a handful of napkins and blowing her nose. "I'm having a hard day."

Georgette didn't quite know what to say. "Would you like a glass of wine?"

The girl nodded and Tony poured her a glass and handed it to her. He turned to Georgette. "The pizza?"

"The pizza!" Georgette, feeling totally useless, fumbled with the oven buttons until the dinging stopped. She was pretty sure the heat was off, she fervently hoped it was. She opened the door ready to reach in and grab the pies, when a blast of furnace-hot air accosted her, reminding her to grab the pot holders. The pizza looked perfect, not burnt, the cheese melted and she felt a jolt of pride as she picked up her newly purchased pizza cutter. She was about to ask Tony how to go about cutting when she noticed neither Tony or Poppy were paying the least attention.

Poppy had seated herself at the table next to Tony and, heads together, they were deep in conversation. Georgette would just have to figure it out—and honestly, it was easy enough. She'd seen pizza before, hadn't she? She wasn't helpless. She cut the pizza, plated it and brought them each several slices.

"Hey, that looks good," Tony said.

Poppy smiled at him and then at Georgette. "I'm starving." She wasn't crying anymore.

"Thank you," said Poppy after they'd eaten. "I'm feeling ever so much better. Now if you'll excuse me, I've got to go call Richard." She kissed Tony on the cheek. "Hang on to this man, he's a wonder."

Georgette watched as she nearly skipped away. "What in the world did you say to her?"

"Not much. I listened mostly." He held up the bottle. "More wine?"

Georgette understood the pang she felt, the little swelling at the center of her heart. It was love, pure and simple, and it was something she hadn't felt for a good, long time. Oh, there had been a line of men parading through her life. She couldn't, in fact, remember a time when there hadn't been a man in her life, or sometimes two or three men. She liked them all, some had made her laugh and some had taken her out for expensive meals and evenings at Lincoln center. Some had been good in bed.

She hadn't loved any of them. Except for Nigel, though she'd been young then and caught up in the dizzy dancing of a romance that made her feel as though she'd walked into the middle of a fairy tale. She had been breathless for the first year of their marriage, in the dream of happily ever after. It had been perfect.

Until it wasn't. She could, with the singularity of a laser light, pinpoint the moment it began to unravel. It was at Hillcrest, the second summer of her marriage, the summer before Richard was born.

She'd been thrilled at the prospect of going to England. Nigel spoke lovingly of his homeland and of the estate in Hampstead. It was her first trip abroad and she kept looking out the jetliner's window, even though there was nothing to see but dark sky.

They stayed at the Savoy in London and went on a yacht cruise down the Thames. He took her to the

British Museum and to Buckingham Palace for the changing of the guard. When she was thoroughly enchanted, he brought her to Hillcrest.

They turned past the gate into a lane lined by aged oak trees, leaves kissing overhead to form a canopy. "It's beautiful." She had sighed contentedly and put her head on Nigel's shoulder. He'd smiled and taken her hand.

"It will be mine someday and then our children's." He put both of their hands lightly to her still flat stomach, where the new baby they had told no one about, not yet, was secreted away.

She might have noticed he said it would belong to this new being they would bring into the world, that he said "mine" and not "ours" as though her part in their family didn't matter, but she was caught up in love and beauty and then the trees parted to reveal a house so large it made her gasp. It was a stone edifice of over eighty rooms, set upon a green lawn that seemed to stretch to infinity.

The butler met them at the door and greeted Nigel as "sir." He eyed her with a frown and said, "ma'am," before escorting them into a marble foyer and up an oaken staircase to a suite of rooms on the second floor. The bedroom had a poster bed made of mahogany and a window with brocade drapes that overlooked a terrace and the grounds beyond. Georgette nearly said, "It's beautiful," but something had changed in the demeanor of the room and she held her tongue.

"His lordship and lady are expecting you for dinner," said the butler.

"Very good, Greer."

"Shall you require assistance with dress?"

"No, Greer. We shall manage."

The butler bowed and shut the door behind him as he left. Georgette giggled and began unbuttoning Nigel's shirt. "Shall you require assistance with dress?" she said in a fake English accent.

Instead of laughing with her, Nigel pulled her hands away and gave her a stern look. "Really,

Georgette, a bit of propriety is in order."

The lord and lady waited to receive them in the library, a room done in elegant dark furniture, with windows tall and wide enough for a horse to gallop through. The two of them stood wordless and expressionless near the fireplace. Georgette was a good actress and so she covered the squealing excitement she felt with her own solemn demeanor.

Lady Benningsworth—and to this day Georgette thought of her as Lady Benningsworth and not just Lydia, came over to them as they entered the room. "Nigel, dear," she said, ignoring Georgette completely as she gave him a kiss on the cheek. "So good to see you."

She felt a small push at her back, Nigel urging her forward. "I'd like to present Georgette."

His mother examined her with eyes as cold as the stones of the manor house. "Ah, yes. Georgette." Her name sounded as though it might have been another word for the gum scraped off her mother-in-law's shoe.

Still, she played her part and did a half curtsey and said, "How do you do?" as formally as she could. She stole a look at her new father-in-law, he hadn't moved a muscle since they'd come into the room.

And that was it, the moment she knew, deep down, she would never be happy at Hillcrest. She feared love couldn't survive the cold shoulder she'd been given. Oh, she held on to hope. She was still head over heels, she carried Nigel's child. When they got back to New York, she thought, maybe, she could keep him happy as long as there was an ocean between Hillcrest and the two of them. She had his son. Then, not long after Richard was born, Lord Benningsworth died, Nigel was called back to the estate, and the fairy tale happy ending she had so fervently wanted to believe in went up in a puff of smoke and ash.

She looked at Tony and realized she'd been a million miles away. Imagine, a million miles when all she wanted was to be right there, in his presence. He wasn't a titled gentleman, he wasn't anything at all but the kindest man she'd ever met, the most caring, and the sort of man she could build a future with—a real future, not one built on fantasy.

She wished his wheelchair away—if he were able bodied, they wouldn't have to think of contingencies, how hard it was for him to stay over with her. He would make do, for her, spend an uncomfortable night. She wouldn't do that to him. "I want to fix it so it'll be easier, for you to stay with me."

"We can do that."

"But you need your rest, so I'm sending you home." She kissed him. "Just so you know I'd rather not send you home. I don't want to send you home ever."

When the intercom buzzed the next morning as she was making coffee, she was surprised and not surprised at all that it was Richard at the door. He was as much her son as he was Nigel's, wasn't he? And her son would not let the small matter of a large estate get in the way of a big matter like love.

The poor boy must have flown all night to get to New York and he looked the part, his clothes wrinkled, his hair askew, dark rings under his eyes. She kissed him lightly without saying a word and went to the still closed door of the guest room and knocked. "Poppy. Someone's here for you."

Poppy opened the door. Despite the comfortable guest bed and the feather duvet, she looked like she hadn't gotten anymore sleep than had Richard. Georgette watched as the girl's face went from perplexed, to surprised, to unadulterated joy.

Richard put down his bag and opened his arms and Poppy sprang into them. Yes, thought Georgette, they're going to make it work, somehow.

"I've been trying to ring you up all night," Poppy said once he'd put her down.

"I saw the messages when I arrived this morning. Sorry, I couldn't call from the plane and I left the flat right after I talked to Mum."

"You did?" Poppy and Georgette seemed to have the same question.

Richard smiled at his mother. "You were right. I have to do this in person." He got down on one knee and took Poppy's hand. "You have to marry me. I'm lost without you. That's all I've got to say."

Poppy's grin faded. "But Hillcrest."

Georgette could not contain a sigh. "For goodness sakes, Poppy. The boy loves you. Hillcrest ruined any chance of happiness I might have had with his father. Don't let it ruin your happiness. Or my son's."

Chapter Twenty One

Tony whistled while shaving, then challenged Vida to an extra two miles in the park, and he was still whistling when he showered to get ready for work. Nothing could break his good mood, not even finding Saul Hammerstein waiting for him in his office.

"Saul," he said, wheeling behind his desk and reminding himself that he liked the guy, even if the guy's wife was a harridan, even if Saul had pulled funding from Helping Hands because of her. Saul's sheepish look, as though he were guilty of murder rather than pulled funding, confirmed to Tony that the guy at least had a conscience.

"Good to see you, Tony. You look good. You doing the marathon?"

The marathon was only a few weeks away and Saul knew damn well Tony was doing it, as Tony had done it every year. "Wouldn't miss it. Why? You want to sponsor me?" He couldn't help needling Saul. He wouldn't have done it in the past, but Saul *had* pulled funding. Vida had said this morning he was getting cocky. Well, maybe he was.

Saul stared at him for a minute and cleared his throat. "Yeah, about that."

Tony did like Saul and he wasn't cocky to the point of not caring about the guy's feelings. "It's okay. We've got the documentary and Georgette is planning a big fundraiser in February. All we've got to do is hold on until then." He loved saying her name.

"The winter gala, yeah, I know."

Tony raised his eyebrows. The gala was still in the planning stages. Georgette was going to talk to the events coordinator at Tavern on the Green in a few days.

"For a big city," Saul said, "New York is a small town. Word gets out." Saul reached into his pocket and pulled out a folded check. He slid it across the desk towards Tony.

Tony unfolded it and nearly fell out of his chair when he read the numbers: a million dollars, made out to Helping Hands. "This is generous."

"Consider it an apology. My old man left us when I was two. I know from poverty, that's why I wanted to support what you do here. I got plenty; it's good to give some back." Saul touched his heart.

"And Mollie's okay with this?" Tony knew he shouldn't poke the pit bull, but there it was.

"What Mollie doesn't know won't hurt her. Though I got a small favor to ask." Saul tipped his head sideways. "I think I can get Mollie to come around if we can get an invite to the gala."

Tony wasn't so sure he wanted Mollie back on the board. Then again, Saul was more than generous. How could he refuse? "That can be arranged. I'll talk to Georgette." Another thought occurred. "She does know Georgette—"

"Is planning this shindig? Yeah. Still, it's going to be a big deal. Besides, I wouldn't mind seeing Ms. Alden in a low cut cocktail dress. Maybe she'll dance with me. That woman—" Saul kissed his fingers.

Tony didn't know whether to be offended or proud. "I'm dating her," he blurted.

"No kidding?" Saul's eyes grew gratifyingly wide and Tony decided on pride.

"No kidding."

"You are one lucky bastard. Electra Holmes, jeez, most guys I know wouldn't mind hitting that."

Tony should have been offended, but pride had

taken over and he was feeling damned good. "It's pretty sweet."

The guest list for the gala was growing like mushrooms in a dark cellar; it seemed everyone wanted a ticket. Georgette was more than pleased, not only because she could plan such an event, but because Helping Hands would benefit from her effort. That Saul Hammerstein had made a very generous contribution made the gala nearly superfluous, but Georgette reminded Tony of all he hoped to do in the future. "Dream big," she told him.

"Is that what you've done?" he asked with a sly smile.

"Yes." She raised her eyebrows. They were moving through Central Park, she was going to Tavern on the Green to meet with the events planner and he was going to do a pre-marathon session with Vida, who was even now making her way towards them.

Vida looked her over, dressed in a Dior skirt and blouse in a dusky fall green with shoes in dark green to match. "I take it you're not running with us?"

"It's too hot to run," said Georgette. It was warm, temperatures climbing well into the eighties and paired with a drenching humidity. It might well have been mid-summer and not late September. "I'm going to meet the events planner."

"She looks good," Vida said to Tony.

"She always looks good. It's a gift, I think," Tony squeezed Georgette's hand. "She's even turned Saul Hammerstein's head."

"Well, poor Saul is married to Mollie," said Georgette.

"Honestly, though," said Vida assessing. "I've seen you with the male population. You do have a knack."

"Sweetheart, I played a man-eater for thirty years. I learned a thing or two."

"Ah, Electra. Tony's told me all about her."

Georgette glanced at Tony. "Has he?"

"Hell, yes. He's been crushing on Electra from way back." Vida gave him a slap on the arm. "Now he's dating her, how great is that? He was nervous, too. Not every guy gets to date the woman he fantasizes over while in bed alone."

Tony's face had gone from red to pale and Georgette wasn't sure how to feel about this. Not long ago, she would have been happy to fulfill some man's fantasy as Electra. But now? She didn't want to be Electra anymore. Vida wasn't a fool; she caught on to the sudden fall in temperature. "Sorry, I shouldn't have said that."

"I've got to go." Georgette walked away from both of them.

She barely listened as the events planner took her through the Tavern, showed her the spaces they'd use, where the band could set up, and went over the menu. Since most of it had already been decided, she could give half an ear, but the woman did ask if she was all right. "I have a terrible headache," Georgette said, hoping that would excuse her absent behavior.

In the cab ride home, she wondered why Vida's telling her about Tony's obsession bothered her. So what if Tony found Electra attractive? Electra was attractive; more than one man had told her just that. Why did she feel as though he had betrayed her? Was she jealous of Electra Holmes? It was ludicrous. She had created Electra, she was Electra. Or was she?

They rode past the plaza and something else came to mind, maybe she was afraid Electra would destroy her relationship with Tony, as she'd destroyed so many relationships on the daytime soap. As she'd had a hand in destroying her marriage to Nigel.

She could still recall the last fight they had, all those years ago. Nigel was set to go back to Hillcrest permanently. She refused to leave the city and her life. They both knew it was over between them, but love doesn't go away because you want it to, it doesn't give up without a fight, and right to the end she hoped he'd chose her and stay.

"You're giving up our marriage for an acting job," he said again, the argument rehashed for the hundredth time.

"I created Electra Holmes. She means a lot to me. This is my life."

He scoffed. "You've become Electra. Or maybe she's all you've ever been. Maybe you're not capable of being anyone besides a character on TV."

Those words had stung then and they came back to slap her now. It was true, wasn't it? She had become Electra. A few of the men she'd dated had even called her by that name in a moment of passion. She'd laughed it off, even been proud of it. But over the past months she'd left the character behind, shed her like a second skin to become Georgette again. Georgette was a living breathing woman who had found a man so genuine she could scarcely believe what they had was real. And now, come to find out, maybe it wasn't real at all.

Her cell phone rang, Tony calling. She didn't answer. She wasn't ready to talk to him.

"It's going right to voice mail." Tony pocketed his cell and shot an accusatory glance at Vida.

"I still think you're making a big deal out of nothing. She's not going to leave you because you lusted after a soap opera character, for God's sake. She just turned off her phone for her meeting."

Tony sighed. "Can you at least be a little bit sorry?"

"Okay, fine. I'm sorry I opened my big mouth. But honestly? Georgette's probably flattered by your fantasies."

"I feel like a friggin' stalker."

"It'll be fine, Tony. Trust me. Why don't we do our workout and then you can go home. Order her up a dozen roses if you feel that bad about it."

"A dozen roses? How cliché can you get? I can't

believe I ever took dating advice from you." He turned his wheelchair onto the course he'd planned through the park. "I'll see you in an hour." And he wheeled away.

He didn't want to be angry with Vida, but there it was. The truth was he had been besotted by the idea of Electra Holmes walking into his life. But now that he'd gotten to know Georgette he had stopped connecting her to Electra. He hadn't thought about the show in months; she wasn't the character she played. She was a far better person, a woman he was falling in love with. And now Vida managed to bring the whole thing back up like a bad hot dog.

He started out on the course, over the bridge and past the fountain, then down along a tree-lined trail. After about ten minutes, he realized he'd forgotten to bring water. It was a warm day and he really should rehydrate, but he'd be damned if he was going to chase after Vida right now. He pushed faster, his arms propelling the wheels, his whole body in sync with the movement. He would push hard, break his personal best and, with some luck, the endorphins would kick in and alter his mood.

By the half way point, the muscles in his shoulders began to ache. He paid them no mind; he had achieved a drippy slightly hypnotic state that allowed him to forget why he was angry. Near the end of the ride, he'd nearly forgotten his own name. The sun beat down and all he could think about was the heat, and then his skin started to feel clammy and cold.

The benches on the south side of the park that marked his finish came into view. His head was spinning, light, and his heart beating double time. A fog began to cloud his vision and he knew he was in trouble. He slowed down and just as he reached the first of the benches, the fog grew dense and thick and then everything disappeared as he slumped forward in his chair.

Georgette stood in front of her building not yet ready to go upstairs. Richard had, finally, convinced Poppy she ought to marry him and this morning he'd gone to see a school friend who worked as a head hunter for Wall Street types. She hadn't thought Poppy would want to move to New York, but the pair had talked it over and decided it was the perfect place to start their new married life together. The biggest advantage being there was an entire ocean between the city and Hillcrest.

This evening, Georgette planned on taking them out to Alfredo's to celebrate. Of course, Tony was invited; she'd chosen the restaurant because she knew it was his favorite. Now though, the prospect of going out seemed like a lot of trouble. Feeling as she did at the moment, she wasn't sure she could go upstairs and face Poppy in her current euphoric and in-love state, let alone dinner with her and Richard and Tony besides. She wasn't ready to see Tony at the moment, and she wasn't sure she'd be ready by dinner time.

Maybe it would help to take a few moments to try and sort through. She could walk the long way around the block to Alahandro's. She'd order herself a cappuccino and a chocolate croissant and she'd sit in the warm shop as she figured out if she and Tony had a future.

Walking worked wonders and by the time she'd reached the coffee shop, she knew what she had to do; she had to talk to Tony. If he was infatuated with Electra, and their relationship was about bedding the character Georgette had been, then she'd tell him goodbye, even though it would break her heart to do it.

No sooner had she settled in at a wobbly table near the window then the store door opened and in walked Peggy Smythe-Bowles.

Peggy looked fit to be tied, and worried besides. Not a good look for her. She marched up to the table and put her hands on her hips. "Why are you not answering your phone?"

Accusatory Peggy was no fun at all, and Georgette

was not in the mood for confrontation. "I forgot to turn it back on after my meeting," she lied.

"Vida has been desperate to reach you. She finally called me. Poppy and I have been combing the city looking for you."

"Well, you've found me." Georgette lifted her coffee cup in mock toast.

"Tony's in the hospital."

Georgette very nearly dropped the cup. As it was, she half-placed half-dropped it on the table, the cappuccino sloshing over the rim. All her thoughts left her and only the word "hospital" remained.

"He was taken to St. Luke's. That's all she said besides that she couldn't get in touch with you."

Georgette's legs felt so rubbery she would have fallen over were she not already sitting. Why was real life so much harder than television? Electra had been through similar scenarios a hundred times over, but it was never, never like this.

Peggy's look softened and she got a napkin and began dabbing up the spilled coffee. "I can drive you to the hospital."

"Would you? Would you please?"

Chapter Twenty Two

The last place Georgette wanted to be was in the lobby of St. Luke's hospital. Yet here she was, running, well striding urgently at any rate, to the information desk.

"I'm looking for Tony Rodriquez's room," she said to the grandmotherly volunteer. The woman had steel wool hair and wore a pink jumper that, had Georgette been in any condition to judge, she would have deemed more appropriate for a kindergartner than a retiree. The woman's lack of fashion sense barely registered with her. If she'd been in a noticing mood, she might also have noted, and been mortified by, the bean shaped coffee stain near the top button of her own blouse. As it was, what she noticed was that the woman moved with painful slowness as she checked the computer register.

She looked up from the task and smiled. "Say, aren't you Electra Holmes?"

"No," said Georgette, giving a slight nod to the computer in an attempt to refocus the woman's attention. "I'm not."

The attempt didn't work and the woman shook her head and smiled. "Well, glory, you sure do look like her. I love *Our Time Tomorrow*, though I'm real upset that they killed off Electra. She was my favorite. Oh well, maybe they'll bring her back."

"She's gone. You have to get over it," said Georgette. Then, deciding she needed a more obvious approach she pointed to the computer and said, "Please?"

"Oh, sure. Tony Rodriguez, you said? Could that be Anthony?"

"Antonio"

The woman stared at the screen. "Nope. No Tony. No Anthony. No Antonio. The only Rodriguez listed is Louisa. I don't suppose that's who you're looking for."

Georgette would have been exasperated if she wasn't so near tears. "Can you check again, please?"

Peggy, who had been parking the car, came into the lobby and, waving to Georgette, walked over to her. Georgette had never been quite so happy to see anyone. "He's not registered."

"He's not? It must be a mistake. Let me text Vida."

Of course, text Vida. Why hadn't Georgette thought of that? Thank God for Peggy. Dear, sweet wonderful Peggy. When this ordeal was over, Georgette would buy her twenty skeins of her favorite yarn.

"You can't use the cell phone here," said the volunteer. She pointed to a corner of the lobby where there were several chairs and couches. "You'll have to go over there."

Once upon a time, Georgette would have argued over here and there, because, really, what difference did it make? Now, she followed Peggy to the area the woman had pointed to and waited anxiously as Peggy typed. She was a fast texter, Georgette wouldn't have thought that of her. Then again, Peggy no doubt had many talents Georgette hadn't considered.

They waited for a long minute and then Peggy's phone began beeping like a news alert. "They're in the ER," Peggy said. "Tony is being treated and released." She looked up from the phone. "He's going to be fine."

Georgette took a deep breath and nearly collapsed onto one of the upholstered lobby chairs. The knot of emotion in her gut came undone and gushed forward to meet her headlong. She put her head in her hands and began sobbing.

Peggy sat down next to her and began rubbing her back. "Hush, now. He's fine. Everything's okay."

"I know," Georgette managed.

"You're good to go," said the ER doctor, much to Tony's relief. He hadn't wanted to come to the hospital in the first place. It was simple dehydration, nothing a quart of water couldn't cure, but Vida decided to be extra cautious and she'd called an ambulance. He'd spent the past hour impatiently watching saline drip into his arm from an IV.

When Vida said Georgette was waiting for him in the lobby, his impatience grew tenfold and he wheeled past the doctor and to the elevator without listening to whatever lecture she would give him on the importance of staying hydrated.

Vida ran to catch him at the elevators just as the doors were shutting. They reopened in the lobby, where Georgette sat in a chair with her head in her hands. She stood up and threw her arms around his neck when she caught sight of him. "Thank God. You're okay." She ran her hands up and down his arms as though she had to check him out for herself and then sat down without letting go of him.

He hated seeing her in distress, but quite honestly, he loved that she was worried about him. He took out a hanky and handed it to her. "I'm fine. I did something stupid, that's all. I decided it would be okay to go rolling through the park without water. Heat prostration and an embarrassing run to the ER were what I got for my rash behavior."

"Yeah, well, I've had a few rash moments of my own." She sniffed and then slapped his arm. "But don't you ever do this again."

"I think I've learned my lesson." They sat looking at each other for a while. Peggy said something about going home and giving Vida a ride, to which Vida asked if he could get himself home.

Georgette stood and gave Peggy a hug. "I'll take care of him," which made his heart feel like it would float away.

There was, though, still an elephant sitting in the middle of the room. He knew he'd have to address it head on if he hoped for any kind of future with Georgette. So, after Peggy and Vida left, he took her hand in his. "Listen, I'm sorry about what Vida said, though really she was just telling the truth. I did lust after Electra."

Georgette didn't say a thing, which made the confession all the more difficult. Tell her what you're feeling, said his heart. She'll understand. She has to. "I did lust after Electra, but then I met you. And you're nothing like her."

Georgette raised her eyebrows, still not saying a thing. He forged on. "I mean, you look exactly like her, which, by the way, is terrific because she's gorgeous. But you—you are warm and funny and my life hasn't been the same since you walked into my office. I love you, Georgette. I want to spend my life basking in the glow you cast over everything. Electra might have caught my imagination for a while, but you've got my heart."

Oh God, she was crying again.

"Say it again," she said softly..

"I love you, Georgette Alden. You've got my whole heart."

She smiled, tears and laughter all mixing together. "I love you, Tony Rodriguez. If I live to be a hundred, I think this will be the best moment in my entire life. Who would have thought Saint Luke's could be romantic?"

Tony drew her onto his lap. "With you, anyplace is magical."

The lobby was busy, people coming and going and talking all around them. Beyond the revolving doors, the city buzzed and hummed with the lives of eight million souls. Many of them knew who Electra Holmes was. A few of them knew who Georgette Alden was, too. Only one of them, though, had his lips pressed to hers, making the room spin and all of those other people vanish into thin air. And, right now, he was the only one that mattered.

About Annie Hoff

Annie Hoff writes comedy and romance. When she's not huddled over a laptop with her 15th cup of coffee, you're likely to find her off watching a play with her hubby, relaxing while listening to music, or out in the woods taking lots of pictures to support her photography habit.